Hurricane in Nicaragua

Hurricane in Nicaragua

A JOURNEY IN SEARCH OF REVOLUTION

RICHARD WEST

MICHAEL JOSEPH
London

MICHAEL JOSEPH LTD
Published by the Penguin Group
27 Wrights Lane, London W8 5TZ, England
Viking Penguin Inc., 40 West 23rd Street, New York, New York 10010, USA
Penguin Books Australia Ltd, Ringwood, Victoria, Australia
Penguin Books Canada Ltd, 2801 John Street, Markham, Ontario, Canada L3R 1B4
Penguin Books (NZ) Ltd, 182–190 Wairau Road, Auckland 10, New Zealand

Penguin Books Ltd, Registered Offices: Harmondsworth, Middlesex, England

First published 1989

Copyright © Richard West 1989

Typeset, printed and bound in Great Britain by Richard Clay Ltd, Bungay, Suffolk

Set in Lasercomp 11½ on 13pt Palatino

A CIP catalogue record for this book is available from the British Library

ISBN 0 7181 3276 9

CONTENTS

PREFACE

MY FIRST VISIT to Nicaragua, in 1966, came as part of a very long journey through Latin America and the Caribbean. This was soon after President Kennedy's confrontation with Cuba, and the United States was still, rightly, alarmed over the spread of Castroism. The new President, Lyndon Johnson had sent troops to repress a revolt in the Dominican Republic. The embittered Argentine revolutionary, Che Guevara, had gone to Bolivia, inciting the Indian peasantry to revolt.

Compared to such countries, Nicaragua at that time was a peaceful place, under the rule of the dictator, Anastasio Somoza Debayle. Although a demagogue and extremely avaricious, Somoza had not yet permitted his National Guard to become as corrupt and brutal as they were ten years later. His bonhomie and his fluent English endeared him to US politicians and businessmen. It was probably of Somoza's father that President Franklin D. Roosevelt is said to have remarked, 'He's a son of a bitch, but he's our son of a bitch.'

Because I was working then for a newspaper, I did not spend long in Nicaragua which was not considered newsworthy. It was almost as tranquil as neighbouring El Salvador. I went to those countries only in search of material on what might be called the underlying themes of Latin America: the influence of the United

States, the cultural divide between Anglo-Saxon and Spanish-Indian, and the increasing rift in the Catholic Church between traditionalists and 'liberation theologians'. A study of these underlying themes emerged as a book, *The Gringo in Latin America.*

About twelve years ago I started to come back to Latin America. Now El Salvador was getting involved in a savage civil conflict, in which both extremists loathed the United States. Under the influence of El Salvador, the Nicaraguan volcano started to give warning of forthcoming eruption. Somoza replied to peaceful protests with general brutality and repression until, in 1979, a full-scale war began and Somoza was forced to flee. The group who then seized power called themselves Sandinistas, after a dimly remembered guerrilla chief from fifty years back.

Although in the early eighties I paid several visits to neighbouring countries like Costa Rica, El Salvador and Honduras, it was not till 1985 that I saw Nicaragua under its Sandinista regime. Right from the start, I was struck by the paradox of this socialist Nicaragua. Here was a group of young, inexperienced ideologues hoping to build a brave new world in a country not only backward and poor but ravaged by earthquake, volcanic eruption and, as I later discovered, by hurricane. And two hundred years after the French Revolution, credulous pilgrims from all over the world were still coming in hope of finding an earthly paradise.

In Nicaragua under the Sandinistas, I saw most clearly revealed those conflicts dividing Latin America, of race, religion and attitudes to the United States. It occurred to me that what I had wanted to say twenty years ago, in a book covering all Latin America, could better be said in a book about one small country. By focussing on Nicaragua, I hoped to be able to add the dimension of history. Nobody would presume to air an opinion on Ireland without some knowledge of Oliver Cromwell, William of Orange, Wolfe Tone and Michael Collins. Yet Nicaragua, just as much as Ireland, is under the influence of her past. And few of the politicians and journalists who speak on Nicaragua, have

2

even the vaguest notion of her history. Although most Nicaraguans can tell one something of Abraham Lincoln or Winston
Churchill, not one in a hundred Americans or Englishmen has
even heard of General Sandino.

The more that I learned of Nicaraguan history, the more it
seemed to come down to three extraordinary men. The first of
these was the most famous bogey figure in Latin America, the
soldier of fortune, William Walker, who came to Nicaragua with a
little army in 1855 and later became its President. Although, like
everyone who has been to Latin America, I thought I knew
something of William Walker, I soon discovered that most of
this was false.

The second great figure is Rubén Darío, the poet. Again, I
knew he had been a diplomat, and I had read some of his poems
in anthologies. Later I found that these rather tinkling verses
gave no indication of Darío's genius. And some of his poems,
expressing the Spanish and Indian fear of the cultural threat from
the United States, make still greater impact today. He was also
typically Nicaraguan in his love of women, alcohol and apocalyptic Christianity.

The third great figure was General Sandino, who fought the
US Marines in the 1920s and was shot in 1934 by the first of the
Somoza dynasty. The truth about his violent career is far from
the version put about by the modern Sandinistas.

The fourth person who figures large in this book is the
novelist Graham Greene, the most famous friend of the Sandinistas. Although he never supported revolution as such, Greene
has for more than half a century stood as a champion of Latin
American peoples against the United States. A Roman Catholic,
he has always been a rebel within the Church and a pioneer of
'liberation theology'.

This is not a history but a travel book in which I have tried to
explain the country today in the light of the past. It starts in
Managua, where I met Graham Greene, then moves to different

3

parts of the country, connected in turn with William Walker, Rubén Darío and General Sandino. I finish with a return visit to Nicaragua in 1988, and an epilogue on Hurricane Joan which struck the country during my stay.

1

MANAGUA

MY FIRST VISIT to Nicaragua under its revolutionary government began with a small disaster. On reaching Miami, where I was due to stay overnight before catching an onward flight to Managua, I found that my US visa was out of date. The black immigration lady was kind but firm. She took me to see a higher official, who turned out to be a Hispanic, like so many people one meets in Miami these days. When I said I was bound for Managua his eyelids flickered, since Nicaragua, almost as much as Cuba, is hated by the Miami Hispanics. Did I have a confirmed flight for Managua the following day? The ticket said clearly 'request'. At this point I recalled that Graham Greene, on his visits to Central America, makes a point of avoiding Miami and taking a slow, circuitous route that always begins with drinking gin at Amsterdam airport — or so he says in his recent book *Getting to Know the General*. Better still, I might have gone to New York, where most of the immigration officials read the *Spectator* and welcome contributors. The Hispanic immigration man was coldly polite, but not a *Spectator* reader. He said I would have to spend the night under guard with two other people whose papers were out of order, a gloomy Indian who spoke no tongue but his own, and a bossy Iranian lady.

We were put in the charge of two young women Hispanics, each wearing the Stars and Stripes on one of her uniformed arms and a gold badge saying 'Security Guard' on the other. We went through customs, then 'agri', the people who check for infected farm produce, where it was found the Indian's luggage was stuffed with edible roots and nuts, wrapped in towels. However, these passed inspection. The two girl guards asked me, by way of conversation, where I was heading and this time when I answered Nicaragua, they scowled. They were themselves from Nicaragua, having left six years ago 'when the communists took over . . . because of the trouble in our country'. Later I understood their antipathy. They thought that a writer bound for Managua was likely to favour the Sandinista Revolution.

Eventually, one of the Nicaraguan guards took the Iranian girl and myself to a place where illegal immigrants stay under house arrest. This was the Playboy Hotel and Bunny Club of the Hugh Hefner organisation. Because this was New Year's Day, the bunnies were taking the evening off, but anyway, as the barmaid remarked to me, 'What man would wanna see girls with a bit of fur on their ass when he can see them nude down the street?' As we began our hamburgers and salad, the Iranian girl said that in Frankfurt, where she lived, there were many live sex shows. The Nicaraguan guard was indignant, 'That is very bad for young people and for the mothers.' The Iranian, who took offence at this, then started to scold the Nicaraguan, 'You shouldn't eat all that salad. It won't make you skinny and it's got crawly insects on it. They don't wash it properly.' She then went to bed, leaving myself and the guard to drink beer and discuss our problems.

The guard said she did not get any overtime but the job was secure because there were so many Hispanics trying to enter America. She told of the hundreds of thousands of Nicaraguans who had left her country because of the Sandinistas, the poverty and the call-up to fight the Contra guerrillas. Since she was, in effect, a US government servant, I thought it tactful not to enquire if she herself supported the Contras. When I said that I had not been to Managua since 1966, many years before the overthrow of Somoza in 1979, or even the earthquake of 1972, she told me sadly that I would find everything changed. What with my jet fatigue, the beer and the dismal stories of Nicaragua, I started to feel depressed, on this my first night out in a Bunny Club.

The next morning, both Nicaraguan guards were once more formal as they escorted me to my plane of the El Salvadorean Airline. The cabin crew regarded me with suspicion for having left Miami under an escort and then for going on from El Salvador to its arch political enemy, Nicaragua. When I at last got to Managua, I met with an unexpectedly genial welcome. It is true that I had to change sixty dollars at the official rate, worth five dollars, but immigration asked no questions, and customs provided a specially fast and efficient service for diplomats and journalists.

Not having been there for almost twenty years, I was taken aback by the sight of central, or downtown, Managua; it does not exist any more. There are square miles of wilderness on the southern shore of Lake Managua on which the roofless Cathedral stands, as well as some recent skyscrapers, an army camp and a broken-down cinema showing a film called *Abortar en Londres* (To abort in London). Far back from the lake shore, round the small hill, Tiscapa, there is a cluster of buildings including the Intercontinental Hotel. This is a cone-shaped edifice in the neo-Aztec, brutalist style, but it makes up in strength what it lacks in beauty and did not fall down in the 1972 earthquake. The millionaire recluse Howard Hughes, who lived in the whole top floor, was one of those who survived unscathed in central Managua. Now the hotel and a number of nearby restaurants, cater for quite another breed of foreign visitor, those who have come to admire the revolution.

7

Among the thousands of visitors to Managua, was a delegation of sixty-four American 'Communicators' of what might be called the liberal or left-wing persuasion. Thirty or forty years ago they would have called themselves 'progressives' and might have called their delegation 'A Congress of Intellectuals in Defence of Peace'. These congresses were in fashion after the Second World War. Such people these days no longer style themselves progressives, certainly not intellectuals. However, they stem from the same tradition. Some of the sixty-four were veterans of such old campaigns as the Vietnam War and the protests against McCarthy and MacArthur, and even the Spanish Civil War. Some of their names were familiar from twenty or thirty years ago. The delegation was led by Mr Abbie Hoffman, a once famous protester on Vietnam. I met Betty Friedan, a veteran feminist lady with what appeared to be cubist earrings; she said she was overwhelmed by Nicaragua. I half expected to see the paediatrician Dr Spock, the archetypal American liberal thinker; later I read in a Sandinista newspaper that he denounced America's role in Nicaragua.

One of the delegates was Harold Kramer, a San Francisco publisher, who wanted to come here after he had met a Nicaraguan woman judge at a party given by Decca Truehaft, the Mitford sister who married a Californian radical after her first husband, Esmond Romilly, died fighting in Spain. The judge had asked for Americans to observe the Nicaraguan general election (held in November 1984) because, she said, it was bound to be misreported. Then Mr Kramer went on, 'I had read a great deal on Nicaragua and Somoza. Our people don't know anything about what's going on here. I'm seventy and I've been in a lot of revolutionary situations but it's the first time I've seen a revolution being made. I was in that place bombed by the Contras. I wouldn't be as fair in my decisions as they are, if someone had killed my brother or sister. We went into a prison. That's an incredible place. One of the men was a former bodyguard of

Somoza. He's a prisoner there. I said to him, "There are no guards and no walls, why don't you leave?" He said, "Why should I leave?" He told me that they had a garden and that they grew their own food. He realised now that he had been exploited by Somoza.'

Another of the sixty-four was Joan Greenbaum, an economics lecturer from New York, who specialises in labour, 'You know, that's rather left wing.' She had been thrilled to meet the Sandinistas, especially the Commandantes, the military and political leaders and some of the youngsters who run the Defence Committees, the CDs, the revolutionary cells in the street or block. 'It's amazing how you'll find the Commandantes of twenty-six, who are not just eloquent but poetic when they talk about a battle plan. You'll find fourteen year-olds who are in charge of their CDs.' After we had been talking some time, Miss Greenbaum asked me, 'Do you think Nicaragua is going to be like the Spanish Civil War in American terms?' I think I know what she meant. She was wondering if Nicaragua might reproduce the heroics of Spain: The Abraham Lincoln Brigade and its anthem, sung to the tune of the *Red River Valley*; the Capa photograph of a mortally wounded soldier clutching a rifle in one of his outflung hands; the war dispatches of Ernest Hemingway; and Paul Robeson's gloating song on the fate of the captured Franco generals, 'They shall be hanging'.

As well as these veterans of the ideological struggle, there were scores, it seemed like hundreds, of young foreign radicals, of whom most were from the United States. Some appeared to be working for student newspapers, or civil liberties organisations. Two pale and serious girls from the Middle West said they had come to Nicaragua after a tour through Guatemala, El Salvador and Honduras; 'We've been making a study of human rights violations.'

'You've certainly been to the right place,' I remarked, in a vain attempt to be funny. They missed the joke. Nor did they get my

9

point that things like murder, torture, poverty and disease were not so much 'human rights violations' as murder, torture, poverty and disease. Some of the less serious girls had picked up Nicaraguan men, perhaps in sympathy with the revolution, perhaps just for kicks. You saw them lounging about the Intercontinental café, the brown arms of the young Sandinistas draped round the shoulders of the excited American girls.

For young American men there is small hope of having a 'Sandinista experience'. The Nicaraguan girls from the middle classes have not yet accepted the Playboy sexual morality. This applies as much to the Sandinistas as to the enemies of the revolution. Those girls would not want to be seen with American left-wing radicals. Nicaragua offers still less joy to visiting foreign homosexuals. Even before the AIDS scare, most Nicaraguans frowned on sodomy. 'Before the revolution', a pious woman told me, 'we used to think that some of the priests were pederasts. That's one of the reasons the Church was not so popular as it is now.' Whispers abound concerning one of the Sandinista leaders, but Nicaragua has not so far started the persecution of homosexuals, or state-run queer-bashing, that goes on in Castro's Cuba.

Some of these young Americans call themselves journalists, though they do not resemble their kind in other parts of Central America. A grinning young man saw me reading the words on his scarlet T-shirt, 'Join the Army, travel to distant places, meet interesting people, and kill them' – or something like that. 'Hi!' he said, shaking my hand, 'My name's Dana. I work for *Mother Jones*. Have you heard of it? Well, it's a paper that kind of knocks you over the head.'

'Does it really?' I said.

This curious foreign press corps of people like Dana from *Mother Jones* had made their informal headquarters at the delightful Mexican restaurant Los Antojitos (the Mexican word for savouries). Most of the outdoor tables are under the shade of a vast, spreading cenizero tree whose leaves rustle and shimmer

10

like silk whenever the breeze comes up from the lake. Occasionally, on religious holidays, Los Antojitos lays on a brass band,
including a 'serpent' which coils round the players. The *tacos*,
leathery pancakes, the dollops of mashed-up bean and the gristly
meat are awful; the eggs on the menu are always off; but who
cares, on a sweltering, scented late afternoon, drinking ice-cold
beer from a pewter mug?

My love of Los Antojitos grew slowly during my stays. On
that first visit, when all of central Managua seemed to be under
the occupation of foreigners, this was the haunt of the journalists.
The young, amateur left-wing reporters listened in awe to those
who made a living out of the journalistic trade. Especially they
listened to one bearded veteran of the troubles in Central
America, an old left-winger and comrade of Graham Greene. He
was holding forth on the new Nicaragua and how much better
the country is than under Somoza. 'It may be inefficient but
corrupt it is not. In the old days in the airport, you'd put a
twenty dollar bill in your passport and you'd sail through.' The
young journalists nodded to show their delighted comprehension.
To me, it did not seem quite so simple. Although I have in the
past had to bribe my way into Honduras and the Dominican
Republic, I had not needed to do so in Somoza's Nicaragua. But
now, in Sandinista Nicaragua, I had had to exchange at a bogus
rate not one but three twenty-dollar bills, making an entrance tax
of around fifty-five bucks.

Not all the foreigners whom I encountered in Managua were
citizens of the United States. Among those I met at Los Antojitos
was an engaging young Ibo woman from what I still call Biafra,
now forcibly merged again with the kleptocratic state of Nigeria.
Like most Ibos she was a Roman Catholic and had come to
examine 'liberation theology'. She was also a feminist. However,
I soon discovered that in Biafra even the feminist liberation
theologians keep their sense of humour. I also met an Anglican
friar I had known many years earlier when he worked as a

11

journalist in South Africa. He had just come back from the Atlantic (Mosquito) coast, with a bad stomach upset and a fit of depression. Like most people who get to the coast (it is hard to get either a permit or transport) the friar had to accept that most of the blacks who live there do not support the Sandinista regime. 'Before I came here', he told me, 'I was a hundred per cent for the Sandinistas. I still support them. But not one hundred per cent.'

I eavesdropped on a couple of English Sandinista supporters. One was a Labour politician, I think an MP, who was out on one of his regular visits. The other was an upper-class lady, the kind who might wear tweeds at home, who acted as guide to the wonders of Nicaragua. She complained of a recent group of women from England, 'As soon as we got near the frontier, they started to quarrel among themselves: the whites with the blacks; the gays with the straights; the CND with the Greenham Common,' (apparently two rival groups of anti-nuclear demonstrators). 'I told them they should forget their differences and join in fighting the common enemy, the United States.'

Not all the foreigners who abound in central Managua are transient ideological tourists, members of delegations and fact-finding commissions, or roving reporters for papers like *Mother Jones.* Many countries, with left wing regimes have pledged their support to the Sandinistas. Foreign charities, many of them with a left-wing orientation, have also collected money for Nicaragua, often intended to help the victims of war against the Contras. At first some of these foreign states and charities gave the Nicaraguans money in cash but soon discovered a disadvantage. The Sandinistas would bank the dollars but allocate to the aid project only the cordobas changed at the official rate which, in 1985, was only a twelfth of the free rate. One British charity collected and sent to the Nicaraguans tens of thousands of pounds, supposedly to rehouse refugees from the fighting. The Sandinistas cashed this money at the official rate, and spent even this on forcibly moving civilians away from the northern border region to stop them providing recruits and food for the Contras. This was the counter-insurgency measure used by the British during the Boer War, of moving women and children to what were called 'concentration camps'.

When foreign countries and even some of the charities found that their money was going astray, they started to give their aid in the form of expert advisers, or projects run by their own personnel. The Russians and their Cuban surrogates train and equip the Nicaraguan army. The Cubans have also provided many civilian advisers, including, at one time, seven thousand teachers. Cuba, one should remember, as well as possessing a massive army at home and fifty thousand troops engaged in a war in Angola, expects its civilian workers abroad to carry arms and keep up military training. When the United States invaded the small Caribbean island of Grenada in 1983, to overthrow its unpopular Marxist dictatorship, almost all the resistance they met was from the Cubans employed on building an airstrip. Perhaps because of their paramilitary role, the Russians and Cubans lie low in Managua. The Cubans, especially, are greatly disliked by the locals.

There are sometimes Czechs and Bulgarians at the Seven Seas Hotel. They are silent and woebegone with the slightly hangdog look of those who work in the interests of their own oppressor. The same feeling no doubt saddened those Irish patriots who served the British in India. They feign ignorance of all languages but their own so I did not discover what they were doing. It is no doubt a lowly job or they would not stay in the Seven Seas. By contrast, the Libyans here live in luxury. I met two of them with Canadian and Nicaraguan friends at a steak house and next day went for breakfast in their villa, a fine home commandeered from one of the émigrés in Miami. The Libyans were still more secretive and afraid than the East Europeans; from what one hears of Colonel Gaddafi I cannot blame them. These Libyans worked on a hydro-electric scheme, which struck me as odd, for as far as I know there are no rivers in Libya.

The Western advisers are quite a different matter. They work for their own governments at enormous salaries, boosted by danger money because of the civil war, in one of the cheapest countries in the world. A foreign adviser stays in the Intercontinental for seven dollars a night compared to the seventy dollars charged to mere tourists. Most have fine cars and a villa. They should be able to bank their salary. Most of these Western aid advisers speak derisively of the Sandinista government. A Canadian fisheries expert told me that often the boats are confiscated for military use. A Spanish adviser on tourism was kicking his heels. The only tourists here are the ideologues. A French engineer complained bitterly of the money his government wasted here in order to strike an attitude with the left, 'Mitterand set up an Embassy here with seventy people. What on earth can they all be doing?'

Socialist Sweden, a firm friend of the Sandinistas, has sent among other things a team of geologists to the capital. They are mainly engaged in earthquake research, but many Managuans think they are looking for gold, and blame this for the fact that the city's water supply is switched off on Tuesdays and Fridays. I met at dinner an English couple working for this research team. Not long afterwards they were found stabbed to death in their house which goes to suggest that working in Nicaragua does deserve danger money. I got a further reminder of this one night when I went with Canadian friends to the Mau Mau Nightclub. I took a seat at the table, only to find that my chair was sliding backwards on to the dance floor. It was only a minor earthquake but nevertheless discomforting in a city that has twice been flattened. The earth tremor made me feel glad I had left my first-floor room at the Seven Seas and moved to one of a row of bungalows at the back. However, this new room lay in the shade of a tree which, if it should fall, was heavy enough to crush all

14

beneath it. That is why most foreigners stay at the Intercontinental, which stood firm during the last earthquake.

During my visit to Nicaragua, in 1985, I met many foreigners
who were neither ideological tourists nor business advisers but
old-fashioned acquisitive businessmen. They are not the same kind
as those hucksters from the United States I met and described on
my trip to Managua in 1966:

> Some of these are ordinary sales representatives and buyers.
> There is also a special kind of prospector or fixer, arrived to
> sniff out the market. These are men with small businesses in
> the United States — especially the South — who have staked
> the price of a plane fare on clinching a sale or a contract. One
> group, with whom I sat in Managua throughout an afternoon,
> had the authentic cigar-chomping, no-flies-on-me bombast of
> American businessmen in a *Krokodil* cartoon. The duty on
> pumping equipment; whom you had to see about taxes;
> whether the drilling team would strike oil, were all discussed
> with furious, sweating deliberation. 'I believe in making
> money,' one of these businessmen remarked after the third
> tentative deal and the sixth whisky. 'What do you believe in?'
> he added to someone across the table. 'I'm a Communist,' said
> his friend, just for a joke. The salesman rose, sat down again,
> turned his back, then exclaimed, 'I shook hands with you.
> Now I unshake hands.'

The American businessmen have gone, since Washington put an
embargo on Nicaraguan trade. The Japanese have largely replaced
them, and most of the cars are Datsuns or Toyotas. Most foreign
businessmen that one meets come from countries in Western
Europe who hope to furnish the goods or services guaranteed by
an aid project, for example a bridge, a lumber mill or some
cotton-ginning machinery. The Nicaraguan government has to
choose between rival bidders. An Englishman, hoping to win
such a contract, told me that it was not essential to offer good
work at a competitive price. His job here was to 'make friends'

in the relevant ministry. 'You mean bribery?' I suggested. Exactly, but bribery in a socialist country, is most often given in perks, especially air tickets and money for travel abroad, ostensibly on official business. A Canadian told me that, from his experience, most of the tools and spare parts paid for by charities and delivered to Nicaragua were instantly seized by officials and sold on the black market.

One European, in 'import–export', told me, 'I import Russian vodka to Nicaragua. They sell it to this country at virtually cost price, as part payment for all the military aid. I buy through a Nicaraguan company from the Russian vodka depot in Hamburg. But if I'm buying a thousand cases, only ten of these actually reach Nicaragua. The rest I sell in Europe, the United States and the Caribbean, at several hundred per cent profit. You should see the business letters we send the Russians – all starting with "Dear Comrade" and ending with "socialist greetings". There's nothing I enjoy so much as ripping off the Russians.'

The phenomenon of a capital city whose centre is populated largely by foreigners depends on the strange topography of Managua, imposed upon it by earthquakes. It is difficult to comprehend, let alone explain.

From my bathroom in the Seven Seas Hotel, I look into the foliage of an exotic tree, inhabited by olive-green birds and a great lizard, its body as thick as a rat's. When the wind brushes the leaves aside, revealing the cityscape of Managua, I see no buildings, only the small volcano on which the present regime has carved the initials of its party, FSLN, for the Sandinista National Liberation Front. The old Managua between the lake and the small hill, Tiscapa, was devastated by earthquake in 1931 and again in 1972, and now has reverted to countryside, dotted with makeshift houses. City streets are now country lanes where pigs, hens and dogs scavenge among the refuse. Directions are given by natural landmarks: lake, sun-up, mountain and sundown, for north, east, south and west, so that the Seven Seas

16

address is 'one block sun-down (from the Intercontinental Hotel) and twenty paces to the lake'.

From when I was first in Managua, twenty-odd years ago, I remember the lobby of my hotel but not the lake, and little about the city except the heat and a wooden drinking-den, where the beer tasted delicious. Now one can walk from Tiscapa down to the lake, enjoying a view of that huge expanse of water and ranks of volcanoes shimmering in the distance. After crossing a field, one passes along the sun-down side of a rambling military installation, ringed by a wall on which are murals after the style of Diego Rivera. Surrealist cane cutters and coffee pickers proclaim the revolution. An Aztec Sandinista scotches the neck of a Yankee dragon. Everywhere are the images of a youth with outstretched arms, one of them clutching a rifle, an image taken, I think, from the photograph by Robert Capa purporting to show the death of a Spanish Republican soldier outside Madrid.

After the military installation, and more wasteland, one reaches the cinema where they were showing *Abortar en Londres*. On the sun-up side of the block is a concert hall in the patio of the Grand Hotel, wrecked in the 1972 earthquake. The hall is actually named the Ruins of the Grand Hotel. Beyond is the main square of Managua, now called after the Sandinista hero, Carlos Fonseca, whose spirit is kept alive by an ever-burning flame. Here, too, is the National Palace which has survived the earthquake and the attack on it, when Edén Pastora kidnapped Parliament to ransom and win the release of Sandinista prisoners. Those whom he freed, like Tomás Borge, no longer talk of Pastora, who broke with the Sandinistas and went into exile.

Nearer the lakeside, where he made love, is a statue of Rubén Darío, the great Nicaraguan poet, in Roman dress on top of a plinth overlooking a pond with stone swans and nymphs. One of the nymphs is headless. The monument is in the style of a greetings card, or a wax statuette of a saint, perhaps of an

Odeon cinema decoration in 1933, the year the work was unveiled. The statue is almost as bad, artistically, as the young man waving an AK-47 assault rifle. On three sides of the plinth are bas-reliefs of a centaur, Caesar's triumphal march and St Francis, illustrating Darío's poems. On the fourth, or mountain side, of the plinth are carved some of the lines from the 'Song of Hope', '¿Oh, Señor Jesucristo! Por qué tardas?' 'Oh Lord, Jesus Christ, why do you tarry?'

The Cathedral stands on the sun-up side of the plaza, but its roof fell in on the night of the earthquake, and grass grows tall in the aisle. One visitor found boys playing baseball there and even a group of squatters, Miskito Indians, but I always find it deserted. This modern church was built by Germans using the latest techniques for resisting earthquakes; however, it did not survive as well as the churches built by simple friars during the Spanish Empire.

Down by the lake there is a radio station, a skyscraper, the Rubén Darío Theatre built by Madame Somoza, and a kind of olde worlde cottage that houses the Ministry of Culture. Most of the life of the old Managua goes on near to Tiscapa, which once was the fortress and bunker of the Somozas, and now serves the revolution. Few civilian Nicaraguans live or work in this neighbourhood. There are airline offices in and around the Plaza España, also a department store and a bakery with a constant queue outside, for bread is scarce. But most of the Nicaraguans that one sees around are part of the People's Sandinista Army, a force with seventy thousand on active service and maybe treble that number in the reserve. It is a large army for two and a half million people (not counting those in emigration), especially when one considers that Somoza's National Guard was only a tenth the size until 1978 and the start of civil war.

Many military men and women come to the Seven Seas for its so-called Chinese lunch of vegetable soup and rice and bits of chicken or beef. Some attend just for the beer or to join in a bottle of rum. It makes me uncomfortable to be in a café where everyone else is armed, especially when they are drinking, and especially when they are women soldiers. Although I do not like to see women armed, I have to admit that these Nicaraguans cling to their femininity, even to wearing the rouge that goes so well with a brown skin and an olive-green uniform. Nor have these soldiers, male or female, abandoned the Nicaraguan swagger: three or four gathered together will automatically group themselves in glamorous or heroic pose, with a foot on the chair, a hat pushed back from the forehead, one hand on a hip or holster. I love their flamboyance; especially that of the women. Rubén Darío wrote that Nicaraguan women love to follow the army, 'More than once they have fought with the bravest, gun in hand. And the same woman, back in her home, is good, hardworking and amorous.'

Even the fiercest women soldiers seem immune to North American feminism. Nicaraguan women do not reject men, nor think them all rapists. It would be impossible here to advance a fad like 'political lesbianism'. Even the wildest Sandinistas hold back from assaults on the family. Watching the girl soldiers relaxing here in the Seven Seas or the outdoor café, Los Antojitos, I thought of the North American girl soldiers I met five years ago in Honduras, where the United States was holding military exercises intended to cow Nicaragua.

In Tegucigalpa, the capital of Honduras, I had spent a few evenings in what had become one of the new 'GI bars', like those I remembered from Vietnam. The proprietor was an ex-Marine who had fought in Vietnam then served as a mercenary, or a 'soldier of fortune', in various parts of Africa. There was much boastful talk between him and his cronies of 'when I was in Angola', or 'when I had Bob Mugabe in my sights for a week'. These older men were perhaps engaged with the Nicaraguan Contras. Most of the guests at the bar were young American soldiers taking part in the exercise. And many of them were women. They were not just drivers or clerks but combat soldiers trained in the toughest of infantry schools, the opposite number of these Sandinistas here in the Seven Seas.

The American girl GIs were homesick and woebegone. One of them told me that most evenings she stayed in her tent and polished her boots. She showed me a photograph of her husband and two children, the boy freckled, the girl with a brace on her teeth. Another lady GI related miserably that all she wanted in life was to be back in New Hampshire. A third wept, literally, into her beer. The only happy girl GIs that I saw were walking, lovingly arm-in-arm, through the streets of Tegucigalpa. The recruitment and training of women as combat troops was started at the insistence of the feminists, who then changed their mind and said it degraded women to teach them to kill. And surely it does.

'Never talk to the military' is a cardinal rule for a country in revolution. They think you are wanting to spy on them or subvert them. This means that as long as you stay in central Managua you meet few Nicaraguans who are not from the new Sandinista élite. Even those that you do meet tend to be very guarded. For example, one evening I fell into conversation with three men at one of the open cafés near to the Plaza España. After half an hour of the usual Nicaraguan small-talk on baseball, earthquakes, women and what I thought of the Queen and Margaret Thatcher, they started to tell me about themselves. Two worked at the airport, one in a government office. All spoke loyally of the Sandinista government, their employer. But then they had to admit that food was very expensive, their standard of living was down, more and more people were off to Miami. After about an hour and a few beers, I asked them how they regarded Archbishop, soon to be Cardinal, Ovando y Bravo, the principal enemy of the present regime. After a few uneasy glances at one another and some hesitation, they ventured the feeling that he was a good man and then, having summoned their courage, they all declared him to be a great man.

Most Managuans are not so much suspicious as jealous and resentful of foreigners. The former middle classes, the people who have been ruined by socialism and, still more, inflation, feel shame about their dingy clothes, the loss of their cars, the lack of money to entertain friends and strangers. They buy dollars from foreigners at the black-market rate, but hate themselves for being touts. What riles them most is to see the young foreign friends of the Revolution, the 'Sandalistas', who live like princes here on the black market, then go away singing the praises of socialism. Understandably, and with good reason, Managua citizens tend to assume that foreigners must be friendly towards the regime; and they detest them for it. This has made Nicaragua much less friendly than other Communist countries, for instance Poland and Vietnam, where people assume that Westerners must be believers in Western freedom.

Although Sandinistas talk of the Revolution, they have not brought in a Terror, with show trials, mass executions and labour camps. They have not persecuted the known opponents of the regime, as Castro has done to the *gusanos* (worms) in Cuba. The new rulers mix with opponents at social occasions, such as the famous parties given by Richard Owen, the British chargé d'affaires until 1987. The most respected diplomat in the country, Owen was ready and eager to sit up all night drinking rum and Coca-Cola with Commandantes, the young and often naïve Sandinista leaders. Such Commandantes mingled at cocktail parties beside the swimming pool with enemies such as the editor of *La Prensa*, the Catholic and Conservative newspaper. At one of these parties, the US Ambassador took me aside and told me a story against the CIA. The CIA had started and funded the Contra guerrillas, but gave their day-to-day running to agents of Argentina's intelligence service. The Argentine agents had filched most of the CIA money and then departed when Washington took the British side in the Falklands War. It was odd to hear this, surrounded by Nicaraguans, beside a swimming pool in Managua.

21

The Nicaraguans that I met at parties, at dinner in restaurants such as La Marseillaise or the Lobster Inn, are generally critical of the Sandinistas, but with the exception of one old lady, who harked back to the age when the streets were washed and cleaned each morning, I have not met anybody who mourned the Somozas. Of course they know they were better off economically; even the Sandinistas have to admit this. But most Nicaraguans wanted to see the Somozas leave, just as most of them now want the Sandinistas to leave.

Political life goes on in Managua but, once again because of the odd topography, this does not express itself in demonstrations, meetings or even café debates. One gets no sense of what the man in the street is thinking because there are no real streets, just lanes or arterial highways. From TV and the government Press, one hears of the latest assault against Yankee imperialism, the comradely greetings from Mozambique or Outer Mongolia, the spirit of joy and resolution with which three thousand volunteers have gone to pick coffee or cotton. One has to wait for *La Prensa*, if it appears that afternoon, to learn more detailed news about what has happened around this sprawling city: a scuffle at one of the open markets, a protest against a government camera crew, arrests, and more dawn raids on those suspected of dodging conscription.

Again, in Managua one gets no sense of what is happening in the churches. In the smaller cities and towns, the church is the centre of social life. The tourist staying in central Managua probably does not see a church; the nearest one to the Seven Seas is a quarter mile away, on the other side of the football stadium. And yet in Managua, just as much as the rest of the country, politics is subordinate to religion. Opposition to the regime, like opposition to the Somozas, is centred upon the Archbishop, now Cardinal Obando y Bravo, backed by the Polish Pope, John Paul II.

The Sandinistas encourage the Popular Church, also called

Church of the Poor, enshrining the notions of Liberation Theology. The dozen or so Nicaraguan (as opposed to foreign) priests who follow its teaching include the Foreign Minister, Father Miguel D'Escoto, the Cultural Minister, Father Ernesto Cardenal, and his brother Father Fernando, another Jesuit Sandinista. The only services of this Popular Church are held in the Iglesia Santa María de los Angeles in a Managua suburb or *barrio*.

Since the word *barrio* now generally means a poor suburb or slum, the word is emphasised by those who support the 'Church of the Poor'. In fact, this is a quite prosperous suburb of Managua. On the one occasion I managed to get there at more or less the right time, I found that the people leaving the church were either foreigners or well dressed Nicaraguans. The young man who showed me round the church had a motor bike which, these days, means he is bound to be a Sandinista. The Santa María Church, like Liverpool's Catholic Cathedral, is built in the round. The Liverpool building, known as 'Paddy's Wigwam', was decorated with photographs of Vietnam wounded and slum children over the slogan: 'Jesus was condemned to die because of the world's sins. He was innocent, like these children, condemned to a life of poverty.' The Santa María Church is covered with murals, again after the style of Diego Rivera, depicting Christ as a Nicaraguan cane cutter, and General Sandino as a disciple. Later, when I had learned a little about Sandino, that mural struck me as still more odd.

The Nicaraguan Popular Church reminded me of the Pax organisation in Poland. The Communists created Pax in the hope of undermining the Polish hierarchy. The head of Pax, was a pre-war anti-Semitic politician, Boleslaw Piasecki, who is said to have taken the job to save himself from the firing squad. The Pax publishing house was given the right to publish translations of foreign authors like Graham Greene, and from this base Piasecki started a thriving business empire, including the manufacture and sale of candles, crucifixes and other religious artefacts, and even established a chemical factory. Pax and Piasecki, in 1968, led the government's persecution of the remaining Jews, especially those in the Communist Party.

If the Popular Church has not yet gone into candles and chemicals, it nevertheless lives well from the state, and Santa María is one of the set pieces for ideological visitors. The Church of the Poor makes no appeal to the genuine poor of Managua, who now exist in hundreds of thousands. They come in multitudes to the feast of Managua's patron saint, Santo Domingo de Guzmán. On 1 August, the effigy of 'Minguito' is carried out of its church, some seven miles from central Managua, and along a country lane to the place where the feasting begins. When I joined the procession at nine in the morning, the crowd was just beginning its journey. Some were on horseback, most on foot and many were painted black as Moors or decked out as harlequins; but there was none of the finery that you see at carnival in Brazil or Trinidad. Many in the crowd looked sickly and ill-fed. The drunkenness was astounding. In a hundred yards, walking along that lane at half past nine in the morning, I stepped over eight men lying insensible. Nowhere else in the world have I seen such drunkenness as in Managua; not in Warsaw, not in Reykjavik; not in the old Liverpool Press Club. A diplomat told me that under the Sandinista regime consumption of spirits had risen five hundred per cent.

The triumphal march of Santo Domingo was marred this year, as apparently every year, by the kind of behaviour *La Prensa* denounced, 'In spite of the clubs that many women carried for self-defence, and the vigilance of the police, groups of oafs constantly managed to bypass the law and do mischief. You could see people going around blatantly with hands covered with hot grease to smear black on the weakest victims.' The degradation and wretchedness of Managua is worse than almost anything I have seen in Central America. The drunkenness, bitterness and despair recall accounts of the Black Death, or Germany during the Thirty Years War.

24

If the first day of Santo Domingo brings out the poor of Managua, the last day, 10 August, sees a gathering of the *caballeros*. Dozens of horsemen and horsewomen parade in front of the Intercontinental Hotel, decked out in stetson hats, shirts wide at the shoulders and tapering to the waist, with their feet in leather stirrups. Some of the horses are trained in dancing steps; one of them shied and kicked in a Japanese car. Later these ranchers, or dude ranchers, lunched in the hotel restaurant to the sound of a Mexican band. Those I spoke to said they had been dispossessed, 'You won't find any Sandinistas here.' I rather suspect, though, that this is a touchy subject; that riding and owning a horse is a mark or proclamation of Spanish rather than Indian ancestry. However, these European Nicaraguans share with the Indians a love of the bottle. A boy of three on the bar stool had just been given a beer and when it was finished, he clamoured for more, '*más, más*', and banged with his little fists on the counter.

Rich or poor, Spanish or Indian, most Nicaraguans go to Mass each Sunday, at one of the churches loyal to Archbishop Obando. Over the last ten years there has been a religious revival comparable almost with Poland. In smaller towns you can see how church after church is crowded on Sunday morning, with frequent processions during the week. Here in Managua, the churches and signs of devotion are spread out over this non-city. The Cardinal's church, or pro-Cathedral, is all of ten miles from the city centre.

The Cardinal is a squat, solid man, whose coppery, sombre features reveal his Indian ancestry. During services at his pro-Cathedral, Obando sits motionless as a carved chess bishop, without a flicker or twitch of expression. Yet when the guitars start up for a hymn, the Cardinal jumps into action as sing-song leader, telling his congregation to link hands, swinging their arms in time with the rhythm. It is all rather jolly and evangelical, though not to my liking; the church is too bright and modern for

25

my taste. On many Sundays Obando says something critical of the government, and after the Mass, is prepared to answer questions from journalists. On this day, he confined his remarks to purely spiritual matters. The only people who went round to see him afterwards were myself and a learned American, who knelt in front of the Cardinal, kissed his ring and began to address him in Latin. Obando cut him short in Spanish. We asked Obando if he was pleased with his recent visit to Rome. Yes, the Pope had always been a good friend, a solid support. When I asked him about the 'popular' priests, the Cardinal sighed; he must have been asked that question a hundred times. They were disobedient, he said, but he had no power to remove them. Once a priest, always a priest.

Obando has been consistent in opposition, first to Somoza, now to the Sandinistas. None of the accusations against him stand up to scrutiny. For example, the Sandinistas claim that Obando took from Somoza the present of a Mercedes car. It is true that Somoza offered the car, but Obando refused it. The Sandinistas suggest that Obando plotted with the United States to protect Somoza. In fact Obando, like many others, was trying to get Somoza to leave and to end the civil war. The Sandinistas wanted to keep the war going in order to win control of the army and its weapons. In this they succeeded.

The Sandinistas claim that, after the revolution, Obando picked a quarrel with them. In fact the revolution followed the end of the war. To quote a Sandinista historian, 'Here class struggle comes *after* revolutionary victory.' Having helped to defeat Somoza, the Sandinistas started another war against real or imaginary foes like the middle classes, the peasantry and the United States. Obando supported the overthrow of the Somozas but not the class war that followed.

The Cardinal neither supports nor condemns the Contra guerrillas. He goes to Miami to speak to his flock in exile, many of whom no doubt are Contras, just as presumably some of his flock at home are Sandinistas. Obando has constantly striven for peace in the civil war. The Sandinistas revile him because he refuses to take their side. They accuse him of partiality to the United States; he denounces the large Russian and Cuban presence in Nicaragua. Otherwise, he is not an ideologue.

The Cardinal is, however, quite uncompromising in his defence of Christian morals, the family and the education of children. He has condemned abortion (a Sandinista cause); pornography, such as you find in the Sandinista humorous weekly; above all the introduction of propaganda to schools. He was one of the signatories of an open letter addressed to the Education Minister, and afterwards published in *La Prensa*, 'With great surprise, the parents of children at church schools have received the circular notice sent out by your Ministry, which obliges all primary school children, in co-ordination with the Association of Sandinista Children, to receive two hours a week of a so-called Plan for Patriotic Education, which includes political and military talks, visits to camps, excursions and games orientated to the installation in children's minds of a partisan mentality, to encourage class hatred, violence, militarism and the warrior spirit.'

This open letter filled me with admiration and envy. If only, I thought, our own bishops in England were half as outspoken against the demands of the Local Education Authorities.

The Nicaraguan government has at times used brutal methods against the Church. When the Pope visited Nicaragua, a mob of Sandinistas shouted him down. The Church's radio station is seldom allowed to broadcast. Those foreign priests who do not agree with 'liberation theology', have been expelled. The Sandinistas attempted to use TV to blacken the name of Monsignor Bismarck Carballo, the Cardinal's right-hand man and press adviser. One day the viewers were startled to see Carballo paraded naked along the streets of Masaya, accompanied by a naked woman of his acquaintance. The news announcer claimed that the couple were found in bed together. The Monsignor said he

27

was paying a pastoral visit when armed men broke into the house and forced them both to undress and go outside, where the cameras were waiting. Most of the faithful took the Monsignor's word, while others joked that he ought to be known as 'Father Caballo' (stallion).

In the sweltering dining place of the Seven Seas, a US professor of history drinks warm Pepsi Cola (he fears the germs in the ice) and recounts the iniquities of William Walker, 'That was one mean son-of-a-bitch and I'm telling you, you've got to admire the Nicaraguans the way that they even speak to us, let alone act so goddam kind to Americans, after the way we've screwed them up.' His listeners murmur 'that's right ... goddam it', expressing the shame they feel over what their country has done to Nicaragua. They have pale, spectacled, sweaty faces, and bitter smiles that reveal their rather enjoyable guilt over the perfidy of Washington.

William Walker is a bogeyman in Honduras, Costa Rica and as far away as Argentina, but most of all here. He was a filibuster, or soldier of fortune, who came to Nicaragua in the 1850s and made himself President. He was shot by firing squad in Honduras. And that is about the sum of popular knowledge. Since the Sandinistas came to power ten years ago, Walker has had a revival of infamy here, in speeches and newspaper articles. Hollywood is to make a film condemning him. But still his career is a matter of legend.

The same is true of Rubén Darío. Years ago I had read two of his poems in an anthology, and knew vaguely that he had been a diplomat. Then I read the startling lines on his monument, here in Managua. A Nicaraguan lady told me Darío was no longer considered to be a great poet, but sent me a book of his early verses. She suggested I look for more at the 'Good Grass' café, a vegetarian restaurant and left-wing bookshop, near to the Plaza España. It is hot, stuffy and thick with flies that seem to enjoy the carrot cutlets. Many books showed on their cover the

28

horrible face of Lenin. All they had of Darío was a collection of newspaper articles, most of them hostile to the United States.

The same frustration greeted my search for knowledge about the third most famous man in Nicaragua's history, Augusto César Sandino. Wherever I go I see his face — thin, cruel and cunning under a stetson hat — but all I could find on him was a hagiographic biography by an Argentine Marxist. I knew he had fought the US Marines and been done to death by the first Somoza. About his motives and his beliefs, I still knew virtually nothing. Here in Managua, the character and the history of the country come down to slogans, speeches, or those ubiquitous pictures after the style of Diego Rivera, crudely splashed on adobe walls. Debate is reduced to a scream of hatred against the United States, and much of it screamed by Americans.

These anti-United States Americans are just as troubling in their way as anti-Semitic Jews. Do Nicaraguans share this hatred? Does it go back to their history, and if so, why? These questions disturb and puzzle me as much as Managua itself, this city of wasteland, surrounded by outer suburbs. Pondering all these questions after the evening shower, I went to the Intercontinental to catch *el happy*, the happy hour.

At the door of the bar, a Nicaraguan grabbed my arm, 'You don't want to go in there. It's full of gunmen. They're Tomás Borge's bodyguard.' Like most of the Commandantes and even quite lowly army officers, Borge, the Minister of the Interior, goes around with a bevy of strong-arm men, like a gangster boss from old Shanghai or Chicago. I went to the bar and bought a drink then, turning round, saw Borge with Graham Greene.

The next evening, Borge and his bodyguard had gone but Greene was there with a young woman interpreter and a bearded, goat-like man who proved to be Chu-Chu, the Panamanian Marxist mathematician and army sergeant whom Greene has described in *Getting to Know the General*. With some diffidence I

introduced myself to Greene, who remembered one or two
things I had written and proved most kind and affable during
several chats in Managua. He talked about friends and a certain
foe in London; about *Getting to Know the General* and Panama;
about Evelyn Waugh and Auberon Waugh who had recently
written that Greene slept with a loaded revolver under his
pillow. 'Absolute rubbish!' He talked about the attempt to get
him to lead a Central American 'peace march', kicking off in
Panama. 'Not on your life!' In spite of a recent operation for
cancer, Greene looked fit, cheerful and vigorous. 'I've had an
extraordinary day,' he said one evening, 'a vegetarian lunch and
nothing to drink till five.'

Although chatting freely on most subjects Greene was reluctant to talk about Nicaragua, although he has written about it in
Getting to Know the General and many letters to newspapers,
defending the Sandinistas. After this visit in 1985, Greene replied
to claims that the Sandinistas were persecuting the Church or
teaching militarism in schools. He described how he and Borge,
walking along the streets of León, had noticed everywhere
pictures and statuettes of the Virgin.

But in conversation with me at least, Greene would not discuss
the Sandinista government. He told me that he was hoping to visit
the 'Popular Church' of Santa María de los Angeles, but would not
enter into a talk on liberation theology. Nor can I blame him for
this. A critic has poured scorn on those who fail to tackle Greene
about his political statements, in 'so-called interviews when a
flabby and deferential "interviewer" (often no more than a
sounding-board, or even a doormat) greets his observations with a
sycophantic silence'. Of course, I had not asked for an interview.
Probably Mr Greene was aware that I do not share his views
about Central America. But even if this had been an interview, I
do not see why Greene should have to be cross-examined. He is
not a politician running for office, in front of a television journalist.
He is a writer, and says what he wants to say in the written word.

Nevertheless it troubled me that a man of whom I have stood in awe since childhood, and now regard as the greatest living English writer, should be such a friend of the Sandinistas, consorting with men like Borge, whom I regard as a terrorist. Although Greene hates to be called a 'Catholic novelist', he nevertheless has written books full of religious meaning, like *The Power and the Glory*. Why does he now support the Popular Church, defying the Pope? His friend Tomás Borge, when asked to define the Christian element in Communism, answered that 'State coercion is love'.

Greene's attitude to Nicaragua baffles me; especially because on most other subjects I share his point of view. He is against all 'isms' and 'ocracies'. So am I. Although he spent many years in Africa, he never campaigned for African self-government. In some ways I share his antipathy to the United States. In general I think religion more important than politics.

These are weighty matters on which to brood in a Nicaraguan hotel bar. Yet somehow, in this obscure country, you find yourself faced by global dilemmas: of Communism versus Capitalism; Religion versus Revolution; Spanish-Indian culture versus the Anglo-Saxon; Morality versus the Playboy Ethic. Nicaragua is a tiny stage on which the rest of the world can see performed its cosmic drama.

With this in mind, I set out on a series of journeys around the country to try and discern not only what is happening now, but the history of the people. In particular I wanted to learn of the three great figures in Nicaragua's past: William Walker, the soldier of fortune; Rubén Darío, the poet; and General Sandino, the partisan. In search of the first of these, William Walker, I went to the south-west corner of Nicaragua, the scene of his major triumphs and infamies.

2

GRANADA

IN THE DRIVE south-west from Managua to Granada, you follow
the range of volcanoes that runs through Central America and
beyond, to the Andes. Here the volcanoes are closely bunched
together and spring from the coastal plain; so they are quite
distinct from ordinary mountains. Nicaragua is also unusual in
having two great lakes. The only other great lake in the Andes
chain, Lake Titicaca, lies in the mountains at ten thousand feet,
but Lake Managua and Lake Nicaragua lie near sea level. Granada,
like Managua, grew at the side of a lake, as did the third main
city León, which later was forced to move by earthquake and
volcanic eruption. Almost everywhere in this land of lakes, you
are conscious of the volcanoes on the horizon. The cones that
are active are naked of vegetation; so, alas, are most of the dead
volcanoes and much of the valley, for soil erosion has followed
the cutting down of the forests. Between the fields of maize and
sorghum lie patches of scrub and stunted trees, but not the
luxuriant growth one might expect in the tropics, and from this
fertile, volcanic earth. Perhaps because there are only three
million people (and probably less, with so many fled into exile)
in what is the largest Central American country, Nicaragua has
not suffered as badly as others from deforestation or soil erosion.
Little El Salvador has six million people, with scarcely an acre of

arable land to spare. The Costa Ricans to the south have almost destroyed their rain forest with its incomparable natural life, to make grazing land for their beef cattle, reared to be hamburgers in the United States.

On the way to Managua one passes Masaya which, like most Nicaraguan towns, is set back from the road. Most of the people are full-blooded Indians, with dark, coppery skin, a piercing stare and often a rather quizzical smile. They are famous for handicrafts and growing flowers, which made Masaya attractive to weekend visitors from Managua. However, the town was severely smashed ten years ago by tanks and planes of Somoza's army, and is still in disrepair. My driver fretted throughout the time I spent around Masaya. 'The people are bad here,' he said. Because they are Indian? No, because they don't like the other Nicaraguan Indians. As usual, when I endeavoured to probe these matters of race and tribal division, I met with evasiveness. Even in western Nicaragua, where most of the population is of mixed Spanish and Indian blood, there are undercurrents of racial hostility. On the Atlantic coast, I learned from those who have got permission to go there, the blacks, Indians and people of mixed race do not care for the Spanish at all.

My driver did not approve of Granada people any more than of those from Masaya. This was not for the reason normally offered, that the Granada people are stuck-up, priest-ridden, mean and reactionary. My driver said that Granada people could not play baseball. Then he said they went in for incest. 'You will see many imbeciles there,' he told me. I never did. What struck me about Granada, as soon as we reached the Jalteva suburb, were fine streets, sturdy adobe houses in the colonial Spanish style, and a great church from the eighteenth century. Only now did I realise how, in Managua, I had been starved of good architecture the sense of history. It was like leaving some hideous housing estate and coming to Oxford.

When it came to finding a place to stay, I turned to the *South*

American Handbook, that legendary guide which every serious traveller, including Graham Greene, carries about with him in this part of the world. In grading hotels by price from A to F, the Handbook will often come up with a charming pension at bargain price, but I did not like the sound of Granada's entries, 'Pension Vargas, F, basic, clean, has an incontinent dog, unfriendly, to be avoided at all costs. Pension Cigarra, F, short stay. Thieves.' I decided to treat myself to the Hotel Alhambra, although it charges in dollars like the hotels in Managua. The shower and the electric fan were working; the chef does a good sirloin of beef, with sauté potatoes and salad that does not give you diseases; above all, there are rocking chairs on the balcony facing the Plaza.

The Plaza is everything I had ever hoped to find in Spanish America. If it does not actually look like Seville, it looks at least like Seville in the set of an old production of *Don Giovanni*, surrounded by houses with colonnades and balconies from which, one imagines, the señoritas flirted and threw down flowers. Since this is also Central America, one can envisage how, from those same balconies, squat politicians issued pronunciamientos, and gold-toothed generals spat contemptuously down on wailing women who followed their dead to church. This Plaza belongs to the age of Conrad's Central American novel *Nostromo*. There are no high-rise buildings because of the danger of earthquakes. Due to the petrol shortage, horsemen and horse-drawn cabs vie with the motor car. The Plaza has all the correct ingredients, such as dust, royal palm trees, cooing or chattering birds, a fountain, a statue of 'Mother, to whom all abnegation and love', cowboys in broad sombreros and schoolgirls eating ice-cream. Although I have never seen the bandstand in action, I frequently heard from a church or a street parade the favourite Nicaraguan brass-band music in three-four time, at once plaintive and harsh and sweet.

At sunset, I took one of the rocking chairs on the terrace, drank beer and studied *Antología*, a volume of verse by Ernesto

Cardenal, the Marxist priest who is now a cabinet minister. He comes from an old Granada family and used to live in a monastery on an island in the lake, from where he started an armed uprising against the Somoza government. The book contains some of the modern-day psalms he wrote for use in services of the Popular Church. Here is a sample of Psalm 15:

> El Señor es mi parcela de tierra en la Tierra Prometida
> Me tocó en suerte bella tierra
> en la repartición agraria de la Tierra Prometida.
> (*The Lord is my plot of land in the Promised Land*
> *There was given to me by chance fine land*
> *in the agrarian distribution of the Promised Land.*)

Or Psalm 34:

> Tu nos librarás del dictador
> de los explotadores del proletario y el pobre
> Alzáronse contra mí testigos falsos
> para preguntarme lo que ni sabía . . .
> (*Oh Lord, Thou wilt deliver us from the dictator*
> *from the exploiters of the proletariat and the poor*
> *False witnesses will arise against me*
> *To question me about things I do not even know.*)

It is comforting, in a way, to find that the Church of England does not have a monopoly in producing tendentious and ugly renderings of the Bible. What surprised me was to find that some of Cardenal's poems were rather good. I like his long poem on William Walker. Although, of course, Cardenal condemns him as an imperialist Yankee, I think I detect admiration as well, from one military man for another.

The cover of the book has a photograph of the author's face in white beard and long hair under a beret and horn-rimmed spectacles. He is looking down in a gesture of modesty, but the mouth expresses self-righteousness. It is the kind of face you always see on marches and demonstrations and very often on television. I put the book face down on the table. As I did so I found I was being observed by a man in the neighbouring rocking chair, a sallow, heavy-lidded man of impassive expression. What did I think of Cardenal, he asked. I answered that I had just been reading Cardenal's poem on William Walker, 'Is it true,' I went on, 'that Walker had people shot in the very Plaza in front of us?' 'No,' said the sallow man, 'he had them shot at the wall behind the Franciscan church. Walker,' he went on, 'shot few people compared with the Sandinistas, who killed hundreds here in the Plaza in 1979.'

'Really?' I asked, intending to show I did not believe the story. The Sandinistas did to death many prisoners in La Pólvora gaol in Granada but none in public. The foreign press would have reported it.

'Perhaps,' I suggested, 'the Sandinistas shot a few of Somoza's National Guard. The ones who might have committed atrocities.' My new acquaintance would not accept this equivocation. He said that eighty per cent of Somoza's National Guard were now employed by the Sandinista police force. He said that most of the Sandinista ruling class were sons and daughters of the Somoza élite.

On a wall nearby, I had noticed bright red graffiti, asking for foreign currency for *Advance* the Communist journal, '*Exigimos Divisos Para Advance*'. Underneath had been scrawled in another hand, '¡*Pídanlos a Reagan!*' (Ask Reagan for them!). 'Can anyone write slogans?' I asked my new acquaintance.

'It's a lie,' he said. 'It's to make the foreigners think that there's freedom of expression. In fact only the government is allowed to write on walls. They wrote both slogans, the one asking for currency and the one blaming Reagan.'

In countries like this, it makes me feel nervous to hear attacks on the government from a stranger. Either the speaker has some kind of sinister motive or he is taking a risk. I decided to shift back to the safer subject of William Walker. The heavy-lidded man for the first time opened his eyes wide. He smacked his right fist into the palm of his upturned left hand and said, 'Walker was a pederast, like Rock Hudson.'

After my dinner at the Alhambra, I joined in the bar with a group drinking Nica Libre, or Coca-Cola with local rum. A man in his forties said he had fought in the civil war in the army of Edén Pastora, the famous Conservative who became a Sandinista and then, more recently, took arms against them. 'I got this scar fighting with Edén Pastora,' he said in English, pulling a sock down to show me his battered ankle. Where had he fought with Pastora? 'On the southern front, fighting across the border from Costa Rica.' This was by far the heaviest of the fighting against Somoza, in which both sides engaged in conventional war. 'What sort of man is Edén Pastora?' I asked. 'A father many times. He loves many women,' was all the reply I got, but everybody agrees that Edén Pastora is much the most original and amusing of all these Central American warrior chiefs.

The man with the ankle wound had been at school and university in New England. 'I knew the Kennedys. I really admire Teddy Kennedy and I hope he will be the next President. I knew the Kennedys at school. I used to play football with them. I got this scar playing football against the Kennedys.' We drank a lot more Nica Libres.

The drunken wife of the scarred man took my hand. I apparently reminded her of a doctor who had done an operation on her in West Virginia. The other woman present became very pious with drink. She said it was wrong that young Nicaraguan women were forced to go to pick coffee up in the mountains without a chaperon. 'Nicaraguan girls always used to be virgins at marriage,' she told me. 'They should not be given the contraceptive pill.' Her husband, who had been watching in silence, afterwards took me aside and said that he too was writing a book, 'Each chapter heading is a girl's name. There are forty chapters, but it is not pornographic. It's very well written but I want to have it published under another name.' Was he frightened of what his wife might think? 'No, but I have certain moral feelings.' The scarred man went on talking about the United States and its present aggressive attitude towards Nicaragua, 'Reagan's a madman. He's making us eat shit. He's going to turn Nicaragua into a Vietnam. I know what Vietnam was like. I fought there and got wounded there . . .' With a fumbling hand, he once more pulled down his sock to show me the scar on his ankle.

Across the Plaza from the Alhambra there stands the ancient Cathedral where William Walker attended Mass; he converted to Rome soon after taking Granada. However, a plaque on the front records that this was one of the buildings burned on Walker's instructions after he left the city in 1856. A priest apparently braved the flames to rescue the monstrance. Every schoolboy here and throughout Central America, and even in countries as far away as Argentina and Chile, has heard of the wicked William Walker and how he planted a spear in the ground with the banner '¡Aquí fue Granada!' (Here stood Granada!) Everyone knows that Granada was razed to the ground and yet, quite clearly, this did not happen. Walker intended to sack Granada. He afterwards claimed to have sacked Granada. He says in his memoirs that most of his army were drunk and no doubt looted many buildings and then set fire to them afterwards. Yet most of Granada remained undamaged or merely scorched. The stone buildings retained their walls and the houses made of adobe brick were easily put together again. The old church at Jalteva, whose repairs were completed only last year (1988), was actually damaged by civil war one year before Walker landed in Nicaragua.

Whereas in Managua you get no sense of the country's history and therefore its character, here in Granada you have an overwhelming sense of the past, in which William Walker appears as a quite recent intruder. One can still see most of the fort that was built when the city was founded in 1524, a mere thirty-two years after Columbus's first voyage. In that same *annus mirabilis*, 1492, King Ferdinand and Queen Isabella of Spain had at last completed the liberation of the Peninsula from Moorish rule, by winning Granada, the city from which this one in America takes its name. Also, in that same *annus mirabilis*, Ferdinand and Isabella passed a decree whose baleful results still trouble the world. This was the expulsion or the conversion by force of hundreds of thousands of Jews who formed the middle class in Spain. Many of the converted Jews went off to the new American colonies, where the Inquisition was not so keen. One or two of the famous old families here in Granada are said to be of Jewish ancestry.

Columbus himself visited Nicaragua on his fourth expedition in 1502. The ship's boats were sent over the bar to get food and water but one was swamped by the surf and two of the sailors drowned. Columbus called the place Rio de los Desastres. The Spanish eventually settled in towns like Granada, near the Pacific coast, because of the great fertility of the soil. And Granada had a still greater importance because, like Panama, it is a natural crossing place between the Atlantic and the Pacific. It is not, measured in miles, the narrowest stretch of the Central American isthmus, but Lake Nicaragua occupies much of the distance between the two oceans. Although the lake is near the Pacific coast, it flows out eastwards down the San Juan River and, ultimately, to the Atlantic. Fish from the Atlantic come up river, so that tourists who bathe in Lake Nicaragua risk getting attacked by man-eating sharks as well as infection from the polluted water.

In Granada, more than anywhere else I know in Latin America, I feel the excitement that comes from a deep awareness of history. After reading the rubbishy Marxist psalms by Father Ernesto Cardenal, one can go to the fortress church of San Francisco and ponder the fact that there preached Las Casas, also known as the Apostle of the Indies, who almost alone in the sixteenth century, championed the interests of the conquered Indian people. That was true liberation theology.

Nicaragua stood out from the rest of Central America because it was almost always engaged not only in wars against neighbouring countries but also civil war between the towns of León and Granada. There had been jealousy between them even in Spanish times. León was the Spanish government town, with the civil servants. It therefore tended to favour high taxation against the interests of the farmers and traders, whose centre of power was here in Granada. This also meant that León people were more Spanish and white than Granada people, who had a larger proportion of Indian blood. Some people claim they can see the distinction today, but I cannot. There may also be ancient divisions between the Indians living in these two regions, hostility dating to pre-Conquest days.

In the first two decades of the nineteenth century, the only demands for independence came from Granada. The Spanish government crushed the rebels by execution, imprisonment and confiscation of property. The citizens of León applauded and plundered Granada's citizens resident in their town. From independence, in 1821, until the arrival of William Walker, the general hired by León, the two towns were constantly fighting. After Walker's departure, in 1858, the two towns patched up their quarrel and built a new capital in Managua, unhappily on an earthquake centre. However, the enmity between León and Granada did not die down and still underlies Nicaraguan politics. The Sandinistas belong to the old León tradition of liberalism, whose heroes were William Walker, Rubén Darío, General Sandino and the Somoza family. The Granada tradition, both clerical and conservative, has found its natural leader in Archbishop Obando. Of course, the followers of Obando are not confined to Granada; they are these days almost as numerous in León. But Granada embodies a certain political attitude which most outside observers ignore or misunderstand.

You can see the history of Granada written on plaques and monuments. You see at once that much of the fighting that has occurred here took place either before or since the cruel boast by Walker 'Aquí fue Granada'. For instance, at the Jalteva Church, you read 'Built in 1781–83 and half demolished during the civil war in 1854'.

There is a monument to 'The Heroes of 1811 and 1821 who fought the Spanish' next to a statue of one who died in 1979 'fighting the beasts', meaning the troops of Somoza. The Post Office is named after Blanca Auzaz de Sandino, telegraphist, revolutionary and wife of the General of Free Men, which is one of the titles given to Sandino.

Most of the plaques in Granada have something to do with the family of the Chamorros who ruled this city and sometimes all Nicaragua. In front of Jalteva church, there is a plaque to General Joaquín Chamorro, President of Nicaragua from 1875 to 1879, 'who brought in the railway, the telegraph, property registration and compulsory education'. The plaque to Dr Evaristo Carazo, President of Nicaragua from 1887 to 1889, a man who 'distinguished himself against the filibuster William Walker ... advanced education and opened important roads', was unveiled in 1976 by the Mayor, Alvaro Chamorro. The Chamorros who came from Seville in the eighteenth century are, by tradition, attached to the land-owning interest, the Church and the Conservative Party, but this last does not signify what it does elsewhere so much as hostility to León and the Liberal Party. The enemies of the Chamorros, like William Walker, Sandino and the Somozas, were all from the Liberal faction. Most of the opposition to the Somozas came from Conservatives like Pedro Joaquín Chamorro, the editor of *La Prensa*, whose murder in 1978 sparked off the final revolt. The most famous Sandinista hero, Eden Pastora, also started as a Conservative.

Although most Chamorros now are in opposition, and some are involved with the Contras, others are Sandinistas. The division within the Chamorro clan divided the family newspaper *La Prensa*. For a few weeks after the Sandinista take-over in July 1979, *La Prensa* gave its blessing to the newcomers. When it went into opposition, some of the left-wing journalists joined the Sandinista organ *Barricada*. Others created *El Nuevo Diario*, a paper that takes the side of the Sandinistas in more subtle language. The strife among the Chamorros is evident in the mastheads of the three newspapers: *La Prensa*, Director General, Engineer Jaimie Chamorro C.; *El Nuevo Diario*, Director, Engineer Xavier Chamorro C.; *Barricada*, Director, Carlos F. Chamorro. The Sandinistas soon made *La Prensa* liable to a censorship so severe and so capricious that often it could not appear. Sandinista mobs threatened to burn down its premises. Newsagents and street vendors were beaten up. Reporters were often arrested on trumped up charges. In a reference to the staff of *La Prensa*, the Minister of the Interior, Tomás Borge, declared that if the Contras ever arrived at Managua, they would find only dead bodies, because the Sandinistas would kill their enemies. 'We will skin them alive,' he said. Another Sandinista leader, Humberto Ortega, said (10 October 1981) that, 'the staff of *La Prensa* will be the first to be strung up along the highways.'

The Somozas never actually shut *La Prensa* because its existence proved there was freedom of speech. The murder in 1978 of Pedro Joaquín Chamorro was widely blamed at the time on one or several of the Somozas, but others think it may have been done by racketeers whom *La Prensa* had exposed in print. The Sandinistas also value *La Prensa* as daily proof of their tolerance. However, their patience is short and in 1986 they closed the paper. Early in 1988, as part of a deal for ending the civil war, the Sandinistas allowed *La Prensa* to start up again. Perhaps conscious of its position as a factor in the peace agreement, *La Prensa* became intemperate in its attacks on the Sandinistas.

The Chamorro family might not care to remember the fact, but Granada once published its own newspaper, *El Nicaraguense*, an elegant weekly in Spanish and English. This was during the rule of President William Walker, himself a talented journalist. Some ten years ago the Bank of America in Managua reprinted in book form a number of articles from *El Nicaraguense* and others from *Harper's Weekly*, a New York magazine whose extensive coverage of this part of the world was illustrated by artists' impressions. They help to remind us that during the two years from 1855, Walker and Nicaragua were the number one newspaper story in the United States, rather as Colonel Oliver North and Nicaragua, were the number one item on television in 1988. The almost eerie resemblance between those two men is one of the things that haunted me during my stay in Nicaragua. The old newspaper articles and drawings also give an impression of Walker and his 'immortals' which is very different from Nicaraguan folklore.

For one thing, Walker actually captured Granada with scarcely a shot fired in anger. He had put his own men and his Nicaraguan allies on to a ship at Virgen, down the shore of the lake, and landed them three miles north of Granada, which was expecting attack from the south. At three in the morning of 13 October 1855, the march on the town began in darkness and silence. The Democrats, as Walker described his men, serving the Democrat town of León, 'had got to within half a mile of the town, and the first rays of the rising sun had begun to warm the eastern heavens, when suddenly all the bells of the city were heard ringing a quick and joyful peal. Some of the Americans thought the bells were a signal of alarm and that their tone showed confidence on the part of the enemy. But the ringing was really to celebrate a victory . . . over the Democrats two days earlier.' The bells were still pealing when Walker's men entered the suburbs, threw off their coats and blankets and rushed the first barricade. The last few shots were fired from the Government House as Walker entered the Plaza in front of my hotel. The only loss to his force was a Nicaraguan drummer boy, killed by a stray bullet.

The citizens of Granada found to their amazement that Walker forbade the murder, looting and arson that normally followed the capture of cities in Central America. His own Nicaraguan allies, the Democrats of León, were most indignant at being deprived of their usual amusement, like dragging their foes behind a galloping horse. Walker released from gaol a hundred political prisoners, for there were Democrats in Granada. He arrested an equal number of the Legitimists, also known as 'Chamorrists', but set them free on bail in the cognizance of foreign residents.

A Protestant born and bred, and once a Freemason, Walker had recently turned to the Roman Catholic Church, and was to die clutching a crucifix in front of the firing squad. The day after he took Granada, Walker and some of his officers attended eight o'clock Mass, where the sermon was preached by what we would now describe as a 'liberation theologian', a priest who had started life as a lawyer and Democrat politician. He praised Walker and scolded his fellow Granadians. 'I have preached peace, liberty and progression to you, and you have cried for more blood. Look at this man, General Walker, sent by providence to bring peace, prosperity and happiness to this blood-stained country. We all owe him and his brave men, many thanks.'

As far as one can make out, Walker remained on good terms with the Church in Nicaragua. On Christmas Eve, he ordered his men to leave the taverns and kneel in prayer outside the Cathedral. He did not drink or smoke but he was not an ascetic.

A correspondent of *Harper's Weekly*, has given us this description of Walker's stay in Granada:

While Granada was the General's headquarters, he lived in an easy, dashing style. He occupied a commodious house; superior French cooks were in his kitchen and his table groaned in a contented, quiet way with all the delicacies of the country. It is said that you only need money in Nicaragua to procure

everything desirable. You can get the finest of beef; venison
can be had almost for the killing; fowls, eggs and delicious fish
from the lake are in abundance, and nearly every variety of
vegetable found in the markets of New York can be had to
order. At Granada, up to the time he left it, General Walker
was accustomed to give *soirées*, sometimes as often as once a
week. A very neat ball-room was fitted up at his quarters and
the music was supplied by an excellent band. The cream of the
native population of the town were usually in attendance, the
ladies being dressed in elegant style. The officers of the 'Army
of Occupation' were present in force, sporting white kid
gloves and bestowing excruciating attentions on the fair sex.
A sumptuous repast was invariably served up during the
evening and champagne and punch flowed freely at all times.

One American historian has suggested that many of Walker's
volunteers had come in search of a Nicaraguan girl-friend, especially the men from California, where women were scarce. Walker
himself was not tempted, certainly not by his hostess in Granada,
a middle-aged widow of a politician. Walker did not fall for the
scented, tropical beauty of Nicaragua.

Apart from razing the city to the ground which, so it seems to
me, did not actually happen, the main crime levelled at Walker
during his rule in Granada was executing some of the local
politicians, including the former foreign minister, Mateo Mayorga. Another victim, General Corral, admitted his guilt but
asked for mercy in order to spare the feelings of his daughters.
The priest who had welcomed Walker a few days earlier, joined
in the plea for mercy. But Walker was unmoved. As he wrote in
his memoirs, 'The daughters of Corral, accompanied by many of
the women of the city, came with sobs of anguish and terror to
attempt what the priest had failed to accomplish.' Corral was led
to the Plaza, in front of where I was sitting, and shot in the
Spanish-American fashion, kneeling and with his back to the guns.
His family and admirers afterwards gathered round the still

45

quivering body, clipped locks of his hair and dipped their handkerchiefs in the blood. The Granada people mourned but were not outraged. Corral admitted betraying Walker. Death by shooting was the conventional fate of political losers; it was dignified and dramatic. If Walker had not been there, the troops from León would have massacred scores of Granada people, as was their custom.

Even his vow to destroy Granada was calculated, so Walker afterwards wrote, to punish political enemies and to satisfy political friends, the Democrats of León, 'While the voice of one party was that of wailing and woe at the loss of its cherished city, the other party could not suppress its feeling of triumph and exaltation.' The actual destruction was probably no worse than that which Granada had suffered from other invading armies, like that which destroyed Jalteva church. It was certainly not as bad as the battering given most Nicaraguan towns during the war ten years ago. Walker is singled out for obloquy because he made the mistake of writing a book to justify his behaviour.

3

SAN JUAN DEL SUR

ON THE SHORE of the lake, about half a mile from Granada, there are signs of a half-hearted effort to make a resort, with open-air cafés, hamburger stalls and strolling marimba players. Some of the children bathe, in spite of the sewage pollution and man-eating sharks. There are herons and egrets to look at and, in the distance, if you have very good eyes, the twin volcanoes on Ometepe island. Although I have heard that Somoza used to race round the lake in a speedboat (and fling his foes to the sharks according to rumour) I have not seen any pleasure boats or, come to think of it, one of the ferries alleged to run to the islands. This may be for security reasons. Father Ernesto Cardenal once launched an attack by boat on the fort at San Carlos, where the San Juan River flows out of the lake towards the Atlantic. The Contras might try the same thing. The length of the river is stiff with Contras and also old-fashioned bandits, who once held up a 'Peace Ship' carrying North American radicals. The former Sandinista hero, Edén Pastora, who later raised a small army to fight them, once held a press conference just on the Nicaraguan side of the San Juan River. Somebody planted a bomb which killed or wounded several journalists. This was blamed, according to taste, on the Sandinistas, the CIA and the Contras, with whom Pastora does not care to be linked.

47

Further down the San Juan River, on the Atlantic coast, the people are mostly Blacks from Jamaica, or Mosquito (Miskito) Indians, who get on well with each other and intermarry, but join in disliking the 'Spanish' from western Nicaragua, especially the Sandinistas. Many are Protestant, English-speaking and fond of the Queen and Margaret Thatcher, at least to judge from those I have met in Managua. For a long time, England ruled the east coast of Nicaragua, as she until recently ruled British Honduras, now Belize, to the north.

Nicaragua's suitability for an inter-ocean route, or canal, lies at the root of her turbulent history, from Spanish times, through William Walker, the years of occupation by the United States Marines, and the recent attempts by Colonel North to throw out the Sandinistas. It explains why England, in 1782, sent Nelson to capture Granada from Spain; why England and the United States came close to war over Nicaragua during the 1850s; and why the Soviet Union is now supporting the army here.

The San Juan River, Lake Nicaragua and then a short stretch of land to San Juan del Sur on the Pacific, form the easiest natural link between the two oceans. Nicaragua was always the favourite site for the inter-ocean canal that was later built at Panama. It is still the favourite site for a new canal. Nicaragua holds in the New World, the same importance that Egypt holds in the Old World, controlling the link between oceans. Just as Britain and France were ready to go to war to hold the Suez Canal, so the United States is prepared to make war, using Colonel North's Contras, to guard what it sees as its interests in Nicaragua. And today, in the age of the automobile, Nicaragua straddles the isthmus and therefore the long Pacific Highway that runs just to the side of the lake.

It was along this highway that I pursued my search for the story of William Walker. But services are erratic and over-crowded, and always seem to begin in a distant suburb. The same applies to the shared taxi service. You may have to wait hours to find enough people to fill up the car. You generally end up getting a freelance taxi driver. It costs very little but nevertheless is a rather furtive operation, and drivers are fearful of leaving their own province and going through the police checkpoints. In Granada, trying to reach the coast at San Juan del Sur, I waited almost all morning in a suburb beneath the volcano.

In the café near to the bus station, I sat down and ordered one of those sickly, gaseous soft drinks that are actually called *gaseosos*. Soon I was joined by two young men whom I instantly took to be 'Sandalistas', the jeering name given to foreign friends of the Revolution. Although they wore shoes rather than sandals, and no slogans appeared on their T-shirts in favour of Fidel Castro or Nelson Mandela, their beards sounded a danger alarm, so that I fully expected to have to listen to half an hour, at least, on the contradictions and sins of 'late capitalism'. But I was wrong. They were not 'Sandalistas', or ideologues of any description, but two Swiss university graduates spending a year in Latin America. They had passed four happy months at a Spanish language school in Antigua, the beautiful and mysterious city of ruins in Guatemala, then made their way slowly through El Salvador and Honduras. All three of those countries, especially El Salvador, are prone to violence and, in the eyes of the left, are victims of Yankee imperialism. These two young Swiss had come to no harm; indeed it was here in Nicaragua, so they told me, that they had for the first time encountered hostility. People would not speak to them. Several times, they said, they had been refused service in cafés or restaurants. Why were the Nicaraguans so unfriendly? Perhaps, I suggested, because they were young and bearded, the Nicaraguans took them for 'Sandalistas', for friends of the present regime, as I had at first done. I tried to explain to them just how much most Nicaraguans loathe the people who come to admire the regime that impoverishes and oppresses them. It is still more galling because these foreigners can exploit the money exchange rate to live in considerable

49

luxury. Even at my age, at which only a few madmen still believe in the Revolution, I find Nicaraguans often suspicious, though I have not encountered the open hatred I did in El Salvador, from those who support the right-wing death squads.

When I at last found someone to drive me to San Juan del Sur, he turned out to be a person of affluence, with a splendid villa and brand-new station wagon. He also turned out to be a Sandinista, the first I had actually met in Nicaragua. He told me that all the economic troubles of Nicaragua were due to the economic blockade by the United States, which, he said, was entirely unprovoked. Of course, I had read this often enough in *Barricada* and *El Nuevo Diario* but I had never actually heard it said in private conversation. The argument simply does not stand up to serious scrutiny. When the Sandinistas seized power after a revolution not of their making, the American President, Jimmy Carter, went out of his way to befriend the regime. The United States was, for a long time, the largest donor of aid. By way of thanks, the Sandinistas called in thousands of Russians, Cubans and Libyans and launched a hysterical propaganda campaign against the United States. They also gave arms to the Communist rebels in El Salvador. Soon they had alienated not just the United States but even the most liberal-minded of Latin American countries, such as Costa Rica. Their only friends in the hemisphere were Cuba and for a short time the preposterous and vicious little dictatorship in Grenada. The driver was rather surprised to meet a foreigner who was not a Sandinista, so for the rest of the journey he did not talk about politics. He talked instead on the favourite Nicaraguan topic of earthquakes and volcanic eruptions, especially the common belief that various animals, especially monkeys and dogs, can sense them coming.

Passing Ometepe Island and coming close to the Costa Rican frontier, we turned off on the road to San Juan del Sur, where there is less than twenty miles between the lake and the ocean. It was here on this little-used and badly maintained roadway that

150 years ago the United States and Britain began their search for an inter-ocean canal, a plan that the Spanish had not even attempted during their three hundred years of empire. The introduction of steam ships increased the interest in the proposed canal. The British thought of it in terms of commercial advantage. Since the days of Hawkins, Drake and Raleigh, the British had tried to get into trade with Latin America, first as pirates, then as colonists in the West Indies and strips of the mainland including Nicaragua. The English statesman Lord Canning was thinking of Spanish-American trade when he talked of 'bringing the new world into existence to redress the balance of the old'. The United States took little commercial interest in places like Nicaragua. Their energy was devoted to the expansion west rather than south. And as they started to dream of capturing California, so they wanted a sea route linking the oceans. The overland route to the west was slow and menaced by hostile Indians. The sea route round Cape Horn was long and troubled by storms. Panama, the eventual canal route, was then considered too mountainous and unhealthy. And so they explored the terrain between Lake Nicaragua and San Juan del Sur.

A retired English naval officer, Captain Bailey, made a detailed survey during the 1830s. He rather unwisely passed his findings to the US diplomat doing research for the opposition. When this American, John L. Stephens, reached San Juan he met with disappointment. The harbour was desolate, bare of shipping and ringed with primeval forest. For miles there was not a house. 'I walked the shore alone,' he afterwards wrote. 'Since Mr Bailey left, not a person had visited it; and probably the only thing that keeps it alive even in memory, is the theorising of scientific men or the occasional visit of some Nicaraguan fisherman, too lazy to work, who seeks his food from the sea. It seemed preposterous to consider it the focus of a great commercial enterprise.'

That description by Stephens is not unsuited to San Juan today. The port has a desolate air. The warehouses are shut. The

51

only ship in the harbour is wrecked and half-submerged. The restaurants on the sea front are mostly shut, patronised only by Scandinavian 'Sandalistas'. According to the *South American Handbook*, there are are some rock caves round the point, and excellent beaches fifteen kilometres away, 'but ask the local authorities if they are safe to visit (Contra activity)'.

A Sandalista told me that in Somoza's time, San Juan del Sur was patronised by the rich bourgeoisie from Managua. He said this with disapproval. But I suspect that in those days plenty of poorer Nicaraguans made their way to the seaside, just as the poor of London or Manchester got to Brighton or Blackpool. In Managua, people complain that they cannot afford the petrol to get to the seaside where, they allege, some of the best beaches are commandeered by the army.

So, even as a tourist attraction, San Juan del Sur disappointed the hopes of Stephens, writing in 1842:

> If the peace of Europe be not disturbed, I am persuaded that the time is not too far distant when the attention of the whole civilised and mercantile world will be directed towards it; and steamboats will give the final impulse. In less than a year, English mailboats will be steaming to Cuba, Jamaica and the principal ports of Spanish America, touching once a month at San Juan and Panama. To men of leisure and fortune, jaded with rambling over the ruins of the old world, a new country will be opened. After a journey on the Nile, a day in Petra and a bath in the Euphrates, English and American travellers will be bitten by moschetoes on the lake of Nicaragua and drink champagne and Burton Ale on the desolate shores of San Juan on the Pacific.

I thought of these words with bitterness as I sat on the beach at San Juan del Sur, a man of neither leisure nor fortune, drinking another disgusting *gaseoso*.

What brought the steamships, fame, prosperity and eventually William Walker to San Juan del Sur had nothing to do with jaded

52

English tourists. It was the Californian gold rush. Adventurers from the United States had already taken Texas from Mexico. They were constantly moving further west. When war broke out in 1846 between the United States and Mexico, the Americans rose up and seized California, months before the Mexicans had acknowledged defeat elsewhere. By the treaty of Guadalupe–Hidalgo, signed between the two countries on 2 February 1848, Mexico ceded to the United States all the country north of the Rio Grande and westward to just below San Diego on the Pacific. In that same month, February 1848, one John A. Sutter discovered gold near Sacramento, precipitating an inrush of diggers and other adventurers. Within a year, the population of California had risen to 250,000.

At about this time, the East Coast shipping millionaire Cornelius Vanderbilt conceived the idea of starting a regular transit service in Nicaragua, using the San Juan River, the lake and perhaps a canal for the short stretch to the Pacific. He went to London in 1850 in search of capital for his venture and, having failed, decided to go ahead with the line on his own, using a road and not a canal for the Pacific stretch. He got from the Nicaraguan government a charter giving him rights in the name of the Accessory Transit Company. He improved the shallow and winding course of the river, built docks at the Atlantic coast, at Virgin Bay on the lake, and here in San Juan del Sur. In 1850 Vanderbilt personally came to Nicaragua and supervised the installation of two small steamers to ply the river, and one large vessel to cross the lake. Three ocean-going steamers were hired to carry passengers between San Juan del Sur and San Francisco, to synchronise with those from New York. A big, bumptious, hard-swearing and hard-fighting go-getter, Vanderbilt had created in Nicaragua the same efficiency as in his line of 'floating palaces', around New York.

As a result of Vanderbilt's efforts, the trans-Nicaraguan route cut two days off the Panama route and the fare was reduced

53

from 600 to 300 dollars. Although the tropical steamers were not 'floating palaces' the unpleasantness of the journey diminished. At first the road between the lake and San Juan del Sur had been 'truly horrible', to quote the account of one traveller:

> During the rainy season, many mules were killed by over-exertion, the road was of a soft, slippery, clayey character and very frequently I have seen mules dashing along, their backs covered by mud, and their heads only visible. Really, it was a swim through a muddy sea. Many travellers perished in this short transit. The hotels at Virgin Bay were composed of tents without floors; and for three coarse meals and a sleep in a hammock, strangers were charged four dollars a day, and very frequently too, were compelled to sleep in the mud all night, or probably for a series of nights, when the steamers did not connect.

The same author, Peter F. Stout, returning a year later, found macadamised roads and here, at San Juan del Sur, 'a large number of broad streets, some fine hotels, good houses and altogether it is North American in its character. The Custom House is located here and the Californian returning to the United States, considerably augmented its revenue.'

Cornelius Vanderbilt made so much money out of the Transit Company that in 1853 he decided to have the first holiday of his life, in his sumptuous steam yacht the *North Star*, taking with him his wife, children, sons-in-law, grandchildren and several guests, including a private chaplain, the Reverend Dr John Overton Goules, who later produced a sycophantic chronicle of the journey round Europe. Southampton was one of the English cities that gave a banquet to 'Commodore Vanderbilt', though, as Dr Goules observed, 'He on no occasion used his appellation . . . if anything, during the whole excursion to Europe, impressed me strongly as it regarded Mr Vanderbilt's deportment, it was his uniform, modest and dignified reserve.' Nevertheless, when a toast was proclaimed at Southampton to the President of the United States, and the audience rose to the band's performance of 'Hail Colombia', the Revd Goules observed that Commodore Vanderbilt and his friends 'were much pleased'.

While the English in England fêted Commodore Vanderbilt, the English in Nicaragua were attempting to wreck his Accessory Transit Company. They made no attempt to conceal what they were doing. Within days of the signature of the treaty of Guadalupe–Hidalgo; within days of the finding of Californian gold, the British had seized the town of San Juan del Norte, commanding the eastern end of the Nicaraguan transit route. That was on the 17 February 1848. The British claimed that San Juan, or 'Greytown', as they renamed it, lay in the Mosquito territory. The United States regarded the seizure as no more than a pretext for wrecking the route along the San Juan River. The settlement of San Juan del Norte was simply a mean collection of fifty or sixty thatched huts sheltering three hundred people, mostly Jamaicans, some outlaws but few with regular jobs. In the eyes of the US State Department, this seizure violated the Monroe doctrine and called for urgent diplomatic negotiations. The British agreed to talk – the seizure of Greytown was no doubt only a bargaining counter – and in 1850 the two countries signed what was called the Clayton–Bulwer treaty after the two statesmen responsible for their countries' foreign affairs. By this treaty, Britain and the United States agreed to join in the construction of a canal and further declared that neither of them would 'assume or exercise dominion over any part of Central America'.

Just before this treaty was ratified, Sir Henry Bulwer added, as an apparent afterthought, that he did not understand it to mean the renunciation of any existing British dependencies. His opposite number, Clayton, rather unwisely agreed, for it soon became apparent that Britain was still determined to keep her spoiling role at the mouth of the San Juan River. On 5 May 1854, Greytown arrested a Company employee and then the Company Agent who wanted to bail him out. On the 16th of that month, the captain of one of the Vanderbilt steamships shot a mutinous

Black boatman, at which the Greytown people attacked the United States minister, cutting his face with a broken bottle.

The squabble in a muddy creek now threatened to get out of hand. The US Secretary of State despatched to Greytown the warship *Cyane* with orders to consult with the US Commercial Agent and then to take any action requisite to preserve the country's interests. On the 12 June, the *Cyane* gave twenty-four hours notice of its intention to shell the village and carried out this threat, destroying everything but the property of a Frenchman who had taken the side of the Company. No lives were lost, but in the words of a patriotic American historian, 'It was a pitiable spectacle to see a great republic wasting its powder on the miserable huts of these outlaws, while the real offenders against its dignity sat quietly by, under the protecting folds of the Union Jack . . .'

The troubles of Vanderbilt with the British at the eastern end of the transit route were slight compared with the turmoil around the Pacific end, where Nicaraguans were engaged in an almost incessant civil war. In the six years leading up to 1855, there had been no less than fifteen presidents. The Transit Company passengers saw deserted fields, wrecked houses and walls pocked by bullet holes. If they visited any neighbouring town while awaiting a steamer connection, they found themselves challenged by sentries or blocked in their paths by barricades, if they did not actually hear any shooting. The more timid passengers cowered away from the violence of Nicaragua. Some of the young men found it exhilarating, and those from California, where women were in a minority of one in five, were thrilled to find a country where the reverse was true; and Nicaraguan women are delectable.

It was here, at San Juan del Sur, that William Walker and his 'Immortals' marched into the cockpit of Nicaraguan history. In 1853 a Nicaraguan president, a Leónese, died a natural death in office (itself an unheard-of occurrence), and in the election that followed, the winner was Fruto Chamorro, the most belligerent of that Granada clan. He exiled his vanquished opponent, who naturally came from León, then altered the constitution to double his term of office from two to four years. The Leónese, the Democrats, called in the help of Honduras and marched on Granada. After knocking down the Jalteva church, they gave up the siege and returned home to León in January 1855. Then the President of Honduras withdrew his army in order to march in the other direction, against Guatemala. The Leónese were desperate, for now they were out of office, they got no pickings from Vanderbilt and his Transit Company, nor the chance of robbing the transit passengers. They had already listened to the suggestion of Byron Cole, a Californian newspaper editor, that he recruit an American force to serve in the Democrat army. The man he suggested was Walker, a lawyer, doctor and journalist living in California, who had already commanded a military expedition south of the border.

Walker was born on the 8 May 1824 to parents of Scottish and Irish descent, living in Nashville, Tennessee. Having been called to the bar as well as being qualified as a doctor, he launched into New Orleans journalism, writing for the *Crescent*. Apparently, in those days journalists were well paid and Walker needed money to marry the girl of his choice, one Helen Martin, of whom we know nothing except her deafness. Walker learned sign language to talk with her. Then Helen Martin died in a yellow fever epidemic. Walker's mother, the only other being he ever loved, had also died, so the sad young man decided to break with the past and leave for California. It was then 1849, and the Gold Rush was on. Like most of the 'Fortyniners', Walker did not intend to pan for gold but to enrich himself from the general prosperity, either as lawyer or newspaperman.

During the six years in San Francisco before coming to Nicaragua, Walker made a name for himself as a combative newspaper writer and politician. In the great debate on slavery which had split California and Walker's Democrat Party, he took the side of the abolitionists. His claim to fame was the expedition he led in 1853 to try and annex the Mexican lands of Sonora and Lower California. Although he and his rag-taggle army were at last driven out, the American public took Walker seriously as a general. His troops obeyed his orders and discipline was so severe that he had men shot for desertion. When he returned from Mexico, Walker was hailed in San Francisco for patriotism and military genius. From someone who met him in Mexico, we have what remains the best description of Walker:

> During the brief visit of this afterwards-noted filibuster, the writer had an opportunity of seeing a good deal of him, and became greatly impressed with his astuteness and determination of character; for although sanguine in temperament, and insanely confident of success, still he evinced such a degree of caution as almost to disarm the suspicions of the Mexicans themselves before leaving them ... His appearance was anything but that of a military chieftain. Below the medium height and very slim, I should hardly imagine him to weigh over a hundred pounds (7st. 2lbs). His hair light and towy, while his almost white eyebrows and lashes concealed seemingly pupil-less, grey, cold eyes and his face was a mass of yellow freckles, the whole expression very heavy. His dress was scarcely less remarkable than his person. His head was sur-mounted by a huge white fur hat, whose long knap waved with the breeze, which, together with a very ill-made, short-waisted blue coat, with gilt buttons, and a pair of grey strapless pantaloons made up the ensemble of as unprepos-sessing-looking person as one would meet in a day's walk. I will leave you to imagine the figure in Guaymas with the thermometer at 100° ...

This was the curious figure who now left for Nicaragua.

William Walker and his fifty-two 'Immortals' or the 'Falanges', as some of the newspapers called them, sailed from San Francisco on 5 May 1855, arriving 1 June at Realejo, now Corinto, the main Pacific port of Nicaragua. They were met by the civilian and military leaders of León, who did not impress Walker — Castellón and Muñoz.

Soon after arriving, the 'Immortals' took Nicaraguan citizenship, which then could be done by a simple affirmation, and marched to León on foot while Walker rode because of a recent duelling injury. Before setting out, Walker had read almost everything that had been published on Nicaragua. What he saw on the journey confirmed his idea of a corrupt and oppressive country, especially that part under the government of his patrons and paymasters, the Democrats of León, 'The road from Chinodega to León passes through a country for which nature has done much and man has done little ... Under the shade of the magnificent ceiba might be seen halted a company of soldiers with their trousers rolled above their knees, but on close observation you could perceive that the sergeants and corporals were keenly watching lest some of their new recruits might have taken advantage of the halt to slip away for a moment and so escape hated service . . .' Walker was probably right to say that the poor of Nicaragua welcomed his foreign troops for easing the tyranny of the press-gang.

The Democrats of León had hired Walker to fight their enemies in Granada and in the other Republics run by Legitimists or Conservatives. But Walker knew that his own best interests lay in getting control of the inter-ocean route, Nicaragua's richest asset, and also a likely source of recruits from among the transit passengers. 'The control of the transit,' he was to write, 'is to Americans the control of Nicaragua: for the lake, not the river, as many Americans think, furnishes the key to the occupation of the whole state.' He therefore wanted to get control first of San Juan del Sur; of Virgin Bay on the western lake shore; and Rivas, a town just north of the road connecting the former two.

59

From July to September 1855, Walker's army spent most of its time drilling and training on their parade ground. The 'Immortals' drank, on tick, at a bar maintained by the French Consul whose bill they never paid, but otherwise they were well-behaved, as mercenaries go. A doctor who served with Walker's army afterwards wrote, 'a filibuster in Nicaragua may be a ruffian, a cutthroat, a thief or a professional gambler, but he is just as likely to be a gentleman and a man of character. I believe that two persons in five of the six thousand who have gone into that country, answer to the name of gentleman, and very commonly deserve it'.

This was the view of most Americans at the time, and of many Nicaraguans.

4

RIVAS

WHILE WAITING TO catch the bus from San Juan del Sur to Rivas, I called at a little shop to buy another *gaseoso*. The lady shopkeeper asked me to sit on the rocking chair on the porch. Across the road a party of schoolgirls were singing hymns to the Virgin Mary. They pinched each other whenever the teacher was not looking. '*Pobrecitas*,' (poor little things) said the shopkeeper. 'Look at them with no shoes. And we don't have enough to eat. We don't eat bread any more. We are hungry.'

The Western friends of the Sandinistas gaily assert that the Nicaraguans are willing to tighten their belts for the sake of their independence from the United States. They even contrast the simple poverty of the country with what they call the materialism and greed of a consumer society. Nothing revolts me more than those well-heeled Socialists living in Hampstead or Holland Park, who claim to admire the poverty of the Nicaraguans or Vietnamese. Why should Nicaraguans not be allowed to enjoy even the modest comforts they had under Somoza, the comforts that most people enjoy in Costa Rica over the border. Perhaps the Sandinistas are ready to make a sacrifice for their ideology; in fact it is they, and only they, who live quite comfortably in the new regime. They face no problems with ration cards; they are in a position to procure food and other supplies; in less than ten

61

years, they have built up their nomenclature. Given another ten years, they may reach the condition of Eastern Europe where the ruling class of Party, Police and Army enjoy a standard of living ten times higher than the masses, as well as privileged education and medical treatment.

On the bus from San Juan del Sur to Rivas, which follows the route of Walker's army, I found myself crushed between a woman holding a chicken and another holding a lobster. The two creatures lunged at me during the journey. Just as we approached the shore of Lake Nicaragua, a thunderstorm broke, illuminating the water in livid colours of gun-metal, purple and putty. Lightning forked behind the volcano Concepción, which rises from Ometepe Island. In Rivas I took a room at the Hotel Nicaragua, costing sixty cents a night, then looked round the sights of the Plaza. There is an old church, modelled upon St Peter's in Rome, a statue of Rubén Darío, and another to honour this 'thrice heroic city', which had the misfortune to be a battleground in 1855, when William Walker beat the Granadan army; in 1856, when he lost to the Costa Ricans; and once again in 1857, when he and his few remaining allies stood against all Central America. The statue honours the Costa Rican soldier, Santamaría, who gave his life in the fight against Walker and now is his country's national hero.

Rivas suffered again in 1979. The rebel army of Eden Pastora pushed from Costa Rica along this narrow isthmus between Lake Nicaragua and the Pacific, engaging Somoza's troops in open country and pitched battles. Fighting in Rivas continued for days after the cease-fire in Managua on 19 July; more than half the houses in Rivas were gutted and much of the town reduced to rubble.

It was Edén Pastora's army, here on the southern front, that broke Somoza's resistance. However, his role is not now emphasised by the Sandinista historians, since afterwards Edén Pastora went into exile.

For the first time since coming to Nicaragua, I felt a little uneasy. Although I had heard no rumour of Contra activities here by the Costa Rican border, I sensed a general fear. Hundreds of young Nicaraguan men leave the country each month to get out of doing their national service; from here they would naturally go to Costa Rica. I was also conscious of being a foreigner in a town where I seemed to be the only one. Not that the Nicaraguans are obsessed by spy mania; they let in anyone who arrives at the airport, and I rather suspect that some of the 'Sandalistas' are really spies for the CIA, or some such intelligence service. To be fair to the present regime, they have not built a police state, much as they might like to do so so. The brats who run the CDs, the Defence Committees, can bully and make life miserable for their elders, but do not constitute a Gestapo. In Rivas, and many other places in Nicaragua, I felt that suspicion came not from the secret police of the Sandinistas but from the ordinary population.

At a Chinese restaurant in the Plaza, I ate noodle soup under the scrutiny of a parrot, and later drank beer under the scrutiny of a sullen barmaid. There seemed to me nothing in Rivas to please the eye or the heart of a visitor. And yet I had hoped to find the enchantment described by Peter F. Stout, who was US Consul in Nicaragua before the Walker invasion. He raved about Rivas, a 'grand old place'. Even before the three battles fought here by Walker the town was a victim of war, but this did not worry Stout, 'There is something in the ruined Cathedral on its plaza, the marks of devastation everywhere to be found, the remnants of antique statues seen in old rubbish and in the songs of the people which remind me of some old legend.' But what had delighted Stout most was the welcome given to strangers, 'The Señorita with her dark olive skin, well washed for the occasion, in her nice *camisa*, not reaching to the waist and with a skirt independent of any contact above, smokes her cigarette and laughs with the bargainer, while her sparkling eyes entice the

unwary foreigner to purchase at an exorbitant rate.' The same
señorita would make a cigarette, puff on it once or twice then
hand it to Stout with a smile to have a 'draw'. From reports of
the time, it would seem that the people of Rivas were just as
friendly to Walker and his 'Immortals', in spite of the war they
brought to the city. Today they scowl.

My visit to Rivas coincided with the celebrations that lead to
Purísima, the Feast of the Immaculate Conception of Mary on 8
December. The Nicaraguans seem to have run together the two
feasts, for in Europe we mark the Purification, or Candlemas, in
February. In Nicaragua, it is second only to Holy Week as a time
of devotion and on the final day of celebration, when families
vie with each other to build beautiful altars to Mary, the children
are given trinkets, toys and sweets, while everyone roams the
streets and asks in front of the altars, 'What causes so much
happiness?' to which the response is shouted 'The Immaculate
Conception of Mary.'

In November 1979, the first *Purísima* under the Sandinistas,
the faithful feared an attack on their feast and therefore decided
to make it the biggest occasion ever, with grander altars and
presents. Wisely, however, the Sandinistas tried to adopt the
feast, so that Tomás Borge and Daniel Ortega joined in a
celebration run by the Popular Church, and even Government
House staged a *Purísima*. While I was staying in Rivas, the rival
papers were doing their best to get *Purísima* on their side. 'Mary
of Nicaragua, Nicaragua of Mary', announced the front-page
headline of *La Prensa*, whose reporter observed that the feast had
begun 'with all the Marian fervour that inspires the Catholic
people who believe in God and Mary'. Thousands of people had
jammed the Cathedral at Granada to witness the taking down of
the Virgin of the Conception, *La Conchita*, which for the next
few days is carried around the city.

The pro-Sandinista *El Nuevo Diario* praised the tact and
leniency of the government in waiving its ban on political

meetings so that the faithful could join the processions. 'The Purification,' *El Nuevo Diario* wrote, 'like the feasts of St Jerónimo and St Domingo, has deep popular roots and has become not only a religious feast but a manifestation of Nicaraguanness (*Nicaraguanidad*).' Unlike those two feasts, the paper went on, 'the Purification has never been spoiled by drunks throwing soot and other deplorable things'.

In spite of these protestations, the government does not approve of *Purísima*, which exalts the Marian side of Christian worship. This veneration, or Mariolatry as its enemies call it, has a special appeal to the Indians here, as it does in all Central America. The apparition of the Virgin at Guadalupe in the early years of the sixteenth century helped to convert some seven million Mexican Indians to the faith of their Spanish conquerors.

The present Pope, John Paul II, whose countrymen pray to 'Mary, Queen of Poland', paid his respects to the shrine of the Virgin of Guadalupe and, when he was in Nicaragua, stressed the value of Marian adoration. In this the Pope has the eager support of the Nicaraguan Cardinal, Obando y Bravo who shares the Marian sentiments of his flock.

The Archbishop, in 1981, inaugurated a Marian campaign, officially consecrating the country to 'the Immacuate Heart of Mary'. In December that year, *La Prensa* reported the 'miracle of the Virgin that perspires'. A wooden image at Cuapa had started to sweat, and some of the faithful had gathered to mop up the liquid with cotton-wool. Later the sweat became known as tears. The Archbishop went to see the statuette, and Bishop Vivas said there was no human explanation. However, Graham Greene says in *Getting to Know the General* that each night the statuette was dipped in water and placed in the deep freeze so that it quite naturally sweated during the day. He added derisively that the 'discovery of the fraud received no publicity from *La Prensa* or from the two Bishops'.

It follows, inevitably, that the Virgin becomes a political issue.

The Pope and Obando are arch-foes of the Sandinista 'Popular Church' of Marxist priests such as the poet Ernesto Cardenal. The 'liberation theologians' regard the cult of the Virgin as superstitious, reactionary and a form of escape from political consciousness. The preaching and ministry of such 'liberation' priests in Mexico and in Guatemala has had the effect of driving hundreds of thousands of Indian peasants into the Protestant sects, like the Baptists and even, in Mexico, the Greek Orthodox Church. In Nicaragua, the government propaganda on behalf of the rational and political 'Popular Church' has had the effect of turning people towards the miraculous, the apocalyptic and if one likes, the superstitious side of Christianity. The Virgin and this, her special feast of *Purísima*, now stand for hostility to the Sandinista regime. The same phenomenon can be found in Poland, where each May some three hundred thousand coal miners march to pray at the shrine of the Virgin Mary.

In a country addicted to bangs and explosions, *Purísima* reaches an ear-splitting volume of noise. From half-past four in the morning, on and off until late in the evening, the neighbourhood of the churches booms with the detonation of thunderflashes, locally known as *petardos* or *bombas*. A brave young man lights the fuse of what resembles a large stick of dynamite, then runs to a safe distance and waits with glee for the blast. The noise of bombardment goes on during the Mass, during siesta time, and long after the children's bed-time. I began to develop shell-shock, and wished I had stayed in Managua or one of the northern towns like León, where they go in for rockets and firecrackers, which make a noise like machine-gun fire rather than heavy artillery.

Although these fireworks are used at religious processions and feasts, the government does not attempt to discourage their manufacture. While I was staying in Rivas, the newspaper *Barricada* published a news item, 'Rockets are ready for Christmas'. It said that in factories making rockets, *bombas* and firecrackers, they were working day and night to meet the demand for 24 December and New Year's Eve. A spokesman, named Walter Scott, for Caiman Rockets said there were thirteen big and six small factories in Managua, working all the year round on explosives, the sticks for the rockets and fuses. He said that in the December period, 'We do not spend even a fifth of the total year's material such as potassium chlorate, white and black aluminium, saltpetre and sulphur.' The same Walter Scott said there were not many pyrotechnic workers now in Managua because of the dangers, but, thanks to the ban on cigarettes and frequent checks on electric wiring to stop short circuits, there were fewer accidents compared to the past. Utilitarians may think it wrong that the capital of a poor backward country has nineteen factories making products that go up in smoke at religious festivals. For my part, I think Nicaragua has its priorities right, like Burma where — so I once read — more than ten per cent of the gross national product is spent on gold leaf to decorate Buddhist temples.

Some people attribute the Nicaraguan love of bangs to the never-ending civil wars. When the revolutionaries took Managua on 19 July 1979 and captured the arsenals of Somoza, they fired off bullets into the air for the next day and night, so that the new regime began without ammunition. Others maintain that the Nicaraguan pyromania has something to do with volcanoes. The connection is clear; indeed, in some European countries they use the word Vesuvius for a conical firework. Nicaraguans love their volcanoes as much as they dread their earthquakes. Every corner of every bar has its own volcano bore.

On my first evening in Rivas, I was already in bed and reading *The Pickwick Papers*, when out in the Plaza the noise of the *bombas* reached the intensity of a civil war. Throughout the *Purísima*, I had not been able to rid myself of the thought that one of these *bombas* might be for real. I remembered how at Tet, the Chinese New Year in Vietnam in 1968, the first machine-gun

67

fire was taken for the explosion of firecrackers. Had not Fidel
Castro led his attack on the Santiago army barracks, in 1953,
after a night of religious feasting? I dressed and went to the
Plaza, but there was no excitement except where a Sandinistan
official lectured the youth of the town on their duty to serve in
the army. The listeners were sullen. Thousands of men of
military age have fled the country rather than serve in the army.
Some have joined the Contras or Edén Pastora's band in Costa
Rica. The government uses patriotic posters and full-page adver-
tisements in the press, like the one that shows a white-haired
mother bidding farewell to her son, 'I don't want to lose you . . .
but duty calls.'

Next morning at half past five, I went to Mass at the church
which has witnessed so much war. About two hundred people
attended this early service in cheerful mood, for Nicaraguans
pray to the Virgin in *alegría*, or happiness. I noticed, as I have
always done in this country, how people relax in church as
though they feel free and among friends. Even the 'Peace', which
is so often embarrassing in England, is here an expression of
comradeship in something deeper than politics, a pat on the arm
of reassurance.

After the service, four strong women placed on their shoulders
the poles that support the life-size figure of the Virgin, shown as
a Queen with a silver crown on a head of human hair, wearing a
white gown and a robe of imperial blue. Our Lady was carried
into the Plaza from where the procession wheeled to the east,
and then the purple figure bobbed and swayed against the
sunrise over the lake and the grey mass of Concepcíon.

The noise of the *bombas* in this Plaza where William Walker
fought three of his greatest battles provided a kind of *son et
lumière* to the story of his débâcle. When he first came to Rivas,
soon after landing at San Juan del Sur, Walker had not yet
learned the techniques of Nicaraguan street-fighting: to burrow
beneath the adobe houses and then set fire to the barricades. The

'Immortals' lost seven men, of whom four were first taken prisoner, then murdered. Here, as always, Walker was scrupulous in his treatment of enemy wounded and prisoners. As he wrote in his memoirs, as usual in the third person, 'To the surprise of the natives, Walker ordered the wounded of the enemy to be as carefully attended to as his own men and none were more amazed than the poor stricken wretches themselves who expected to be shot or bayoneted, according to the Nicaraguan custom.' This kindness shocked his own allies, the Democrats of León, who complained of Walker's leniency to Nicaraguans, who could be governed only 'with silver in one hand and a whip in the other'.

However, Walker and his Americans had created a good impression by their discipline and their coolness under fire. When Walker reported back to León, he was widely acclaimed as a hero. Puffed up by success, Walker obtained the authority of León to settle all differences and accounts with Vanderbilt's Accessory Transit Company. Thus Walker, on behalf of León, was claiming the right that had belonged to the more lawful government in Granada. He could have formed an alliance with Vanderbilt but, as always, something in Walker's character made this impossible. He was quite without tact, charm, humour or simple companionability. He quarrelled with men of power and worth, and put his trust in rascals.

Thus it was that, after taking Granada, Walker made an enemy of the English. They feared him as an American and also because he threatened to bring strong government to the region. It suited the English to deal and trade with a number of weak little republics. They therefore armed and equipped the Costa Ricans to lead an army on Rivas. The Costa Ricans took the town and slaughtered any Americans who might be Walker's men. Walker counter-attacked and captured the Plaza, but came under withering fire and a siege. Many Americans deserted, or asked for leave and then failed to come back. In a speech in the Plaza, Walker admitted that they had nothing left to support them in their struggle 'save the consciousness of the justice of their cause'. Whatever one thinks of Walker, he was not a mercenary or a vulgar pirate; he really believed in his destiny as a statesman; and stranger still, his army of ruffians and adventurers were willing to die for nothing more than his rhetoric.

After the battle of Rivas, the Costa Ricans had bayoneted their prisoners and the enemy wounded, then made the mistake of chucking the corpses down a well. Cholera broke out and destroyed the army, leaving only a few hundred to stagger back to Costa Rica. Walker surveyed the plague with satisfaction, even when it spread to his own army and struck down one of his own two brothers who had joined him in Nicaragua. He attended the funeral with no more emotion than he would have displayed for anyone else. As usual, the only feeling that Walker allowed himself to indulge was self-righteousness at his own behaviour compared with that of his enemies. 'The victims of the murderous court-martial at Santa Rosa; the bayonet stabs inflicted on the wounded prisoners found near the altar of the church at Rivas; the insults to the bodies of the brave dead who gave up their lives on 11th April for a country, theirs by adoption; were to be avenged by mercy, by care and attention bestowed on the sick and wounded of those who had done wrong.'

The cholera epidemic had made Walker a hero again to the Nicaraguan people. Taking advantage of this, he went in June to see his original patrons in León, where he was met with crowds, music and feasting.

Although Walker succeeded in getting elected President in June 1856, his time in office was less than a year, or about par for the course in Central American politics. The English and Vanderbilt had joined in financing an expedition against him, with troops from all the other republics. The cholera which had destroyed the Costa Ricans, now struck Walker's men in Granada. Sick men filled the makeshift hospitals in the churches. A siege army assembled outside and made forays into the city. Among those wounded in battle were Walker's judge and the editor of *El Nicaraguense*.

When Walker departed, making the brutal boast '*Aquí fué Granada*', he sailed to La Virgen and then to Rivas, where he remained under ever-increasing attack through the first few months of 1857. Vanderbilt had blocked the supply of arms, ammunition and of the new recruits who still, amazingly, wanted to join Walker. Many Americans gave themselves up to the Central American Allies, who scattered leaflets over the suburbs of Rivas, promising kindly treatment to those who surrendered. In a battle here on 29 January, eighty Americans lost their lives. The Allies brought up howitzers to shell the town, whose defenders now ate mule flesh. The women and children left on 24 April, followed by more Americans. 'But while Americans were thus proving false to themselves,' Walker afterwards wrote in his memoirs, 'the native Nicaraguans in Rivas were giving an example of their fidelity and fortitude worthy of the race which had been naturalised in their midst. The natives of Rivas were mostly Democrats.'

The end came for Walker when the United States Navy started to show the same hostility on the Pacific coast that the British had always shown in the Caribbean. Commander Davis, aboard the US *St Mary*, sent a message to Walker saying the game was up, and offering him and his soldiers safe passage to Panama and then home. Walker surrendered and never again came back to Nicaragua, though this was not the end of his violent story.

On my last evening in Rivas, the beer ran out. The only drink in the Nicaragua Hotel was rum and pineapple juice which, oddly enough, was the favourite tipple of Mr Steggins, the hypocritical preacher in *The Pickwick Papers*. But reading became impossible, what with the *bombas* outside in the Plaza, and also the blare of the hotel's only record, called 'Money, money, money'. The only other customer in the bar was a quite spectacular drunk. Three times in twenty minutes, he walked to the door and then fell over backwards, keeping his body rigid from head to toe, so that he hit the floor like a plank. I have seen such an act by circus clowns, but never so naturally. While he was talking at the bar, he sounded, if not sober, certainly in control of himself. But when he got near to the door, his eyes closed, he fell into a trance and keeled over backwards. During my time in Nicaragua I have seen more hopeless drunks than anywhere else in the world, more than in Iceland; but never an artist like that.

Laying aside *The Pickwick Papers*, I started a letter to my wife and wrote of the noise of the *bombas* and my still persistent fear that one of them would be real. As I wrote, there sounded what seemed to me a louder than usual bang in the Plaza, but I could not be bothered to investigate. This time it was a real bomb which went off on the steps of the church during Mass, seriously wounding fourteen people. It was the 3 December 1985.

Next morning, the seventh day of the Feast of *Purísima*, the doors of the church were locked and four armed soldiers stood on guard. The police had drawn a circle in chalk at the place where the bomb had exploded; a trail of blood showed where one of the victims had run away. Those who had come in the hope of attending a service were frightened. 'They are trying to kill us,' a lady told me and added, 'This is what they mean by "They shall not pass",' a reference to the slogan now frequently used by Sandinistas. They sneered at my suggestion that the bomb might have been set off by a drunk, a quite common occurrence in this country. The Sandinistas afterwards blamed the CIA.

5

LEÓN

WHEN DRIVING NORTH to León, along the Pacific side of Lake Managua, you soon grow aware of the grey, looming presence of Momotombo, the mighty volcano that means as much to the Nicaraguans as Fuji does to the Japanese. The Conquistador, Hernández de Córdoba, founded León in 1524, close to the foot of Momotombo. During the sixteenth century, brave or acquisitive friars climbed Momotombo and other volcanoes and had themselves lowered in cages into the crater; they thought that the walls of the cone were lined with gold. Several perished, and those who came back with lumps of metal found it dross. In the nineteenth century, a North American writer told this tale in a book that was read by the French poet Victor Hugo. The anticlerical Hugo wrote that the friars had died because Momotombo disapproved of the Inquisition:

> Trouvant les tremblements de terre trop frequents
> Les Rois d'Espagne ont fait baptiser les volcans
> Du Royaume qu'ils ont en-dessous de la sphère;
> Les volcans n'ont rien dit et se sont laissés faire,
> Et le Momotombo lui seul n'a pas voulu.
> Plus d'un prêtre en surplis, par le saint-père élu,
> Portant le sacrement que l'église administre
> L'oeil au ciel, a monté la montagne sinistre,

Beaucoup y sont allés, pas un n'est revenu . . .
(Finding the earthquakes too frequent, the Kings of Spain decided to
baptise the volcanoes of their kingdom across the globe; the volcanoes
said nothing and let it go on, and only Momotombo was opposed.
More than one surpliced priest, sent by the Holy Father carrying the
sacraments of the church, his eyes raised to heaven, has climbed that
sinister mountain; many have gone there, but none has returned . . .)

Momotombo showed its displeasure still more drastically on 31
December 1609, when it shattered León with an earthquake. The
survivors moved to the present site, twenty miles to the north-
west, next to the Indian village of Subtiava.

The new León has always been conscious of its position,
ringed by volcanoes. In 1869, the year of the birth of Rubén
Darío, two great volcanic fires, with smaller ones scattered along
the northern plain, lit up the skies of León at night and cast a
roseate glow on the roofs and spires of its churches. Perhaps
because of this portent, Darío grew up to be much in awe of
volcanoes, earthquakes and cataclysms. He learned Victor Hugo's
poem by heart, and because of it loved the journey by boat from
León to Managua.

There is now a cocktail actually called 'Momotombo', a rum
drink much like a 'Planter's Punch'. The girls who hang out in the
bar of the Intercontinental (not prostitutes, not police informers,
perhaps just a bit of both) prefer 'Momotombos' to foreign
whisky or gin. Momotombo once featured in Nicaraguan foreign
affairs. At the start of this century, the US Congress was split on
whether to cut the inter-ocean canal in Panama or in Nicaragua.
There were lobbyists and public relations men acting for both
sides. The most ingenious was the Frenchman, hoping to get the
canal in Panama, using the assets left from the previous French
workings twenty years earlier. He sent to every member of
Congress a Nicaraguan stamp showing Momotombo. This helped
convince Congress that Nicaragua was constantly menaced by
its volcanoes and earthquakes.

Four centuries after the Spanish friars, the Somoza family suffered the curse of Momotombo, which was their private property. The first of them, Anastasio Somoza García, was killed in León in 1956. His son, Anastasio Somoza Debayle, was President during the world fuel crisis of 1972–3, when Central American countries began to explore the prospect of thermal power, or 'plugging in' to volcanoes. Somoza set up two geothermal research companies, which then were given a contract by the Nicaraguan government, i.e. himself, to explore the lower slopes of Momotombo. Although this terrain was stony and barren, and populated largely by poisonous snakes, Somoza as landowner claimed compensation for losses to agriculture caused by the drilling. Because the exploration was meant to save on imported fuel, the compensation was linked to the everrising cost of petroleum. Somoza finally sold his Momotombo exploration rights to the Japanese for a million dollars. The volcano got its revenge when Somoza was overthrown in 1979, and later murdered in Paraguay. Other politicians still have not learned to respect the sensibilities of the volcanoes. In neighbouring El Salvador, so I read in *Barricada*, the Marxist guerrillas claimed over their radio that the volcano Guazepa 'continues to be the territory of the people and the victorious symbol of revolution'. However, the Sandinistas here have not yet dared to call Momotombo a 'people's volcano'.

In the presence of Momotombo and lesser volcanoes the mind tends to dwell on the prospect of natural disaster, so when we approached León and spotted the rubble and broken houses, I asked the usual question, 'Earthquake?' getting the usual answer, 'No, señor, civil war.' It was here in León that it started to dawn on me that the town of Granada, famous for being destroyed by Walker, is almost the only place in Nicaragua with no sign whatever of military strife. In León, one sees the result of bombing from the Somozan air force and shelling by the Somozan tanks, the gutted and charred buildings and twisted steel girders, as well as the pockmarks left on the walls by machine gun bullets. The film *Under Fire* showed reconstructions, actually shot in Mexico, of planes coming low over streets of adobe houses, and Sandinista marksmen holed up in the tower of the Calvary church.

The centre of town is covered with martial posters, slogans and pop-art representations of men waving assault-rifles. One of the posters shows a disembodied eye over the statement, *Yo estoy el dia con la vigilanza revolucionaria. Y vos?* Roughly translated this means, 'I'm full of revolutionary vigilance. How about you?' In a country where thousands of teenagers, members of Sandinista Defence Committees, are ever on the alert for enemies of the revolution, these words suggest a political terror. Yet most people I meet speak freely against the regime, even before they have asked me my own opinion. 'Are you American?' a plump man calls out in English, and when I answer, he goes on, 'We like the Americans here. Don't you believe that crap the Sandinistas give you. Just look what those bastards have done here.' 'Before we had poverty,' says a university lecturer, 'now we have misery. Just look how little there is in the markets. And don't think I'm a Somoza man. I had the National Guards come round to my house. They looted it. Burned my books. And I don't support the Contras. In fact I'd fight the Americans if they invaded. But we're really frightened of all these Russians here, and the Cubans. That's what really worries people, although they may be scared of telling you that.' The barber, cutting my hair, leans close to my ear to whisper, 'Do you know the Contras are getting close? They blew up some trucks in Libertad. Did you hear that?' I said I had read that in the papers.

One building that has survived intact is the famous León Cathedral, the largest and some say the ugliest church in Central America. I love it. It achieves its size not by towering into the sky — there are no high-rise buildings here in León — but sprawling out on its massive walls. When I saw it first I thought of one of those giant sea lions or walruses, flopped on the beach. Stone lions (León is the Spanish for lion), guard the West door. These sculptures are not as beautiful as the lions over St Mark's in Venice, or those in Trafalgar Square; but they are more forbidding.

The Cathedral here is one of the finest exhibits of earthquake architecture. Some say that the eighteenth-century Spanish sent to León, by mistake, the plans for a church in Cuzco, high in Peru near Lake Titicaca, where pilgrims pray to the Lord of the Earthquakes, *El Señor de los Temblores*. The bulk and solidity of León Cathedral, planned to defend it from Nature's assaults, have also resisted the works of man. An English visitor in the 1860s, who regretted that William Walker had not blown up 'that colossal altar of deformity', León Cathedral, claimed there had been 'more murders committed within sight of that holy building than ever were wrought before a temple of heathendom in the same time'. Certainly, in the 1820s, León was infamous, even in Central America, for its carnage. When the Indians from the Subtiava suburb went into the town in 1824, 'the blood of women and children cascaded down the steps of the Cathedral', according to one European. On another occasion, a Scottish trader said that the very churches of León 'were flooded with the blood of victims who had taken refuge in them, such being (as might be expected) principally the old and infirm, women and children . . .'

And yet in León Cathedral lies buried Rubén Darío (1876–1916), one of the most kind-hearted and gentle of poets, whose only enemy was the whisky bottle. His statue in the Cathedral shows him above a lion couchant. His sad, frightened but likeable face, with its dark, Indian eyes in a forehead creased in frowns, appeared as well on the five hundred cordoba note, before inflation.

Rubén Darío's life was volcanic, catastrophic. He suffered torments from women, from whisky, from superstitious terror and from the love and fear of God. Most of his life resembled that of a poet in burlesque or opera, like that of Rudolfo in Puccini's *La Bohème*. He was happiest, as was Rudolfo, in Paris where he was often broke and seldom went to bed before dawn. Darío loved women but (or because of this?) he was the opposite of a macho man.

Despite his failings, Darío led an active and even successful career as a journalist and diplomat, both jobs he performed for other countries besides Nicaragua. He was a famous public figure in Buenos Aires and Madrid, the two great capitals of the Spanish world, and he relished consorting with presidents, kings and, still more, their wives and daughters! As a journalist, even more than as a diplomat, Darío was heard on the great political issues facing Latin America, especially in its relationship with the United States. In modern Nicaragua, there have been efforts to show Darío as a strident foe of Yankee imperialism. Certainly he wrote on this matter. Moreover, he was alive at the time when the US imposed Marine Corps rule on Nicaragua.

Darío expressed the agony of his country during the second crisis of independence, between that of the Walker invasion and General Sandino's revolt. However, it would be wrong to think of him as an ideologue or a politician, still less as a premature Sandinista. We can learn from his life how Nicaraguans felt about their position then, as ever, under the shadow of the United States. But we can also learn from Darío, a writer of genius, what it is like to be a Nicaraguan; for the history of that country owes much to a national character recognised as distinct by the other Central American peoples. In his poetry, his romantic passion, even his tendency towards drunkenness and disaster, Darío was a true Nicaraguan.

Darío's father, a tailor by trade, had married too late in life to cure himself of the bachelor habits of firewater, beer and visits to 'dens of girl-friends' out in the Indian suburb, still the most lively part of León. Darío's mother, Rosa, had been in love with another man when she was bullied into this match with a much

78

older cousin. When she was eight months pregnant she left to stay with friends in the highlands. Darío was born en route, at a village since renamed Ciudad Darío. She took the baby to join her previous lover across the border in Honduras. Darío afterwards claimed to remember sitting beneath a cow in that farm in Honduras. But when he was still a baby, his mother sent him to live with rich relatives in León. Later in life, he felt upset at meeting his natural mother. As a boy he used to visit the tailor Manuel 'who had a liking for black English beer' but did not know till later that this was his natural father.

The relatives, who became his foster-parents, were a Colonel Remírez, a veteran of some of León's many wars, and a younger wife, who almost outlived Darío. They belonged to the turbulent era of Walker's wars, and most of Darío's relations had died violent deaths. One grandfather was dragged to death through the streets of Granada. One uncle was knifed in a gambling den. Another was shot in an ancient vendetta. But Colonel Remírez, in old age, was glad to enjoy one of the few eras of peace in Nicaraguan history. He taught little Rubén to read, to ride a horse and to get a taste for Californian apples; perhaps also champagne, say some biographers.

Rubén grew up in the fine corner house on the main street Calle Reale (now Calle Darío), which still survives as Darío's Museum. Like most León houses, it is a one-storey adobe structure, with red tiles and wooden shutters, surrounding a courtyard or garden. That courtyard and its sweet-smelling plants enchanted his growing imagination, 'I remember the big calabash tree, beneath whose boughs I used to read; and a pomegranate which still exists; and another tree that gave a perfume which I called oriental . . .' He remembered hearing the fireworks outside the Calvary church on the eastern side of León, and songs from the nearby Franciscan church: 'When somebody died in the district, the bells in this church rang out the slow dirge that filled my boyish soul with terror.'

Darío started to write poetry when he was quite young:

In front of our house at the crossroads, there passed the processions of Holy Week, a famous Holy Week, "Holy Week in León and Corpus in Guatemala", and the streets were adorned with arches of green branches, palms of bananas, bright stuffed birds, carefully painted Indian paper; and on the ground there were mats coloured especially with sawdust of red Brazil or Cedar, yellow "mora" wood; with popcorn, with flowers ... From the centre of one of the arches by our house there hung a golden pomegranate. When the procession of God in Triumph passed on Palm Sunday, the pomegranate opened to drop down a shower of verses. I was the author of these. I cannot remember them but they were verses in bud, instinctive. I never learned to write verse. It was something organic, born inside me. In those days it was the custom – I believe it still is – to print and distribute at funerals, what were called "epitaphs" in which the bereaved lamented the dead in public verse. Those who knew of my rhythmic gift, used to get me to put their lamentations into verse.

An old woman servant used to fill the ears of the young Rubén with tales of a headless monk, a witch who pursued unfaithful husbands and, worst of all, of a hairy hand that came along the street as a spider. Like many children, Rubén was frightened of the dark and suffered from nightmares. He was different because these nightmares grew worse as he grew older. They came to him while still awake in the dark, filling the room with phantasmagorical horror. These fits produced alarming physical symptoms such as nose bleeding. He was morbidly superstitious.

Superstition, in Darío's mind, was never a bar to religious belief or practice. At an early age he entered the congregation of Jesús at León, where he won the blue sash and the medal of the brotherhood. About the time that Darío was one of the congregation, the Jesuits of León were involved in a noted scandal. Before the feast of San Luís Gonzaga, they put a box on the high altar in which anyone who wanted to get in touch with San Luís or with the Virgin, could drop their letters. The Jesuits took out the letters and burnt them in front of the public; but not without reading them first, so it was said. 'In this way the Jesuits knew many family secrets and greatly increased their influence by this and other means. The government decreed their expulsion, but not before I too had taken part in the rites of Saint Ignatius Loyola, rites that enchanted me and which I could have prolonged for ever, just for the scrumptious food and delicious chocolate that the priests gave us.'

León had always inclined to be anti-clerical. At various times in the nineteenth century, the city fathers disbanded the nuns and forced them to marry. Returning home to León in 1908, Darío rather sadly observed that 'liberalism triumphant' had meant the banning of ritual, ceremonial manifestations outside the churches. 'According to what I have heard,' he wrote, 'Nicaragua and Mexico are the only countries in the world in which priests are not allowed to wear their distinctive clothes in the street.' He was glad to see that the old bishop ignored this rule and still wore his vestments as he was carried around León in a coach pulled by oxen.

The hostility between the Church and what Rubén Darío described as 'liberalism triumphant', is still more stark and ferocious today. The bishops and virtually all the priests in León support Cardinal Archbishop Obando y Bravo. When the Sandinista President Daniel Ortega wanted to hold a service of mourning for mothers of soldiers killed by the Contras, he had to bring in a left-wing Brazilian bishop to say that 'the God of the Poor will not let people destroy the Sandinista revolution'. It is not that the León clergy favour the Contras; they will not lend the Church to political propaganda.

The bookshop in Plaza Jerez, in front of León Cathedral, is now devoted to Marxist literature, most of it from the Moscow

Foreign Publishing House. There are books by Marx, Lenin and Sholokov and even a volume called *La Libertad de Prensa en la Unión Soviética* (Press Freedom in the Soviet Union). The Church in León, as everywhere in the country, was worried when, shortly after the Revolution, the government sent many young Nicaraguans to study for six years in Cuba, where Fidel Castro has tried to destroy Christian belief. At the same time, thousands of Cuban teachers and workers poured into the Nicaraguan countryside, some of them mocking religion and taking over the village churches.

The most famous publicist for the Sandinistas, Omar Cabezas, expresses their enmity to the Church and the Christian idea of the family. Now deputy minister of the Interior, working for Tomás Borge, he started in politics as a student radical here at León. His breezy memoirs, published abroad as *Fire from the Mountains*, is claimed to have been the best-ever selling book in the nation's history. Besides his duties running the country's enormous police force, Cabezas frequently travels to international conferences, and greets delegations to Nicaragua, especially those from friends of the Popular Church. His boastful memoirs tell one much of the character of the people who now run Nicaragua. He recounts how the Sandinista students, during the 1970s, stole stationery from the university stores to pay for their propaganda. On the feast of the Virgin of Mercies, the patron saint of León, when everyone sets out lighted candles in front of the house, Cabezas thought of a joke to play on the University Dean who was, and is, a very religious man. 'With a bold flourish and tremendous conviction, I quickly painted in capital letters on the spotless white of the Dean's house "Through these doors one enters the 15th century".'

Darío, eighty years ago, had rejoiced that people did not want to know about Malthus, the great Victorian advocate of birth control. By the 1970s, Nicaraguans such as Cabezas were able to buy contraceptives at the chemist or, as he preferred, to steal them. Under the Sandinistas, abortion is all the rage. *Abortar en Londres*, the film, was showing here in León, as it had been on my first trip to Managua. From a look at the stills and a few inquiries, I gathered that this was a drama about the Spanish women who travel all the way to London to get rid of their babies, combining this with a bit of shopping and maybe a new romance. From someone who keeps these odd statistics, I learned that the number of Spanish women who get abortions in London rose from eleven in 1968, to 38,000 twenty years later. Abortion might be described as Britain's leading growth industry.

The demand for abortion is one of the favourite campaigns of the Sandinista *Semana Cómica* (Comic Weekly) which claims to present a mixture of humour, erotica and Marxism. It appears only intermittently. The numbers I saw were weak on humour, strong on Marxism and strongest of all on obscenity. The most famous issue of *Semana Cómica* came out on the anniversary of the appearance, naked, on TV, of Monsignor Bismarck Carballo, to which I referred in chapter one. The cover drawing showed Monsignor Carballo once more naked, and serenading beneath the balcony of a house. Inside there were more obscene drawings and fake congratulatory messages from the United States. When the papal nuncio raised a protest, the government said that the issue in question had somehow slipped past their censor. Few believed this, especially since one of the chief contributors to *Semana Cómica* is the flamboyant Rosario Murillo, wife, or *compañera*, of President Daniel Ortega, and mother of five of his children.

It is intended not to arouse desire but to pour scorn on the subjects ridiculed. It is a frontal attack on the teachings of the Church. It is also, perhaps, an attempt to incite the young against their parents; perhaps against the very idea of the family. In this way *Semana Cómica* rather resembles Hitler's *Der Stürmer* which used sexual obscenity, of an often sadistic nature, to stir up hatred against the Jews and other enemies. We should all steer clear of state-supported and subsidised humour.

The Sandinista attacks on the Church and the Christian idea of the family, have helped to create an upsurge in piety. An historian at León University told me, 'The strangest phenomenon of the last ten years in León, is the religious revival. It's partly because there are so few cars and motorbikes these days, so people don't go to the beach on Sundays. They go to processions instead. Before the war [he meant the Civil War 1978–9] there would be only fifty people at a religious procession. Now there are thousands. It's because people are frightened that the Marxists want to take their religion away.' My own observations bear out what the historian told me. The Calvary church, the nearest to where I was staying, was full at the early Mass on Sunday. So were the other churches I visited on a Sunday. The only church which seemed to be little patronised was the one that advertised 'liberation theology' functions. One weekday, out in the eastern suburb, I came across a religious procession, a huge throng moving across the railway lines behind the figure of Jesus, his back hideously bloodied in paint. Red carnations and white and green lilies were piled high on the float. Three priests led the way to the blare of a dirge from a brass band.

I have heard it said that liberal León now outdoes clerical Granada in manifestations of piety during Holy Week. No less a witness than Graham Greene has told in a letter to the press how he and his friend Tomaś Borge had seen the cult of the Virgin Mary displayed in León during the feast of *Purísima*.

One morning in the America Hotel, I joined a group in the courtyard which forms a haven of greenness and shade from the hot streets outside. All five men actually introduced themselves as poets. One was from the United States and talked about Allen Ginsberg, the 'beat generation', and poets against the Vietnam War. He appeared to be much more left wing than the Nicaraguan poets, who did not like the influence of the Russians on their town, especially the Soviet literature in the bookshops. I asked if any good poetry had emerged from the war against the Somozas and now the Contras. They said it was mostly propaganda and seemed to agree that the best war poetry came from those who detested war. One of them spoke good English but he was not very much interested in American or English writers and called Graham Greene 'patronising' on Nicaragua. He was at the time writing a play about Rubén Darío's death and maybe a novel set in Somoza's time. All four of these Nicaraguan writers were interested above all in their own country, the rest of Latin America, Spain and then France. For although Nicaragua has always been under the influence of the United States, and England as well, its cultural links are with Latin America, Spain, and what one might call Latin Europe. In the eyes of the Anglo-Saxons, Nicaragua may be just a paltry and troublesome 'mini-republic' (*Republiqueta*, a word that enraged Darío), but in Spanish literature Nicaragua has a distinguished and honoured place, as Ireland does with regard to English. And just as Ireland has brought to the English language a richness derived from her Gaelic ancestry, so Nicaragua adds something of Indian culture to Spanish. It was almost entirely through Rubén Darío, his poetry and his wanderings, that Nicaragua won importance on the world map.

The house where Darío grew up, the present museum, was a meeting place for León politicians, lawyers, teachers and other literati, including a radical Polish émigré. However, the grown-ups decided that the precocious boy should try to advance his career at Managua, which had become the capital in 1858, after the William Walker wars. The President at the time was one of the many from the Chamorro family, the Catholic Conservatives from Granada. Although Darío belonged to the rival liberal faction, the President took an avuncular interest in the young man, who was looking for money to go to Europe. Darío was summoned to read some of his verse and, whether from innocence or a sense of mischief, he chose an anti-clerical piece, no doubt under the influence of Victor Hugo. President Chamorro, who was reported to be a religious bigot, heard it out, then placed his hand on Darío's shoulder and told him, 'My son, if you write like that now, against the religion of your parents and country, what will happen if you go to Europe and learn even worse things?' Nevertheless, Darío got work writing articles for the government press, and later became an assistant at Nicaragua's new National Library.

It was in Managua, when he was still fourteen or barely fifteen, that Darío encountered his *femme fatale*, almost literally, for she was present at his death-bed. This girl, who later became Darío's second wife, was called Rosario Murillo, the same name, oddly enough, as the wife of the Sandinista President, Daniel Ortega.

This is Darío's description of her, written when he did not love her at all, 'She was an adolescent with green eyes, chestnut hair, pale cinnamon complexion with that pale sheen one finds with eastern women of the tropics. She was gay, laughing, full of sauciness (*frescura*), talked deliciously and sang with a voice of enchantment.' He and she would walk together beside the lake, which in those days was a promenade and not an industrial site; or they would sit in the evening in a hammock, listening to the doves and smelling the perfume of the exotic shrubs and flowers. They kissed, and Darío was transported with joy and erotic desire. One day he announced to his friends, 'I'm going to get married!' His friends answered reasonably, that Darío was barely fifteen, he had no money or job, and no experience of the world. They insisted that he must get away for a time, from the heady, erotic spell of Rosario. The government had refused to help with money to send Darío to Europe, so at last it was decided that he should go instead to El Salvador, the tiny state to the north which was said to enjoy a richer intellectual life than Nicaragua.

Perhaps his patrons hoped that a move from Managua might

also help to check Darío's growing fondness for alcohol. An English visitor to Managua during this period, the 1880s, described the city as noisy, turbulent and immoral, 'Congress was sitting as we arrived and well that it was, for many of the members were unable to stand.' Even at fifteen, the young Darío had started to write his newspaper articles in the bar, a habit he kept up all his life. Until quite recently in León, there were bars where the patron would show snatches of verse that Darío had dashed off to pay for a round of drinks.

On the way to El Salvador, Darío stopped off at the north Nicaraguan town of Chinandega, where a girl he knew was about to marry a man whom she did not love. Darío got drunk, recited some verses derogatory to the groom, and was thrown out of the hall. He also could not pay his bill at the Hotel Moderno. He therefore left Nicaragua under a cloud, but appeared to be in the best of spirits on reaching San Salvador. He asked a cab to take him to the best hotel, an establishment run by an Italian baritone, Petrillo, whose macaroni and sparkling Moselle were liked by visiting theatre people. Darío was immediately summoned to meet the President of El Salvador, who had heard of the Nicaraguan prodigy. 'What do you want here?' he asked Darío, who answered, 'I want to hold a good social position.' This reply from a boy of fifteen did not disconcert the President. When Darío got back to Petrillo's hotel, he was visited by the Chief of Police bearing a gift from the government, of five hundred silver pesos. Darío, in the style he would keep to all his life, promptly invited some of his fellow guests to drink, and later that night he attempted to enter the bedroom of an actress. The last escapade seems to have tried too far the tolerance of the El Salvadorean government. The next day, the chief of police returned and took Darío to stay with the headmaster of a boarding school, where he was kept virtually prisoner for the next nine months. This did him good, for he used the time to read. He taught at the school and wrote articles for newspapers.

The following year, Darío composed and read at a ceremony, fifty-one verses in honour of Simón Bolivar. As a reward for this, he was freed from the school and given another five hundred silver pesos, which he employed in the same way ... He went to the Grand Hotel and ordered champagne to be served for himself and four distinguished guests, Homer, Virgil, Pindar and Cervantes, to each of whom he offered appropriate toasts as he emptied his and their glasses!

Darío was at last allowed back to Managua and to his 'brown heron', Rosario Murillo, who was now with another man. Grief-stricken, Darío decided to seek his fortune in Chile, which then was enjoying a period of expansion. His leave-taking in 1886 was thoroughly Nicaraguan. A civil war had just broken out in most of the country, with proclamations and shooting. The day before his departure there came a volcanic eruption and an earthquake, 'While I was visiting a house, I heard a loud noise and felt the earth shake under my feet; instinctively I took in my arms a girl who was standing near me, a daughter of the house, and went into the street; seconds afterwards the walls fell in on the place where we had been standing. The enormous Hugoesque volcano boomed, then poured down ashes. The sun was darkened so that at two o'clock in the afternoon, people went down to the streets with lanterns ... Later, looking out from the ship at Nicaragua, I saw a black cloud over the land and a great sadness fell upon me.'

In two lonely years in Chile, Darío made his name as a journalist and published his first volume of verse *Azúl*, which was highly acclaimed by the leading literary journal in Madrid. He had also obtained an enviable job as roving journalist for the Buenos Aires *La Nación*, the richest and most esteemed of Latin American newspapers. All this before he was twenty-one. On returning from Chile in 1889, Darío went to live in El Salvador, probably for fear of meeting the dreaded Rosario. There he became editor of a daily newspaper *La Unión*, whose policy, as the title suggests, was Central American unionism. For once, Darío agreed with the politics of his paper. A young Costa Rican, Tranquilino Chacón, complained that he had to do most of the work, as Darío went out each evening to the casino. But on the other hand, 'when I could get him to write, he was tremendous; what rare facility he had for his pieces.'

Chacón was one of the witnesses at Darío's first marriage, to Rafaela, the younger daughter of one of the leading Liberal citizens of El Salvador. They had some connection with León, and Darío had actually known his bride as a child, although they had not been sweethearts. Not much is recorded about Rafaela, the 'white dove' of some of Darío's later poems. They met in formal, possibly rather stuffy, circumstances, where it was customary to exchange gallant verses, perhaps to flirt under the eye of older relatives or dueñas. It was not the same as the hot kisses exchanged at night with Rosario Murillo beside the lake at Managua. Yet, although Rafaela's parents were friends of Darío's foster parents, this was not an arranged or forced marriage. It seems that Rafaela admired and adored Darío and, like many young girls, she thought her fiancé was a genius; unlike many girls, she was correct in this. Darío was also handsome in a Byronic fashion; thin, pale, intense with a brooding melancholy stare.

The civil wedding of Rubén and Rafaela took place in El Salvador on 21 June 1890, a day that also witnessed one of the more spectacular *coups d'état* in the blood-stained history of that little republic. Characteristically, the editor of *La Unión* had passed out and slept through the revolution and change of government.

Because Darío supported the losing side in the *coup d'état* in El Salvador, he fled to Guatemala, where he got a job on a paper that was both Conservative and 'separatist' on the question of Central American union. However, Darío got on well with the President, General Sánchez. One evening, when General Sánchez took his drinking companions on to the roof of San José Castle and then ordered his troops to open cannon fire on one of the towers of the Cathedral, Darío persuaded the General to halt the bombardment and drink a bottle of brandy instead.

In Guatemala, Darío and his bride took the religious part of their marriage ceremony and they then went to live in Costa Rica. In those days, Central Americans moved from country to country almost at will. In 1892, the 400th anniversary of the discovery of America, Darío was sent as Nicaraguan delegate to the celebrations in Spain. However, one of his earliest poems with a political message, 'To Columbus', expressed contempt for Latin America and its constant bickerings:

> Plugiera a Dios las aguas ante intactas
> no reflejeran las blancas velas;
> ni vieran las estrellas estupefactas
> arribar a la orilla tus carabelas . . .
> Cristofero Colombo, pobre Almirante
> ruega a Dios por el mundo que descubriste!
>
> (*Would that it had pleased God that the unspoilt waters had never reflected the white sails; that the astonished stars had never seen your caravels arrive at the shore . . . Christopher Columbus, poor Admiral, pray to God for the world you discovered!*)

Darío came back, intending to go to Managua to get his expenses from the government, but he was frightened of meeting Rosario Murillo. He could not go to El Salvador, where his wife was awaiting a baby, because he feared for his life from the new political leaders there. At a reception here in León one evening, Darío got a telegram saying his wife was very ill. He said he knew by intuition that she was dead, and shut himself up to drink in his hotel room.

His wife was indeed dead. Before the fatal operation she had asked that the child be entrusted to her mother and the education put in the care of a banker friend of the family. The child, a boy, survived and grew up with foster parents, as had Darío.

Darío did not wait to hear the confirmation of Rafaela's death. He got blind drunk on the first night and did not return to his senses for eight days, when he found his natural mother among the anxious people around his bed. That upset him even more. The tragedy of his wife's death was followed by another disaster, perhaps even more serious. When he was sober enough to get out of bed in León, he took it into his head to go to Managua and make the government pay him the money they owed him for his expenses in Madrid. He was crazy with grief and alcohol when he arrived in Managua. Almost at once he met Rosario Murillo whose reputation was now blackened by sexual scandal. Her brother was determined that she should somehow restore the family honour by getting married to Darío. What happened is not quite clear. It seems that Darío, very drunk, was alone with Rosario when her brother came in, pulled a revolver and threatened Darío with death if he did not marry the woman he had compromised. Darío got drunker still and found himself married a second time, only four weeks after the death of his first wife.

A few weeks after this shot-gun wedding, Darío took leave of his wife and country for what was almost a lifetime in exile. Although he loved his own small country, Darío regarded himself as a kind of citizen of the world, or at any rate the Spanish- and French-speaking world, and took up the job of Colombian Consul in Buenos Aires, at that time a prosperous and exciting city. In Argentina, he published a volume of poems, *Prosas Profanas*, whose language and rhythm broke all the established rules of Spanish verse, and caused a sensation. To us today, *Prosas Profanas* sounds almost genteel and a little tinkling; at the time it was thought to be revolutionary, sensual, tropical, Indian and strange. Darío was a famous man when he sailed for Spain in 1898 as correspondent in Europe for *La Nación*.

Although still in his early thirties, Darío became the adviser and confidant to even younger poets like Miguel de Unamuno, Antonio Machado and Juan Ramón Jiménez who wrote of him as 'like some human monster from the sea, uncouth yet exquisite'. He was to become the idol of two of the greatest poets in Spanish of this century, Federico García Lorca and Pablo Neruda. In 1900, his newspaper sent him to Paris to write on the famous Exhibition. As a boy, on the lake shore, Darío had prayed to God not to let him die without knowing Paris. His manner of life there brought death closer. In spite of newspaper work and serving as Nicaraguan Consul, Darío spent most of his life in cafés, seldom eating his supper, of sole and whisky, till six o'clock in the morning. He met such heroes as Paul Verlaine, 'he was in fact sad, grotesque and tragic', and Oscar Wilde, who was also drinking himself to death. By the time they had died, Darío himself was the most famous poet in Paris's Latin Quarter, clad in a frock coat, his dark, Indian eyes staring out of a white mask-like face.

His fear of the dark had now developed into a terror of all public places, including railway stations. When he was not in a bar, drinking Prince of Wales cocktails, Darío would be in a church. The finest poems he wrote from now on, were cries of despair and prayers to God. He went to Lourdes to pray for the soul of Verlaine. In Madrid he had taken as mistress a servant girl by whom he had three children, only one of whom survived. His only child by Rosario had died too, but she would not divorce him. Instead she arrived in Paris demanding a share of the wealth which, she wrongly believed, Darío must have made from his poetry. After some nasty scenes, she accepted two thousand francs and agreed to return to Nicaragua. By this time Darío, also, was longing to revisit his homeland. He had also heard that the Liberal President, General Zelaya, had recently introduced laws offering easy divorce. And so he returned for the visit he later described in a charming book, *El Viaje a Nicaragua* (The Voyage to Nicaragua).

On coming back to America after ten years in Europe, Darío discovered that he was famous, not just as a poet but as the champion of a cause. He was the voice of Latin America in opposition to the United States. And it is in this way that the Sandinistas proclaim Darío today. The Sandinista President, Daniel Ortega, made reference to 'the divine Rubén' in his speech at inauguration. The Sandinista poet, Father Ernesto Cardenal, has called Darío 'not only the greatest poet in the language, but the most anti-imperialist.' The Marxist bookshop on Calle Darío has only a small selection of his verse, with none of the great religious poems, but gives much prominence to a book of his 'anti-imperialist' articles. Of course, Darío has always been claimed as one of their own by all Nicaraguan politicians, including the last Somoza, whose wife built the Rubén Darío Theatre in Managua. And, in a way, Rubén Darío *was* the foremost champion of the Spanish American people, not because he was very 'anti-imperialist' but because he wrote very beautiful Spanish. Indeed, I have found in Darío's poetry the clearest expression of why so many Nicaraguans feel such antipathy to the United States.

The Sandinista publicist, Omar Cabezas, who also believes in Darío as a leading 'anti-imperialist', claims that the US has invaded Nicaragua fourteen times, starting with Walker's adventure in 1855. It is not, of course, true that Walker came here on behalf of the US government. Moreover, the first US intervention in Nicaragua took place in 1909, more than a half century after Walker's expulsion. Oddly enough, most of Darío's 'anti-imperialist' writing, up to the end of the nineteenth century, is directed not against the United States but against England. With the United States still busy expanding westwards and healing the wounds of the Civil War, they had little energy to expend on Central America, where England was still the dominant trader and banker. It was then the English, not the Americans, who employed gunboat diplomacy, often to clear up debts.

When Rubén Darío was twenty-three, he wrote an article on the British bankers who were demanding interest on their loans to Guatemala. It was entitled *Voyage to the Land of the Pound Sterling* and consisted largely of an account of 'that great tower of gold named Baring Brothers of London', a tower in danger of tumbling down.

Two years later, Darío was moved to write, in *La Nación* of Buenos Aires, a protest entitled in English, 'John Bull For Ever!' The occasion was the dispute starting in 1893, between Nicaragua and England over ownership of the Mosquito coast. Britain had sent an ultimatum demanding £15,000 idemnification for the expulsion of her Consul in Bluefields. This was not the first time that one of the European powers had tried to bully small Latin American nations. 'But of all the European countries', he continues, 'none is like that red-faced, pot-bellied England!' He recapitulates some of the history of the Bluefields region and quotes Lord Palmerston on having called the Mosquito Kings, 'No more Kings than you or I.' The English, he said, were irremediably deaf to the truth about Latin America, 'If someone had dared in the English Parliament to compare the large and prosperous land of Argentina with Turkey or the Barbary coast, then Nicaragua in the eyes of the British must be similar to the land of Cetewayo!'

As a matter of fact, we do have an impression of how the English thought about Nicaragua at this time, in a novel by Darío's near contemporary, also a poet and a Roman Catholic, G. K. Chesterton. Nicaragua plays a part in *The Napoleon of Notting Hill*, a political fantasy published in 1904, but set at the start of the twenty-first century. At the opening of this futuristic novel, the two English characters encounter 'a tall, stately man, clad in military uniform of brilliant green, splashed with great silver facings,' who turns out to be the former President of Nicaragua. 'But Nicaragua is no longer a country,' one of the Englishmen protests, to which President Juan del Fuego answers, 'Nicaragua has been conquered like Athens. Nicaragua has been annexed like Jerusalem ... the Yankee and the German and the brute powers of modernity have trampled it with the hoofs of

94

oxen. But Nicaragua is not dead. Nicaragua is an idea.' Later in the novel, one of his characters finds a newspaper poster from fifteen years earlier – the end of the 1980s – reporting the country's overthrow by the United States:

> LAST SMALL REPUBLIC ANNEXED.
> NICARAGUAN CAPITAL SURRENDERS AFTER A
> MONTH'S FIGHTING.
> GREAT SLAUGHTER.

The United States was nearer than Britain to Nicaragua and came to be more influential; yet it does not figure large in the hundreds of articles Darío wrote from Nicaragua, El Salvador, Guatemala, Costa Rica, Chile, Argentina, Spain, France and the United States itself. Unlike many Latin Americans, Darío was not obsessed with fear or dislike of the Yankee. He had the political attitudes of the average, easy-going liberal. He was against commercial exploitation, tyranny and war, though he did not object to Nicaragua's own militant foreign policy. He was a Nicaraguan patriot who also believed in Central American federation. He was, in a more general sense, a Spanish-American patriot, even a patriot of the Latin race against Anglo-Saxons, but in a defensive, not in an arrogant fashion. He loved the Spanish and French languages but did not, on that account, hate English. He lacked the chauvinism that later appeared in Hitler's Germany and Mussolini's Italy, though never in Franco's Spain.

It was in a defensive spirit that Rubén Darío opposed the growing involvement of the United States in Caribbean affairs. Towards the end of the nineteenth century, when the Europeans were joined in the 'Scramble for Africa' and other adventures in eastern Asia, the United States had begun to look south to pursue her 'manifest destiny'. In particular, she had started to challenge the role of other imperial powers like England and Spain. The United States took the side of Nicaragua in 1893, against British claims on the eastern, Mosquito, coast. A few years later, Britain and the United States came near to war over a claim by Venezuela to part of British Guiana. The United States had once more started to press for an inter-ocean canal, either in Nicaragua or Panama. Politicians revived the 'Monroe Doctrine' that the United States had the right to police the rest of the continent. The warlike and restless Theodore Roosevelt, who later became President, dreamed up the 'Roosevelt Corollary' to that doctrine: 'Chronic wrong-doing, or an impotence which results in a general loosening of the ties of civilised society, may in America, as elsewhere, ultimately require intervention by some civilised nation, and in the western hemisphere, the adherence of the United States to the Monroe Doctrine may force the United States, however reluctantly, in cases of wrong-doing or impotence to the exercise of the international police power'. The one single event that expressed the new Yankee imperialism, and outraged men like Rubén Darío, was the Spanish American War of 1898, which wrested from Spain most of her few remaining colonies, such as Cuba, Puerto Rico and the Philippines.

Like most Nicaraguans, Darío had formerly sympathised with the independence movements in Spanish colonies, especially in Cuba and the Philippines, where the two revolutionary heroes, Martí and Rizal, were also distinguished poets. But when Spain was defeated, not by the independence movements but by the United States, Spanish American sympathies turned to the 'Mother Country'. The first manifestation of Spanish American feeling against the United States appeared in 1900 in an essay (a short book really) called *Ariel* by a young Nicaraguan, José E. Rodó.

It was published in 1900 when Rodó was twenty-eight, though from his writing, he might have been ten years younger. The title comes from Shakespeare's *The Tempest*, the author himself taking the role of Prospero, and lecturing us on the two opposing principles in the modern world, represented by Ariel, standing for 'beauty and virtue', and Caliban, 'symbol of sensuality and crassness'. Needless to say, Ariel stands for Latin America and Caliban for the United States. The book is so pompous and over-blown that one comes away warming to the United States; but it had an effect at the time, helping to soothe the hurt of the Spanish American War.

Rubén Darío felt the same way. In particular, he was sorry for Spain, the Mother Country that had lost so much of her pride and confidence with the Empire. When he went to Madrid in December 1898, to become the correspondent there for *La Nación* of Buenos Aires, Darío expressed the idea that Spanish Americans ought to cheer up Spain. Not all former colonies feel this way about a former colonial power. Even the old dominions of Britain, like Canada and Australia, have not always felt so warmly about the Mother Country; the Irish question has something to do with it. Asian and African peoples have never regarded Britain as a mother country. Darío's loyal feeling to Spain was all the stranger because he was largely Indian by race; and mostly Indian in appearance. Nicaragua is one of the Spanish American countries where Indian characteristics outweigh the Spanish. In Central America, only Costa Rica is really European. But in Nicaragua, unlike for example, Guatemala, there has never been great social division between the races, or exploitation of Indians by the whites. Darío was free of resentment on the question of his race.

In the first few years of the century, Darío wrote several poems intended to show the loyalty of the Spanish Americans to Spain and her culture. In *Los Cisnes* (The Swans), the poet enquires of the Sphinx:

> ¿Seremos entregados a los bárbaros fieros?
> ¿Tantos millones de hombres hablaremos inglés?
> Ya no hay nobles hidalgos y bravos caballeros,
> ¿Callaremos ahora para llorar después?
> *(Shall we be handed over to the wild barbarians?*

97

Shall those millions of us be speaking English?
Already there are no noblemen or brave knights.
Shall we stay silent now and weep later?)

One of these patriotic poems, *Salutación del Optimista* (Salutation of an Optimist), was to be read aloud at a public meeting, so Darío decided the theme required the fourteen-syllable Spanish Alexandrine, which closely resembles the classic hexameter, 'A Spanish of America and an American of Spain, I chose for my instrument the Greek and Latin hexameter; and declared my faith and confidence in the resurrection of the ancient Hispanic ... in the chorus of nations which make a balance and counterpoise to the strong, daring race of the North':

Inclitas razas ubérrimas, sangre de Hispania fecunda,
espíritus fraternos, luminosas almas, salve!
Porque llega el momento en que habrán de cantar nuevos
himnos lenguas de gloria.
(Illustrious, fertile races, blood of fecund Spain,
fraternal spirits, luminous souls; greetings.
Because the time is coming in which there will have to be sung new
hymns in the tongues of glory.)

There are presages of catastrophe, perhaps wars and revolution:

La inminencia de algo fatal hoy conmueve a la Tierra
y algo se inicia como vasto social cataclismo
sobre la faz del orbe.
(The imminence of something deadly shakes the earth;
and something is starting like a great social cataclysm
over the face of the globe.)

One image looks forward to Mussolini's *Fasces* or bunch of rods:

Unanse, brillen, secúndense tantos vigores dispersos;
formar todos un solo haz de energia ecumenica.
(Join, shine, help one another, all those scattered strengths;
form into one bundle of ecumenic force.)

98

Darío had to read his salutation at a meeting in Madrid in 1905. The poet's friends had given him more whisky than usual, which may account for the cloudiness of *Salutación*. It does not read as well as the more precise and vigorous poem, *A Roosevelt*, addressed to the President of the United States and leading advocate of an aggressive Latin American policy:

> Es con voz de la Bíblia, o verso de Walt Whitman,
> que habría de llegar hasta tí, Cazador!
> Primitivo y moderno, sencillo y complicado,
> con un algo de Washington y cuatro de Nemrod.
> Eres los Estados Unidos,
> eres el futuro invasor
> de la America ingénua que tiene sangre indígena
> que aún reza a Jesucristo y aún habla en español.

(*It would need a verse of the Bible, or of Walt Whitman to describe to you, hunter, primitive and modern, simple and complicated with something of Washington and four parts of Nimrod. You are the United States, you are the future invader of the simple America that has indigenous blood, that still prays to Jesus Christ and still speaks Spanish.*)

The poem contrasts the wealth of the United States, combining 'the cult of Hercules and the cult of Mammon', with the ancient America of the Aztecs and the Incas, now Spanish and Catholic.

> . . . esa America
> que tiembla de huracanes y que vive de Amor,
> hombres de ojos sajones y alma bárbara, vive.
> Y sueña. Y ama, y vibra; y es la hija del Sol.
> Tened cuidado. Viva la America española!
> Hay mil cachorros sueltos del León Español.
> Se necesitaria, Roosevelt, ser Diós mismo,
> el Riflero terrible y el fuerte Cazador,
> para poder tenernos en vuestras férreas garras.
> Y, pues contáis con todo, falta una cosa: Diós!

(This America which trembles from the hurricane and lives on love
– oh men of Saxon eyes and barbarous soul – lives on. And dreams
and loves and pulsates, and is the daughter of the sun. Take care!
Spanish America lives. There are a thousand eager cubs of the
Spanish Lion. Roosevelt, you would need to be God Himself, the
terrible Rifleman and the brave Hunter, to be able to hold us in
your steel claws. And since you count on everything, one thing is
lacking, God!)

The poem *A Roosevelt*, had a huge success in Spain and
Spanish America from its appearance in 1905 in the collection
Cantos de vida y esperanza. Darío quite displaced Rodó as spokesman of Latin resentment against the American eagle, 'with claws
of steel'. Then, in the following year, Darío upset his admirers by
writing a poem in praise of the United States, entitled, of all
things: *Salutacíon Aguila* – Salutation to the Eagle. In that year
Darío had been chosen as Nicaraguan delegate to a Pan-American
congress at Rio. The salutation was given as a poetic after-dinner
speech to delegates of all the American countries, including the
United States. The poem begins with some windy bombast,
'Welcome magic eagle with huge and powerful wings', but ends
with a pertinent quatrain that Rubén himself would have done
well to heed:

> E pluribus unum! Gloria, victoria, trabajo!
> Tráenos los secretos de los labores del Norte,
> y que los hijos nuestros dejan de ser los retores latinos,
> y aprenden de los yanquis la constancia, el vigor,
> el carácter.
> *(E Pluribus unum! Glory! Victory! Work!*
> *Bring to us the secrets of the labours of the North,*
> *so that our sons may cease to be latin speech-makers,*
> *and learn from the Yankees; application, effort and character.)*

Darío was here advocating the Protestant, Anglo-Saxon work
ethic. When some of his friends reproached him for having

turned soft, Darío explained that while he was at the conference, he had met delegates from the United States who were friendly and idealistic. He might declaim in the abstract against the United States or Britain, but when he encountered individuals of a country, his feeling was always good-natured and courteous. His attitude to the United States had more of alarm than hostility. The United States and New York in particular filled Darío with terror.

Returning to Nicaragua after a troublesome stay in New York, Darío experienced joy that bordered on ecstasy. There were feasts and celebrations, palms and bouquets of flowers, 'days filled with sun and happiness' though, as he later added, 'In those hours of gold and fire I never thought . . . how close to Palm Sunday there follows Good Friday.' Here in León, his fellow citizens pealed the Cathedral bells and carried their hero through the streets. He went to his old home on the corner, prayed at some of the churches and went to the lake to recite Hugo's poem on Momotombo.

The greatest delight I got from reading *The Voyage to Nicaragua*, here in León, was finding how little has changed since publication in 1909. There are still no skyscrapers or even high-rise buildings like those that depressed Darío in New York, and now uglify most Latin American cities. There are not many cars, thanks to the fuel crisis. For meccanophobes such as myself, this is one of the few good features of life in bankrupt, socialist countries. What makes León so delightful is simply the absence of change or progress, the failure to keep up with the twentieth century. People still live in graceful and cool adobe houses with tiled roofs, instead of the new cement boxes where life is insupportable without constant air-conditioning. Léon is a town for strolling and sitting about in cafés to gossip. I especially like the café near the Cathedral on the Plaza or, when the beer runs out, some of the rackety places down in the Indian district Subtiava. Although I was told that Subtiava was not safe, I never encountered any hint of aggression there, or anywhere else in Nicaragua, nor for that matter the dope peddlars, beggars, prostitutes, race fanatics and militant 'gays' that abound in New York and Miami. To me it is not surprising that Rubén Darío greatly preferred Nicaragua to the United States. So do I, and this has nothing to do with politics. It is simply that Nicaragua, especially León, is one of those rare places that have not got worse in the course of the twentieth century.

In his *Voyage to Nicaragua*, Darío wrote rapturously of the women, especially here in León, where girls of as young as twelve are ready for childbearing, 'splendid girls like roses or fruit'. At feasts by the side of the lake or on the seashore, he watched women sing and dance to folk rhythms or quick fandangos, learned in the Spanish times. 'All this is very patriarchal, very primitive if you like; but for me an irreplaceable delight.' Darío affected to find an eastern mystery in the Nicaraguan women who, though not a different physical type from others in that region, had something special, 'a kind of Arabic language, or creole nonchalance combined with a natural grace and an uninhibited movement and stride'. He quotes Havelock Ellis (Darío dabbled in psychological writers, including Freud) on how the special anatomy of the Spanish women comes from carrying burdens, as women do in Albania and parts of Ireland. He especially admired the simple peasant women, as against those who had studied in the United States and aped the 'manner of Amazons'.

Unfortunately for Darío, there was one particular Nicaraguan woman who shared certain qualities of the Amazons. This was Rosario Murillo, his second and still his legal wife. She knew that he wanted to get a divorce, using the new legislation; but this did not apply to couples who had had any kind of connection during the last two years. Accompanied by two of her friends to act as witnesses, Rosario bearded her husband, 'Do you deny having had anything to do with me? And don't you remember the ten thousand francs you gave me recently in Paris?'

'But, Rosario,' wailed the unhappy Darío, 'it was two thousand.'

'That's what I wanted you to admit,' she crowed. 'You are my witnesses, gentlemen.'

Virtually no unpleasantness is to be found in *The Voyage to Nicaragua*, which gives the impression of a country peopled with beautiful, laughing women and filled with the scent of roses. Yet Darío was writing in Nicaragua just before the calamitous civil war that led to the occupation by US Marines. An anguished postscript tells of Darío's reaction to the overthrow of the Liberal President, General Zelaya. Darío had written a handsome account of Zelaya's Presidency, his achievements in building railways and schools, the introduction of *habeas corpus*, the kindly treatment of minorities and still greater achievements in war and peace. He had even written a flattering poem in praise of Señora de Zelaya, the First Lady. In return he was given the plum diplomatic job of Minister to the Court of Madrid. And even if this was, as Conservatives said, a political posting, it hardly could be denied that Darío was an eminent citizen, whose name would honour his country in Spain.

But it has to be said that Zelaya was venal, brutal and bellicose. He had sold to foreign capitalists all the country's natural resources including the gold mines, the timber, banana plantations and most of the coffee, the port of Corinto and even the ice-making plant. Most of these foreigners were American; but Zelaya had quarrelled with the US government. He was furious when the Americans decided to build the canal at Panama, and he started plans for a rival canal, to be built by the Japanese. He threatened to put Nicaragua hopelessly into debt by getting a loan from Britain at an exorbitant interest. He invaded Honduras, exacting hideous casualties with the first machine guns used in Central America. Citing the 'Roosevelt Corollary' to the Monroe doctrine, the United States backed a revolt against Zelaya, beginning as usual on the Atlantic coast. In the words of one of Darío's more sombre poems:

Un gran vuelo de cuervos mancha el azul celeste
Un soplo milenario trae amagos de peste.
Se asesinan los hombres en el estremo Este.
(*A great flight of crows darkens the blue heavens. A warning breeze
brings threats of pestilence. They are killing men in the far east.*)

Now was the time for Rubén Darío to take up the cause of his
nation's freedom as two fellow poets had done, Martí in Cuba
and José Rizal in the Philippines. Both paid with their lives and
are now enshrined as national martyrs. Darío, the author of
poems like *A Roosevelt*, was looked upon as the voice not only of
Nicaragua but all the Latin American countries now under threat
from the United States, including Cuba, Haiti, Panama, the
Dominican Republic and, above all, Mexico which, in 1910, was
once more on the verge of revolution. And Darío was sailing
from Spain to Mexico to join in the celebrations of Mexican
independence. When his ship, the *Champagne*, arrived at the
Mexican port of Vera Cruz, Darío discovered himself to be the
man of the hour. The corrupt dictator, Díaz, who had the support
of the United States, was frightened of the effect of Darío's
arrival at Mexico City, the capital, especially during the visit
there of US delegates. He therefore said that since Darío had
been appointed as Minister to Madrid of a government that had
since been overthrown, he could not attend the celebrations. An
immense crowd that had gathered at Mexico City railway station
to greet Darío from the coast was enraged to find he was not on
the train. They marched to storm the President's Palace. Another
immense crowd gathered outside Darío's hotel in Vera Cruz. He
could, had he so wished, have uttered a proclamation against the
interference of the United States in Nicaragua, Mexico and the
rest of Central America. It was his hour of destiny, the chance to
win fame that would have been irresistible to a more self-important person. But Darío, timid, diffident and no doubt drunk, was
appalled by the hubbub and passion. He went back quietly to the
same ship, the *Champagne*, which was leaving for the return trip

104

to Europe. He got off at Havana, Cuba, and had to stay there two months, unable to pay his hotel bill.

This Cuban episode is a sad, comical coda to Darío's week of destiny in Central American politics. During his first few days in Havana, Darío drank himself into a state of delirium, in which he tried to jump off the hotel balcony. His friends locked him up, got a doctor and after three days Darío was recovered enough to go for a drive along the Malecón, to a place where he had a rendezvous with a woman he knew from Paris. After a frantic search through his pockets, Darío discovered that he had lost her letter. To make up for this, Darío was visited by a lady called Mrs Davis, who said she had read of his story in the papers and wanted to remake his acquaintance. This turned out to be his cousin Inés whom he had known and adored as a boy in León and hymned in an early poem, 'White Doves and Brown Herons'. In fact, in his recently published *El Viaje a Nicaragua*, Darío had confessed he had felt for Inés his first erotic passion. Now here she was in Havana, a mother, perhaps a grandmother, and married to an Anglo-Saxon. She taxed him with his indiscretion, 'Why did you give the impression that we were lovers, when that is not true?'

'Certainly,' replied Darío, 'it is not true and I am aware of it. But would it not be better if it had been true, and both of us had experienced love in its finest hours, in the heat of adolescence and in the fiery springtime of the tropics?'

The visit of Inés provided Darío with a day of relief from his sickness. The next knock on the door came from the manageress with the bill. Apparently on his first day in Havana, Darío had hired a motorcar on what he thought were excellent terms, 'I got a great bargain,' he told friends, 'it's normally rented for fifty dollars and I got it for forty-five.' Needless to say he did not have forty-five dollars. He had been picking up the restaurant bills for sumptuous meals with hangers-on. He moved to a boarding house in El Vidado suburb and there waited in vain for money from friends to meet his debts, which increased the

105

longer he stayed in Havana. Meanwhile, Darío had discovered a black nightclub where he was made welcome, supplied with whisky and soda and even given a formal diploma declaring him an honorary Negro. At last Darío obtained the money to go back to Europe, where he spent most of his time in Paris, Barcelona and Majorca.

In Majorca, Darío stayed at the Carthusian monastery which had once been the home of Chopin and George Sand. It inspired a poem about his failing battle against the excesses of the flesh,

> Darme otra sangre que me deja llenas
> las venas de quietud y en paz los sesos,
> y no esta sangre que hace arder las venas
> vibrar los nervios y crujir los huesos.

(*Give me new blood to fill my veins with quietude and my brain with peace, and not this blood that boils in the veins, shakes my nerves and cracks my bones.*)

Darío was now saying Mass as often as twice a day. His drinking had developed into alternating bouts of delirium tremens and even more frightening abstinence. He had grown stout and was maybe already suffering from the cirrhosis of the liver that eventually killed him. He stayed for a time in Barcelona with Francisca, his mistress, and their surviving daughter. He also met there his son by his first marriage, whom he had never seen. Their meeting was cordial but it did not lead to the kind of deep affection that Darío craved. Also in Barcelona he met ex-President Zelaya, who was living in grand style, no doubt from all the bribes he had taken while in office.

Darío made another visit to Argentina where he was coaxed into dictating his brief but delightful *Life of Rubén Darío by Himself*. Like his *Voyage to Nicaragua*, this autobiography sings the happy memories of his life and is quite free from the envy and rancour that often accompany age. Darío was always generous in his praise of friends and colleagues and never seems to have borne a grudge. In the end he made his peace, even with the vindictive Rosario Murillo. Darío was as near as a man can be to lacking in malice.

Spain, where Darío was living, did not enter the war in 1914, but nevertheless he felt oppressed by the horror that had afflicted the rest of Europe, including his beloved France. In November that year, he agreed to go to New York to give a series of lectures on Spanish America and the crisis. Darío was cold and ill in New York. In February 1915 he sailed for the warmth of Cuba, from where he went in April to Guatemala. There he was joined by, of all people, his second and legal wife, Rosario Murillo; she seems to have had a return of her old affection for Darío; she cannot have wanted money, for he was as poor as ever. She had arranged for this reconciliation through the offices of the Bishop of León, who in turn wrote to the Archbishop of Guatemala.

Rosario was determined that Darío should go home to die, and so he arrived on the 25 November 1915 at the main Pacific port of Corinto. A Nicaraguan biographer, Eldeberto Torres, is eager to show how the country had changed since the US Marine occupation, 'Silence reigns in Corinto . . . How different from that arrival in 1907. There is no reception committee; no national anthem pierces the air; it is a country that has suffered a profound transformation. After the civil war at Zelaya's overthrow, there followed a second; the United States has mutilated national sovereignty; debased the governing class and turned the economy into a madhouse which has enriched the sane men of Wall Street.'

Perhaps the government did not know that Darío was coming, for when he arrived on the train at León, the great cathedral bells started to toll, and once more his carriage was pulled through the streets by the crowd.

When Rubén Darío died, on the evening of 6 February 1916, the bells of León Cathedral, accompanied by the firing of cannon, spread the news around the city and the world. He was buried in the immense, ugly Cathedral, that he loved.

6

CHINANDEGA

ONE AFTERNOON, in the café by León Cathedral, I fell into conversation with an American friend of the Sandinista Revolution. He was too old to be called a 'Sandalista', belonging more to the generation which fought in the civil rights campaign and later opposed the Vietnam War. He had seen some of the Nicaraguan sights, like the Popular Church in Managua, the open political prison whose occupants want to stay, and victims of Contra attacks. He asked me whether I did not agree that the Revolution was overwhelmingly popular. I said that I had not found it so. Then what of the general election in 1984? Had it not been quite fair and democratic? No, there were countless reports of harassment of opposition leaders and the intimidation of voters, mostly by threats of cutting their food supplies. When I said that the Sandinistas got most support from the young, this American was triumphant. 'You've said it yourself! And the young are the great majority of the population.'

In vain, I attempted to tell him what was wrong with a revolution that made its appeal to the martial, fanatic instincts of youth, like the Comsomols in the Soviet Union, who took as their hero a boy who had his own father shot by the secret police; the Chinese Red Guards, subjecting a mighty nation to terror; the pitiless Khmer Rouge children, still armed and lusting to kill in their camps in Thailand; ferocious brats in the South African townships, jeering at those whom they burn to death with the necklace. All of these, like the Sandinista Defence Committees, were organised into cells, and dedicated to 'revolutionary vigilance', or spying and sneaking on parents, teachers and other grown-ups. These revolutionary youth movements are not necessarily on the left: witness the Hitler Jugend and the riotous mobs of Iran and Libya.

George Orwell, in *1984*, converted the Scouts into young spies and informers. He had also grasped that a secret police state needs to maintain the populace in a state of constant fear and loathing of outside enemies by propaganda which he envisaged as 'Hate Week'. He took as his model, Stalin's campaign against Trotsky during the thirties. The Red Guards in China indulged in hatred against the Russians, Americans and the old. The Sandinistas, after the Cuban fashion, struggle to keep up a hate week all the year round against the CIA, the Contras and the emigrants in Miami. The threat from outside is used as a justification for the suppression of opponents, the revolutionary vigilance, the shortages and above all the army of seventy thousand men and women. The Nicaraguan Revolution has followed the course of the one that started in France two hundred years ago, moving from lofty talk of liberty, equality and fraternity, to persecution, terror and finally war against surrounding countries. Socialism and militarism are just two sides of the same bad coin. In this century they have reappeared in the still more virulent forms of Communism and Fascism. Darío was certainly right when he said about Nicaragua in 1909, 'Although living conditions are different from those which bring such protests from the workers in Europe and the United States, we have not avoided a gentle breath of the socialist spirit; but it did not find a responsive atmosphere, here where nobody dies of hunger.' Whereas the Nicaraguans badly wanted to rid themselves of Somoza, they felt little hatred against the United States. They are, on the contrary, well disposed to the North Americans. The anti-Yankee feeling is more pronounced in the Marxist middle classes. Both socialism and hatred for the United States inspire the foreign admirers of Sandinismo, not least the rich United States citizens.

These foreign admirers of Sandinismo, like George Bernard Shaw and the Webbs who drooled over Stalin's Russia, continue to fill me with irritation and scorn. It was therefore a pleasure to meet up in León with a foreign visitor who is quite the reverse of a friend of the Revolution, a veteran anti-Communist. This was Peter Kemp, whom I first got to know in Vietnam, and still see from time to time in his favourite pubs in London, and was not surprised to encounter here in Nicaragua. For Peter has spent more than half a century fighting in, or observing civil wars, guerrilla wars, revolutions and counter-revolutions. On leaving Cambridge in 1936, Peter went off to fight in Spain but, unusually in his generation, he joined the Franco side, first with the Carlists and then in the Spanish Foreign Legion. He survived almost three years, was hideously wounded, and once had to supervise the execution by firing squad of an Irishman from the International Brigade. With the British Army during the Second World War, Peter was sent on raids into occupied France, then dropped into Albania, to give support to the Communists, like Enver Hoxha, whom he detested. It was here in León, in a café, that Peter happened to notice the news in *Barricada* that Enver Hoxha was dead, whereupon he rose to his feet, hoisted his mug of beer and gave the toast, 'Stoke well the furnaces of Hell!'

After Albania and Yugoslavia, where he had gained much skill in guerrilla war, Peter was dropped into German-occupied Poland to fight on the side of the anti-Communist Home Army, whom he admired as much as he loathed Enver Hoxha. When the Russians advanced into Poland, they threw Peter in gaol and murdered his Home Army companions. After a narrow escape from death at the hands of the Russians, he flew to Southeast

Asia to join in the war against Japan. He was dropped into north-east Thailand where, after Japan's surrender, he allied with the French for six months fighting the Vietnamese Communists, who put a price on his head. From there he was sent to supervise the liberation of Bali, surviving skirmishes with the Indonesian nationalists. A bout of TB put an end to his active soldiering, but Peter embarked on a new career as a writer to get to the scenes of post-war conflict. He was in Budapest during the 1956 uprising, Algeria, the Congo, Laos, Vietnam, Czechoslovakia, Rhodesia (Zimbabwe) and more recently Guatemala, where he has the advantage of speaking perfect Spanish.

Even by his appearance, Peter stood out from the rest of the foreigners in León. A tall, stooping figure of seventy, he was wearing a well-tailored safari suit and a Guatemalan shoulder bag, which I knew from experience must contain such essential kit as maps, pipes and tobacco, a bottle or two of beer and a paperback copy of *Right Ho, Jeeves*. He appeared as sprightly as might be expected, considering that he had just had heart bypass surgery, and had broken his arm in a fall; on top of the numerous wounds to his head and body. He limps, partly from gout, partly from bungled parachute jumps. His senses of hearing, sight and taste have suffered, not from age but explosions, such as the mortar bomb that blew out his teeth and much of his jaw over fifty years ago.

As soon as we started to drive north towards Chinandega Peter's spirits rose. He eyed the surrounding landscape, no doubt searching for natural cover, a good field of fire or a suitable gun position. At the sound of reports or distant thunder, he pricked up his ears in excitement. The rush of air through the car windows scattered the burning pipe ash over his face and safari jacket, but Peter ignored it all, grinning hugely. He was enjoying himself, hopeful of hearing the guns again.

In this he was disappointed. In spite of the war hysteria, and scares of a US invasion, the Contras have never attempted to make real war in this western seaboard, where nine tenths of the people live. The open terrain does not lend itself to guerrilla warfare, especially now that the Sandinistas have planes and helicopters. The Contras have not gone in for bombs or other terror attacks in the western cities. The bomb that went off in Rivas when I was there was a freak occurrence and, anyway, could not be blamed on the Contras. Except for that stay in Rivas, where I had felt uneasy even before the bomb, I never had any awareness of civil war, which is quite remote from the west of the country. Even later, up in the hill country, I did not feel that nervousness which is part of life in El Salvador, or even in Northern Ireland.

The struggle against the Contras has been from the start a rather phoney war, affecting only the north and east of the country, whose mountains and forests are suitable for guerrilla fighting. The confrontation was all of the Sandinistas' making. Right from the start, ten years ago, they tried to provoke the United States. They set out to challenge the Monroe Doctrine by bringing a Russian presence on to the mainland of America. However much some Latin Americans may resent the Monroe Doctrine, it has protected them from the international conflicts in Europe, Asia and Africa. The Sandinistas also proclaimed their intent to spread the Revolution to other Central American countries. They armed and supplied the rebels in El Salvador, whose favourite weapons are mines called 'limb-removers'. Not surprisingly, the United States began to arm and supply the Contras in Honduras. Some of this army was made up from the exiles in Miami. Probably more came from eastern and northern Nicaragua, whose Indian and Negro population has always been hostile to rule from Managua. As Rubén Darío wrote, '*Asesinan los hombres en el estremo Este.*' (They are killing people in the far east.) Here in the western part of the country, most of the people may not like or respect the Sandinistas, but have not been driven to take up arms.

Peter Kemp and I argued on whether or not to support the Contras. He tends to favour all opposition to Communists. I favoured aid to the Contras in order to force the Sandinistas to stop supplying the Communists in El Salvador. It would also put pressure on them to grant more freedom within the country, like raising the ban on *La Prensa*. However, supporting the Contras also helps the Sandinistas. They need the Contras as justification for their army and for their constant state of emergency. Nor do I quite agree with Peter in thinking the Sandinistas Communists. They lack the training and discipline of the Communist Party in Europe. Most of their rhetoric comes from Fidel Castro, Juan Perón and various 'third world' gasbags. They want revolution not to achieve any social aims, but just for its own sake. They want to live in an atmosphere of constant rallies and loudspeaker screams. Their favourite slogan, borrowed from the Italian '*La lotta continua*', is '*La lucha sigue*', 'the struggle continues'. The Sandinistas have little in common with old-fashioned Communists in Russia, China or Vietnam. They are more like the people you find in Liverpool City Council or one of the more left-wing polytechnics.

Discussing the case for supporting the Contras, we passed through the flat and not very attractive cotton country of Nicaragua. The Somozas and other farmers started these cotton plantations during the 1950s and soon developed a thriving business, often held up as a model to other Latin American nations. Nicaraguan cotton was sought by textile manufacturers all over the world because of its extra fine quality. Although cotton enriched the farmers and the Somozas, it also contributed to an economic boom which everyone in the country enjoyed. It also caused social problems. A writer I met in León, whose own father was one of the early planters, said that the new plantations had tended to break the traditional bonds between farmers, or ranchers, and their employees. 'Cotton turned them into share-croppers, as the Americans say, though I've never quite under-

stood what the word meant. It deprived them of their own land.
They felt rootless, like industrial workers out in the countryside.'
The Sandinistas nationalised most of the plantations, and brought
in 'volunteers' to pick the cotton. Production declined. A Dutch
textile buyer I met in Managua said that his firm had recently
discontinued certain lines for want of the good Nicaraguan
cotton.

Peter and I had wanted to visit Chinandega partly because of
its curious claim to fame as the first town in history to be
bombed during a civil war. That was in 1927, more than ten
years before the bombing of Guernica in Spain, a subject on
which Peter holds strong views, denying the left-wing version of
an attack on undefended civilians.

The bombing of Chinandega occurred in one of the civil wars
that continued on and off in Nicaragua, from the overthrow of
General Zelaya in 1909 until the rise of the first Somoza in
1934. For most of this time, the US Marine Corps kept law and
order, at any rate in the western part of the country. The
Americans even held fair general elections. But as soon as they
left the country, the old feuds re-emerged: Conservative versus
Liberal, Granada versus León, the Chamorro clan against the rest
of the politicians. The United States Congress, then as now, was
split on whether to intervene in Nicaragua. The Reagans and
Bushes of those days were all in favour of sending in the Marines.
The liberals disapproved of intervention in general, and in par-
ticular of intervention to help the Chamorro family. Senator
Borah, the equivalent at that time of someone like Senator
Kennedy now, paid special attention to the Chamorro family in a
speech in 1922:

'. . . It is a well-known fact that Diego M. Chamorro is President of Nicaragua, Rosendo Chamorro Minister of the Interior;
Salvador Chamorro President of Congress; . . . Augustín Chamorro Financial Counsellor; Filadelfo Chamorro Commander of

the capital's main fort; Leandro Chamorro Commander of Corinto, Nicaragua's main port; Carlos Chamorro Military Commander of the northern zone; Dionisio Chamorro Administrator of Customs; Octavio Chamorro Member of Congress; Augustín Bolanos Chamorro Nicaraguan Consul in New Orleans; Fernando Chamorro Nicaraguan Consul in San Francisco; Pedro J. Chamorro Consul in London; Emiliano Chamorro Nicaraguan Minister in Washington.'

After many years of Chamorro family rule, the Nicaraguan voters in 1924 elected in the rival Liberal Party. The Americans, satisfied at having brought back democracy, withdrew in August the following year. Two and a half months later, the leading Chamorro launched a successful *coup d'état* by seizing the army barracks in Managua. Early next year, 1926, the Liberals counterattacked in traditional style, by raising revolt on the eastern coast. *'Se aseninan los hombres en el estremo este.'* The Liberal columns, one of them led by the self-styled 'General' Sandino, advanced slowly westward towards Managua. The fighting took an unusually gruesome turn in February 1927 when Liberal troops captured Chinandega, a town of twenty thousand inhabitants. What happened next created a world sensation and *cause célèbre* of the left until it was overshadowed by Guernica. Like Guernica, it is still the subject of claims and counter-claims by partisans of the two sides. All are agreed that Chinandega was held for three days by the Liberals. Then a Conservative army arrived, backed by two aeroplanes of the Nicaraguan Constabulary, whose commander was an American. Two American pilots flew their Laird-Swallow biplanes over the town of Chinandega, dropping their home-made dynamite bombs, with fuses lit from cigars. Their intention was to stampede the Liberal forces, throwing them out of the town. A fire broke out in which many civilians died, although Chinandega was crowded with Liberal troops. Some historians now believe that the Liberal soldiers and other looters started the fire that gutted the town; the Sandinistia historians put all the blame on the bombers. Photographs of the charred and bloated corpses in Chinandega appeared all over the world as anti-American propaganda. They had much the same effect as more recent pictures of napalm victims in Vietnam.

Chinandega was once more battered by civil war in 1979 but here, as opposed to León, you see little trace of it. Most of the town consists of one-storey adobe buildings which can be rebuilt in weeks. The scars of a civil war, like those of an earthquake, are visible only where there were tall buildings of stone or cement. Chinandega is rather a lifeless town. Even Rubén Darío found little to praise here but for the oranges, which were not in season at this time.

The heat of the afternoon was overpowering, so Peter and I went into a little shop selling beer. The proprietor and some of his neighbours sat us down in rocking chairs, and saw to our comfort, but it was clear that they themselves were uneasy. Looking out from the dark shop into the midday sunlight, we saw just over the street the offices of the Sandinista Defence Committee, the youngsters who are the 'ears' of the Party. Two of them stared at us. The shopkeepers seemed to be terrified that the 'ears' would hear them, in spite of the noise of the radio and electric fan. They insisted on speaking in whispers, so that Peter, because of his deaf ear, could not hear them, and I had to do the talking in my bad Spanish. These Chinandega people spoke to us about the shortages and the poverty; the great number of Cubans, and the disastrous cotton crop. They said the pickers were students, conscripted against their will under threat of losing their place in school or university.

It was obvious that these people were frightened of something more than the Sandinistas over the road. They were also suspicious of Peter and me. I found out why when one of them shyly asked me, nodding as well at Peter, if we were Germans. In León, we had been asked if we were Russian, and once, if we were Swedish, which angered Peter still more. No, I explained, we

116

were not Germans but English, the country of Queen Elizabeth and Margaret Thatcher. For once, those names brought no reassurance. Doubt remained on the questioner's face, as she went on 'Please could you tell us, are you from Federal England or from the English Democratic Republic?'

7

CORINTO

AT THE TIME of the Nicaraguan Civil War, in which Chinandega was bombed from the air, the United States was obsessed by the danger of Communism. 'The Bolshevik leaders have set up as one of their fundamental tasks, the destruction of what they term American imperialism as a necessary prerequisite to the successful development of the international revolutionary movement in the New World,' said Frank B. Kellogg, the Secretary of State, addressing the Senate in January 1927. The country uppermost in his mind was Mexico, which then, like Cuba today, had a pro-Soviet government. But then, as now, the United States saw a secondary danger that Communism might spread to Nicaragua.

The Soviet threat is not just a 'Red scare', as I saw when I made a trip to Corinto, the main Nicaraguan port on the western, Pacific coast. Getting as near as I could to the docks without raising suspicion of espionage, I spotted a Soviet freighter and one other ship, whose colours I did not recognise, but no doubt came from the eastern bloc. It was here at Corinto that, during the early 1980s, arms and supplies poured in from the Soviet and Arab countries. The US Defense Department estimated that by late 1984 the Sandinista Army had 150 Soviet T54 and T55 tanks, 200 other armoured vehicles, multiple rocket launchers, long-range artillery, early-warning radar, anti-aircraft rockets, and high-speed helicopter gunships. In November 1984, the United States warned that Soviet vessels approaching Corinto might be carrying MIGs, the Soviet jet fighters, an escalation of military strength that would be unacceptable. As it turned out, the crates at Corinto did not contain MIGs. However, Corinto became a potential flashpoint of war. American battleships cruised in the Gulf of Fonseca, their rockets and long-range artillery targeted on the port. The harbour was mined. The Contras sabotaged Corinto and even attacked it with planes.

The port, which once prospered from commerce with the United States, or shipping coffee to Hamburg and cotton to Rotterdam, does much of its business still in armaments from the Soviet bloc. This may account for the quite unusual hostility of Corinto people. They avoided the simplest questions. I could not find a café with soft drinks on sale, or even a cup of coffee, in Nicaragua, one of the world's great coffee producers. The only prospect of entertainment came from a cinema, showing, of course *Abortar en Londres*. After León, or even Chinandega, Corinto looks woebegone and decaying. Instead of adobe houses with red arabic tiles, there are rickety huts of unpainted wood, or bits of debris. The railway track is overgrown and littered with rubbish. The whole town pongs.

The Sandinista newspaper *Barricada* had recently published a story about a meeting to honour the Beatles at 'Liverpool, the once great port of north-west England, which is suffering a financial crisis'. The article did not mention that Liverpool, the once great port of north-west England, is now the 'twin town' of Corinto. Shortly before my visit, a delegation of Liverpool dignitaries and assorted Trade Union officials came here on a visit financed by the Liverpool ratepayers. At least one of them changed all his money at the airport at the official rate of twenty-eight cordobas to the dollar, when he legally could have obtained at least three hundred in town.

A West German doctor coming to work in Corinto was

interested and envious to hear of this friendship with Liverpool. 'Do they have many of these twin towns between England and Nicaragua?'

Yes, I explained to him, London was twinned with Managua, Sheffield was due to be twinned with Estelí and León with its fellow university town of Oxford. The doctor sighed, 'That would never happen in West Germany where the Social Democrats who control the cities are very right wing. But in England, I think, it is different. You even have bleck burgomeisters, ja?' It was my turn to sigh as I thought of some of our more exuberant 'burgomeisters'.

Some of the English cities and left-wing boroughs conduct what amounts to their own foreign policy. The London borough of Lambeth, including the very Jamaican suburb of Brixton, is 'twinned' with Bluefields, on the Atlantic coast of Nicaragua, where there are many English-speaking Blacks. Unhappily, for the twin-town arrangement, most of the Bluefields Blacks are opposed to the Sandinistas, and therefore to the ideals of the Lambeth politicians. Some Bluefields people kidnapped a Sandinista official. When this happened, the British chargé d'affaires in Managua, Richard Owen, was startled to get a telephone call early on a Sunday morning demanding to know what action he planned to take. The caller was an official of Lambeth Council. When Mr Owen said he had written a memorandum about the matter, the caller from Lambeth wanted to know why he had not lodged a protest. A protest! Where? To the United States Embassy. When Mr Owen refused to do this, the caller said she would make a report on him to Neil Kinnock, the Labour Party Leader.

Gone are the days when Britain would send a warship to show the flag at Bluefields or Corinto. British policy on Nicaragua is formulated not in the Foreign Office, but in the council chambers of Lambeth and Liverpool.

The sight of a Soviet ship at Corinto, possibly bringing the latest weaponry, brought home the imminence of the danger described by Kellogg sixty years ago. It explains why the US Government wanted to intervene in Nicaragua during the eighties, and why it did intervene in the twenties. What happened then has a direct bearing on what is happening now, and helps to explain the crisis in Nicaragua. The United States, in 1927, supported neither side in the Civil War as she supported neither side in 1979. She had tried in vain to bring together the different factions in peace talks, under the chairmanship of a US diplomat in Managua, or senior naval officer from a ship at Corinto. Then, early in 1927, Kellogg sent as his representative a senior and distinguished public servant, Henry L. Stimson, who later went on to be Secretary of State and, later still, the confidant and adviser to President Franklin D. Roosevelt. Although Stimson had no Spanish, nor any previous knowledge of Nicaragua, which he pronounced 'Nickeragewya'; he gave an impression of wisdom and sincerity. His very ignorance of the country was taken as reassuring proof that he was free from prejudice on the ancient quarrel between the Liberals of León and the Conservatives of Granada.

His impartiality and his shrewdness appear in the book that Stimson wrote immediately after his mission was over, *American Policy in Nicaragua*, an object lesson to all United States diplomats on how to approach a violent, quarrelsome and suspicious nation. The book is agreeably free of the liberal guilt that affects more recent American writers on Latin America, many of whom seem to believe that all the faults of the continent can be blamed on the United States. This was not Stimson's view:

> The central cause of the breakdown of popular government in these countries, lay in the failure in their hands of the system of popular election. The percentage of illiteracy among the voters in each of the countries was overwhelming, and great masses of the Indian population had for centuries occupied a position little, if any better, than serfs or slaves. It was easy

121

therefore for them to be controlled by fraud or threat of force . . .

The heads of departments who correspond to the governors of our states, instead of being elected by the voters of the departments, are in Nicaragua, and I believe in most, if not all of the other four nations, appointed by the President of the Republic; and this is true of most of the other officers. There is therefore very little local self-government, that great school of democracy . . . I believe it remains literally true that no Nicaraguan election has ever produced a result which was contrary to the wishes of the man or party which was in control of government.

The same could be said of recent Nicaraguan elections. The only exception that Stimson might have recalled, was the election of 1924, when the US presence ensured a fair vote.

When he arrived in Corinto in April 1927 and took the train for Managua, Stimson saw from the window signs that 'the country was in the grip of war . . . The portion of land through which we passed was evidently of great fertility. There were long stretches of open farming country interspersed with park-like vistas of beautiful trees, but the fields were uncultivated and little farming was going on. A large portion of the city of Chinandega was in ashes. Almost every man or boy whom one met, either in the country or the city, were armed . . .'

This account of the region around León has an odd similarity to the accounts of travellers in the same region one hundred years earlier. Like William Walker before him, Stimson remarked that, 'the armies of both sides were largely recruited by conscription among the lower classes of the population . . . I myself saw boys of eleven and twelve side-by-side in the ranks with men old enough to be their grandfathers. Even women were to be found in both armies.' It sounds like Nicaragua now.

Having seen the effects of civil war, Stimson was more than ever determined to bring about peace before the planting season began in June. All the politicians that Stimson met were 'seeking our intervention and asserting the permanent interest of the United States in the establishment and maintenance of orderly and responsible governors throughout Central America.'

Early in May 1927, Stimson got a message through the lines to General Moncado, the leader of the insurgent Liberal army that now threatened Managua, the capital. The two men arranged to meet at Tipitapa, a spa and resort town. During the conversation, which took place sitting under a blackthorn tree, General Moncado agreed to stop the war if the United States would supervise the elections next year, which, he correctly believed, would mean the return of a Liberal government, and, as it so happened, with General Moncado himself as its President. After the talk at Tipitapa, Stimson recorded that, 'He [Moncado] then retired to his army and the following day I received a telegram signed by him and all his Chieftains except Sandino, formally agreeing to lay down their arms . . .'

It was thus that Stimson introduced the name of the man, Sandino, who was to spoil the otherwise successful peace talks; and lead his guerrilla army for six undefeated years. To Stimson, writing in 1927, Sandino was merely an obstinate troublemaker, 'one of Moncado's lieutenants who, as Moncado told me, having promised to join in the settlement, afterwards broke his word and with about one hundred and fifty followers, most of whom he said were Honduran mercenaries, had secretly left his army and started northwards towards the Honduran border. I was told that Sandino lived in Mexico for twenty-two years, where he served under Pancho Villa, and only came to Nicaragua at the outbreak of the revolution in order to enjoy the opportunities for violence and pillage which it offered . . .' The truth about Sandino was not as simple as that.

123

8

MATAGALPA

IN HIS *Voyage to Nicaragua*, published in 1910, Rubén Darío spoke fulsomely of the coffee country up in the highlands, north of Managua. 'From the plantations up in the hills one can see Lake Managua; the huge volcanoes frozen against the sky by a trick of the light.' He told how coffee was brought from Europe to Martinique and then, after a century, to Costa Rica and so to this country. 'Such was the story of coffee told in his *History of Nicaragua* by Don José Dolores Gámez, whose father of the same name, cultivated the first coffee plantation from 1845–6 in the hills above Managua. These days, Nicaraguan coffee is some of the most sought-after in the world. It was not for nothing that Jinotega coffee recently won top prize in the international competition, for taste and quality.'

Darío felt proud of the trees laden with red berries; he wanted to see more Europeans arrive as planters. 'Agriculture is really the source of life, and coffee is what grows best here.' He tried and greatly enjoyed the life of a planter, 'Excursions on horseback, walking, dances and those sensual and almost languid women who go to spend a few days in the country, out in their haciendas. You might imagine them as the resident spirits, the goddesses, living and in the flesh.' One guesses he might have enjoyed the bibulous and erotic life of the 'Happy Valley Set' in

Kenya during the 1930s. Rubén Darío presented an equally cheerful impression of working life on the coffee plantations, whose scent evoked the poetry of the West Indies, and in whose cottages he observed 'dark wenches, tall with supple bodies, bronze, cocoa-coloured or pale mestizas, who offer one a cup of water, with beautifully turned shoulders and arms, and a gracious smile ... It is mostly the women who do this work [picking coffee], and in the little camps that arise under the branches of the coffee shrubs, one sees flocks of children, confirming the fertility of the race. There are hammocks slung under the red fruit, and people sing as they work ... And what glorious vegetation, what a triumph of life confronts the eye at the height where the climate changes. The air is fresh and the valleys stretch out before you as in a vision of Eden; and everywhere an expanse of green and a vast murmur goes up from the plantains and the bananas and the huge fantastic trees where grey squirrels leap, the soothing pigeons fly, the woodpeckers and all winged creatures ...'

The countryside around Matagalpa is just as beautiful as it was in Darío's time; but man has brought sorrow into this Eden. Perhaps if Darío had not been so carried away by the tropical scents and the gracious smiles of the pale mestizas, he might have observed that the old Nicaraguan quarrels of Liberal versus Conservative, and León versus Granada, had already found their way into the coffee country. The old feud helps to explain, although I did not at first understand this, a rare and significant lapse in the *South American Handbook* (1987 edition). For years it has been singing the praises of the Hotel Santa María de Ostuma, 'a fine mountain inn at over 1,200 metres, 10 km along the scenic paved road from Matagalpa to Jinotega; good food, superb scenery ... with hiking, riding and fishing.' In fact the hotel was already shut in 1985, two years before this last edition. In Matagalpa I heard that the closure had something to do with politics. Later I found that the trouble revolved around the

Salazars, a family of Conservatives who came to this region during the 1900s. A glance at their story gives a revealing insight on how the old Nicaraguan quarrels have lasted from independence, and William Walker, through to the present dispute between Sandinistas and Contras. When the Salazars first came here, and bought six thousand acres of pasture from some of the local Indians, the President of the country was General Zelaya, the patron of Rubén Darío. Being a Liberal, he looked on Conservatives such as the Salazars as enemies to be plundered. When President Zelaya visited Matagalpa, he had already acquired the volcano Momotombo and many farms in the Chinandega area, owned by Conservatives, whom he plundered and exiled. The Salazars heard that Zelaya was planning to do the same for their property round Matagalpa and took the precaution of passing the deeds to US citizens, before themselves leaving for exile in California, which then had the status Miami now holds as a centre for émigré Nicaraguans. Long after the overthrow of Zelaya, when the Conservatives were enjoying a spell of power, one Leo Salazar bought an estate at Santa María de Ostuma, where the hotel now stands. In the subsequent struggle between the US Marines and General Sandino, Salazar became an officer in the National Guard, under the first Somoza. He became a manager of the Somoza family estates in the Matagalpa region. For this reason he thought it prudent to leave the country before the Sandinistas took power in 1979.

The Sandinistas nationalised Somoza's property. But here in the coffee country, Leo Salazar's only son, Jorge, led the resistance to any further expropriation of land by organising some seven thousand private farmers into a Matagalpa cooperative. The quarrel between the coffee farmers and Jaimie Wheelock, the Sandinista Commandant for agriculture, led to the first open conflict in Nicaragua after the Revolution. Fighting broke out between Sandinista gangs and those of the opposition. One day, in November 1980, a carload of Sandinistas pulled into a petrol station and shot dead Jorge Salazar. This was one of the incidents that sparked off the Contra movement. It also explains why the Hotel Santa María de Ostuma, the former home of the Salazars, no longer takes guests.

Visitors to the region now have to stay in Matagalpa itself, a dreary town; unless they prefer another mountain inn, the Selva Negra (Black Forest). It was built and named by the Germans who came here around the turn of the century to clear the forest and plant their coffee. In the hall of the Selva Negra there is a mural showing their pride and joy, a steamroller, surrounded by portraits of Uberzezig, Kuhl, Dr Josephson, Zeys, Vogel, Kraudy, Boesche, Maser and (odd man out) Travers, all in stiff collars and long moustaches. The hotel and restaurant and the surrounding cabins are set in what is indeed a black forest of dense, almost jungle-like vegetation, loud with the shrieks and whistles and pings of wildlife. The restaurant faces a pond where you can watch frogs, dragonflies, kingfishers, humming birds and a kind of golden oriole or finch, that looks all the more splendid against the dark forest. The pond also supports the very aggressive hotel geese, who guard the way to the outside gents with all the vigilance of their ancestors by the citadel in Rome.

By day, there are walks from the Selva Negra around the hills, from which you can see several miles down in the valley the glinting tin roofs of Matagalpa. At night, the forest is not so cheerful. The restaurant closes early and afterwards there is nothing to do but retire to the cabin and try to read by a feeble light, or drink a few glasses of rum or listen to the forest sounds, before settling down between dank sheets under two insufficient blankets. The Sandinista officers and their girl-friends in the surrounding cabins go everywhere with their machine guns; for this is Contra territory. The Canadians who work on a project at Jinotega say they have issued their names and photographs to the local Contras, to make it known they are neutral and not to be mixed up with, for instance, the East Germans. However, they add that the main danger they have to face comes from drunken Sandinistas who sometimes chuck a grenade at a car that will not stop to give them a lift.

The coffee pickers now come to the mountain in uniform, armed to the teeth, for reasons explained by the Sandinista newspaper *Barricada*. The report makes it sound like a military operation:

> Of the 30,500 voluntary pickers needed to mobilise for the battle of coffee, just over 24,000 have so far enlisted and the first contingent left yesterday for coffee production centres in Region VI. 'To pick coffee. To strike blows at the counter-revolutionaries. To destroy imperialism. And to Defend the Revolution.' These were the words used by commandante Jaimie Wheelock to send off thousands of workers who have turned themselves into production soldiers ... The General Secretary of the National Union of Clerical Workers, Mercedes González, told the contingent that they should remember as they picked the red beans, the hundreds of Nicaraguans who, in the course of their duty, had shed their blood for the Revolution.

The battle of coffee may have encouraged the Revolution but has not produced good crops. A Matagalpa man, who once had a smallholding and may, for that reason, be biased against the government, told me, 'The coffee plantations are short of pesticide, fertiliser and labour. There are few private estates left and the government doesn't know how to run a plantation. The people they bring from the towns don't know how to pick. They damage the trees by picking the wrong way. There are a lot of German volunteers who are good at drinking beer, but that's all.' One of these German internationalists admitted the truth of the accusation. We were drinking rum rather than beer and soon he became pleasantly cynical, 'The West German internationalists don't get on with each other, they are all very individualistic in a typically German way,' then added '. . . typically of the young West German. Some of the three brigades are Social Democrats, some are Greens, some are New Left, some are Communist Party. But none of them speak to each other. Even the West German Communists won't talk to East Germans, they call them "state bureaucrats".' This young West Berliner, an economics graduate, was one of the few really amusing foreigners that I have met in Nicaragua. Perhaps under the influence of the rum, I found myself wholeheartedly sharing this young man's opposition to Friedman's economic theories. We discussed the possibilities for the recolonisation of Africa. He said it was good fun living in Nicaragua, with plenty of cheap tobacco and alcohol and beautiful women. His carpentry job was never demanding.

'But what about picking coffee? Isn't that hard work?'

'Yes,' said the young German, 'it's terrible work because the beans are all different heights and sometimes quite low, so that you have to stoop. But there's an easy way of getting through the day's stint. I just hire some of the local children to do the work for me.' Did I sense the disapproving stares of Uberzezig, Kuhl, Dr Josephson, Zeys, Vogel, Kraudy, Boesche, Maser and even Travers?

Among the guests at the restaurant of the Selva Negra were Yugoslavs from a Bosnian timber company working nearby. Although they had previously served in Angola, Mozambique and Bangladesh, they were not in Nicaragua for socialist or philanthropic purposes, but to make money.

Forty years ago, young 'internationalists' of the kind that now pick coffee in Nicaragua would spend their summers in Serbia or Croatia building the motorway, 'Brotherhood and Unity', to link the six nations of Yugoslavia. Many Yugoslavs told me that they resented the foreign students because they were given less work, because they were flattered, and, above all, because they were free to return to the West. Then, in 1948, Tito quarrelled with Stalin and no more 'internationalists' went to Yugoslavia. Two decades later, a new generation of left-wing students from Western Europe went to Cuba to cut cane. Then Cuba lost its glamour. Also, cane cutting is painful work. Now a third generation of youngsters from Western Europe has come to Nicaragua to pick coffee.

Yugoslavia, Cuba and Nicaragua have something else in common. In each country, the ruling party honours a revolutionary hero, a partisan who took up arms against, and defied a great oppressor. There was Tito, up in the snowy mountains of Bosnia; Castro in the Sierra Maestra; and General Sandino, here around Matagalpa. But while the rest of the world knows something about the careers and personalities of Tito and Castro, little is known of the man whose name is used by the Sandinista rulers of Nicaragua. His gaunt features, with a mouth suggesting the cruelty of which he was all too capable, appear on the one thousand cordoba bank note, under a broad stetson hat and over a bow tie. The face, which also appears on the one cordoba coin, on hundreds of thousands of posters and stamped in red paint on adobe walls, does not reveal the size of Sandino. He was barely five foot, possibly even smaller than William Walker, a man he resembled in many ways. Like Walker, Sandino ended up in front of a firing squad. Unlike Walker, Sandino triumphed after his death, in the sense that his name lives on in the Sandinista government, the main political party – the Sandinista National Liberation Front (FSLN) – the uniformed Sandinista police, and the plain-clothes Sandinista Defence Committee, charged with the task of smelling out and punishing enemies of the Revolution.

Sandino was not the first of the twentieth-century partisan leaders; that title belongs to the Filipino, Emiliano Aquinaldo, who fought for three years against the United States army. The revolution in Mexico in the second decade of the century, produced such guerrillas as Pancho Villa and Emiliano Zapata. In 1927, the very same year that Sandino began his struggle against the US Marines and their Nicaraguan allies, Mao Tse-tung led an uprising in China.

Perhaps because of Nicaragua's small size and obscurity, the name of Sandino did not enter the folklore of the world, like Tito, Castro or Ho Chi Minh, until the present troubles of Central America brought it back into vogue. Sandino, today, is better known as an anti-Yankee freedom fighter, than ever he was in his lifetime. He has become a cult. Yet at the same time, he remains obscure. Left-wing historians do not venture too deeply into Sandino's career. He was not wholly a bandit, as the Americans, such as Stimson, said at the time, but he was not a Communist either. Although he is now held up as a symbol of poor 'third world' people fighting 'imperialism', Sandino thought of himself as a Nicaraguan patriot. Sandino's quarrel with the United States, which has persisted into the 1980s, had much to do with Nicaragua's special and sensitive place on the map. And in spite of his reputation now as an ideologue of the left, Sandino was very Nicaraguan, involved in the country's ancient feuds.

Augusto Calderón Sandino was born on 18 May 1895 at Niquinohono, fifteen miles west of Granada, to Don Gregorio Sandino, a farmer of Spanish descent, and Margarita Calderón, an Indian servant girl in the house. Both parents were under eighteen, but Gregorio did not shirk his responsibility to the bastard son. He recognised Augusto as his first-born child and gave the mother a house with a roof of tiles rather than thatch. When he later took a legal wife, he brought Augusto into the house where he got on well with his half-brothers and half-sisters. The village was neither surprised nor shocked when Margarita Calderón had three further children by another man to whom she was not married.

It is said that Sandino learned from his father a love of classical history and he was overjoyed to find that his Christian name was that of the Emperor Augustus. For this reason, so family legend goes, he changed his middle name from Calderón to that of another emperor, Caesar; or he could have been ashamed of his mother's surname.

131

After studying at commercial school in Granada, Sandino returned to work on his father's estate, then set himself up as a grain jobber, buying corn and beans to sell on the market. Twice during Sandino's adolescence, in 1909 and 1912, there were brief civil wars in Nicaragua, but there is no proof that he took part. One story, credited by Sandino's Marxist biographer, says that he saw the corpse of the Liberal Party hero, Zeledón. Another story says he was once knocked down in a drunken fight over politics. In any case, he became a life-long Liberal and teetotaller.

Deeper mystery hangs over the fight which compelled Sandino to leave his home and the country in 1920. The Marxist, Gregorio Selser, says that Sandino, 'saw himself obliged to kill a man; some say because of an insult to his mother; according to others, for political reasons.' To the end of his life, Sandino rather enjoyed surrounding himself with legend and mystery. He went in for shooting those who offended him.

After the shooting, Sandino fled to León and then to Honduras, where he became involved in another quarrel involving the use or threat of guns. He left in haste for Guatemala, continuing on to Mexico where he got a job in the oil town, Tampico, then very much under the influence of the American Standard Company.

Mexico, in 1923, was in one of its more stable, rational spells between the peasant uprisings of Pancho Villa and Zapata and, later, socialist militancy against the Church and foreign capitalists. Among the fifty thousand immigrant workers at Tampico, there was every brand of communist, socialist, anarchist and trade union militant, many of whose ideas were no doubt studied by Sandino. He was also attracted to Spiritualism, Theosophy, Yoga, the Freemasons and Seventh Day Adventism. His left-wing admirers say that Sandino's experiences of a lock-out in Mexico gave him an understanding and hatred of Yankee capitalism. However, Sandino's anti-American feeling was racial rather than ideological. He gloried in his Indian blood and in Mexico, which had rejected the Spanish side of its heritage. He said that he felt ashamed because Mexicans called the Nicaraguans traitors, selling their country to the United States.

Sandino afterwards talked of himself as a simple worker, a plain mechanic, yet nevertheless he became the head of the gasoline sales department of Huahtaca Petroleum Company, saving up five thousand dollars against the day when he thought it was prudent to make his return to Nicaragua. This time came in May 1926, when the Liberals rose in armed revolt against the usurper Chamorro; Sandino's father, also a Liberal, wrote urging him to return.

After visiting home, Sandino went to the Nueva Segovia region, close to the border with Honduras, getting a job as a pay-clerk at the San Albino gold mine. This was owned and partly managed by citizens of the United States. In talking with his American bosses, Sandino fantasised about his career. He said he had served eleven years in Pancho Villa's army in Mexico and he also claimed to have been a circus acrobat.

Throughout his career, Sandino was fond of telling tall stories, especially to admiring journalists. Nor is it always clear that he said or wrote some of the stirring and quotable statements now attributed to him. The youth who changed his name from Calderón to César, retained to the end of his life a love of fantasy and mystification, to which was added the pleasure he felt in laughing at those more trusting and frank than himself.

The San Albino gold mine lay in the north-eastern hinterland of Nicaragua, comprising nine-tenths of the territory of the country, but less than a tenth of its population, and these mostly of Indian and Negro race. In 1926, as always, the inhabitants of the hinterland were revolting against the politicians of the Pacific coastal strip where most Nicaraguans live.

The opposition party, in this instance the Liberals who had been ousted by a Conservative *coup d'état*, had set up their base on the Caribbean coast and from there were dispatching armies against the west. Sandino, observing events in his job as assistant paymaster at San Albino, decided to join the civil war in October 1926. He spent his last five hundred dollars on rifles bought from Honduran smugglers to arm the twenty-nine men who had volunteered to join his first army. He led them in an attack on the government garrison at Jicaro. Nobody was killed, but his troops were downhearted; therefore Sandino decided to march them off to the east coast town of Puerto Cabezas, there to enrol in the Liberal army of Dr Sacasa and General Moncado. Both distrusted Sandino, a gasoline salesman and a gold-mine clerk who talked of himself as a veteran in the wars of Pancho Villa. However, Sandino commanded a body of men with rifles and so he was hired by the Liberal army.

Early in 1927, the US Marines arrived again on the Caribbean coast and imposed what they called, 'a neutral zone', which meant, among other things, that the Liberal faction had to surrender its weapons. The Liberal leader, Dr Sacasa, agreed to these terms which gave him a *de facto* recognition in Nicaragua and in the North American newspapers.

But one of the Liberal warlords, Sandino, did not mean to hand over his precious weapons. He broke into and looted the Liberal armoury on the night before it was due to be occupied by the US Marines. The Sandinista version of these events was later told to a journalist by young Colonel Colindros, who had worked at the San Albino mine before joining Sandino's army:

One day when we were still in Puerto Cabezas, American battleships anchored and three hundred marines landed without asking anyone's consent. The port, the seat of Sacasa's government, was declared a 'neutral zone' where the Liberal forces were successful. Sacasa was ordered to deliver up his arms to the American forces ... this though Sacasa was the only legal President ... When the marines appeared in Puerto Cabezas, Sandino was all for repelling them. Sacasa calmed him down. Thereupon, Sandino instead of delivering his arms, retired into the mosquito-infested marshes where every drop of alkaline drinking water had to be secured by digging wells and straining out the mud. To him here, the women of the town, even down to the prostitutes, smuggled out rifles. He secured some twenty-five Mosquito Indians to carry what he had salvaged down to Prinzapolca through the most terrible marshes. From there he made his way to Cabo de Grácias, and suffering untold hardships with a small group, ascended the Rio Coco into the mountains of Nueva Segovia.

In later years, Sandino gave the impression that when he purloined the rifles he had started up on his own. In fact he was still counted as one of the leaders of Dr Sacasa's Liberal army. He was the right flank of General Moncado's main force, heading west to threaten Matagalpa and Managua. It was during these early months of 1927 that, somehow or other, Sandino acquired the title of 'General', while some of his underlings, like Colindros, rose to be Colonels. Nevertheless, it appears that even before he became an outlaw, a Robin Hood, Sandino displayed the qualities of a leader. In March 1927, his men took the important town of Jinotega, where he was later visited by a party of six US Marines, headed by Major M. S. Berry. According to Marine archives, 'As Berry was bidding his host goodbye, Sandino remarked that the American horses looked tired. The Liberal General offered the Marines their choices of any six of his mounts, including his personal mount. Berry declined the offer but noted Sandino's friendly attitude in his report. He informed his superiors that Sandino claimed to have three thousand men and that he had personally seen "three-hundred well-mounted, well-equipped and well-shod men. They were the highest type I have seen in Nicaragua and all seemed to have the fighting spirit".'

Two months later, in May 1927, Stimson obtained a settlement of the civil war between the Liberal and Conservative factions. The troops of both armies responded well to the call to hand in their weapons for cash. The US mission set itself to the next task of organising a fair election in 1928, and training a National Guard to serve as a joint army-police force, free of party feeling.

In spite of the peace agreement, fighting continued, especially in the Liberal region around León. The mob at León were a nuisance, but far more danger faced the Americans in the highlands, eighty miles to the north-east, where General Sandino still commanded his army. After the capture of Jinotega, he made his base at a nearby village called San Rafael del Norte, largely because he had fallen in love with Blanca Auraz, the telephone manager's daughter. Even at this time, he did not trust the Liberal leaders and said that General Moncado would sell out at the first opportunity. After the peace agreement arranged by Stimson, General Moncado tried to persuade Sandino to lay down his arms in return for the governorship of Jinotega province. Sandino agreed to disband his troops but refused to hand over his arms which he oiled and buried in the forest. Further negotiations were held, during the course of which Sandino said he would hand over his arms, provided that the United States formed a military government, dismissing all the Nicaraguan ministers till the election the following year. He was not opposed to American rule as such; only American rule through puppets. Then General Moncado asked Don Gregorio Sandino to reason with his son. Augusto Sandino explained to his father his doubts and anxieties over the peace agreement. He swore that if the Americans did not keep their promise to hold a free election, and 'kicked us in the arse', he would kill himself. Gregorio Sandino went back to Managua empty-handed; but he had seen his new daughter-in-law, Blanca, who had been married on 18 May, Augusto's birthday.

In May, some of Sandino's men had handed their rifles in to the government in return for ten dollars, so he thought it prudent to get them out of temptation's way by moving north to the mountains and jungle near the Honduran border. He named one of his officers, Francisco Estrada, as governor of the Department of Nueva Segovia, with its capital in the village of Jicaro, which he renamed Sandino City. He made his base high in the mountain of El Chipote (bump on the head) in an area so remote that his enemies did not at first believe that El Chipote existed. The base had thatched living quarters, stores for food and ammunition and a corral for horses.

In June, a force of US Marines was sent to Nueva Segovia to persuade, or, if necessary, to force Sandino to end his revolt. Their commander, Captain Hadfield, offered a personal meeting to which Sandino replied (29 June 1927) that he would not come for a conference and 'die like a dove' deceived by 'a few grains of rice at the door of the trap'. (This was a curious premonition of how he did eventually die.) He added, in answer to Hadfield's rather insulting message, 'I remain your most obedient servant, who ardently desires to put you in a handsome tomb with beautiful bouquets of flowers.' In his reply, Captain Hadfield still further lowered the tone of the correspondence, 'Bravo General! If words were bullets and phrases were soldiers, you would be a field marshall instead of a mule thief.' He told Sandino to write again, 'when you have something more to contribute than the ravings of a conceited maniac.' Hadfield's Marines and the Nicaraguan National Guard were based at the town of Ocotal, which Sandino now resolved to attack. But first he needed to strengthen his fire power, to which end he raided his old employers, the San Albino gold mine, taking five hundred pounds of dynamite, with fuses and caps to serve as bombs. He also issued his first manifesto, designed to show 'the Indo-Hispanic race, that on a spur of the Andean mountain range there is a group of patriots who know how to fight and die like men.' A few recruits came in. Captain Hadfield had not the means of publishing manifestos, but wrote to Sandino urging him to follow the lead of Emiliano Aquinaldo, the Philippine guerrilla who had fought against the Americans, then made his peace and later became a devoted ally. Five days after this letter, on 16 July

1927, Sandino gave his reply by sending his troops in a mass attack on Ocotal, supported by eight hundred local peasants eager for loot. The Marines defended their headquarters, meanwhile calling in five De Havilland planes that dive-bombed and machine-gunned the dense ranks of the Sandinistas, inflicting heavy casualties. It was the first dive-bombing attack in history.

The attack on Ocotal and especially the use of dive bombers, provided Sandino with much needed publicity, even if some of it was unfavourable. The American Secretary of State, Frank B. Kellogg, felt obliged to declare that, 'Sandino's activities cannot be considered to have any political significance whatsoever,' and his forces were 'common outlaws'. The United States peacemaker, Henry L. Stimson, whose efforts had been frustrated by the obstinancy of Sandino, blamed him for 'an attack on a much smaller group of Marines and constabulary ... his forces augmented by other lawless individuals who had drifted ... to him.' The Liberal General Moncado accused Sandino of having robbed merchants in Jinotega, after which he went to the mountains, 'took foreigners into his army and dedicated his time to murdering his enemies, both Conservative and Liberal.'

Sandino's base at El Chipote was near the Honduran border town of Danli, through which he could publicise his thoughts and achievements, using as intermediary, the Honduran poet, Froylan Turcíos, the editor of the left-wing fortnightly *Ariel*. Sometimes Sandino's propaganda backfired, as when he sent to the press of the world a photograph of a captured American airman, Lieutenant Thomas, who had been shot and hung from a tree. The picture provoked and enraged other American pilots, who afterwards were merciless in their air raids. Again, this may have been what Sandino wanted, for the bombing attacks on women and children were later to win much foreign sympathy for his cause, as well as providing recruits in Nicaragua.

It was through *Ariel* that Sandino received the best publicity of his life, from the journalist Carleton Beals of the weekly,

Nation, who had arranged with Turcíos to be taken to see Sandino in his jungle hide-out. The vivid and stirring account of this journey which Beals wrote in his articles and a book, *Banana Gold*, was to make Sandino an international figure and remains by far the best picture we have of him. The very few Spanish or Spanish American writers who met Sandino, offered accounts with more rhetoric than reporting. Over the next fifty years, dozens of journalists were to make their names by trekking into the mountains or jungles or deserts to meet guerrilla leaders in China, Spain, Abyssinia, Yugoslavia, Vietnam, Malaya, Cuba, El Salvador and Afghanistan . . . but Beals was perhaps the first. From his own book of memoirs, *Glass Houses*, it seems that Beals had arrived in Mexico in 1920, an adventurous young graduate, and had wandered about, taking odd jobs, living rough and learning Spanish. He was a man of left or liberal sympathies, but he was not an ideologue, and he wrote clean, vigorous prose, probably influenced by the abrupt, macho style of Hemingway. Oddly enough, parts of *Banana Gold* bring to mind the scenes of guerrilla life in *For Whom the Bell Tolls*, though, of course, the Spanish civil war came ten years *after* Sandino's revolt and Beals's book.

The Honduran poet, Turcíos, suggested that Beals should travel with General Santos Siquieros, 'nervous and arrogant', a Nicaraguan exile anxious to join Sandino. Even before leaving Honduras, Beals encountered another Sandino officer, General Torres, coming the other way, 'taking his family, cattle, asses, household goods and concubines to safety; a large cavalcade winding its way down through the pine woods. He was bursting with stories of marine atrocities – looting the hacienda El Hule; pillaging; brutalities to women and an old grandmother dragged with a rope round her neck.'

On entering Nicaragua, Beals was given a mounted guide, Captain Herrero, wearing a tattered shirt, with his bare feet in stirrups of rawhide. Referring to the reports that the Sandinistas were just marauders, Beals made the sarcastic comment, 'Surely banditry should have brought him a better return here, where the meadows are full of cattle and horses, and the cribs are overflowing with corn; and coffee is piled high, ready for the shelling.' Beals recorded with every sign of belief, that Herrero had 'received his Captaincy for an attack single-handed on a patrol of four marines. He had fallen on them with machetes, no gun, and had cut them to pieces.' Perhaps he had, but I think Beals should have put this claim in quotation marks, rather than stating it as a fact.

At last Beals arrived at Sandino's camp in the village of San Rafael del Norte. They were challenged by sentries and then, at the barracks, they found an entire company lined up at attention. 'Their rifles snapped from ground to shoulder as we passed. After sundry haltings, we arrived to the sound of a night-splitting skirl of bugles. Sandino's troops were excellently disciplined.' Beals found a message from Sandino saying he was unwell but would give an interview next morning at four o'clock. He spent the evening with Colonel Rivera and his wife, talking and looking at snaps in the family album. Among the photographs were some on the bombing of Chinandega. Beals accepted the Sandinista version, blaming American bombers, 'An entire street laid in ruins and sprinkled with mangled bodies; the tumbled walls of the hospital; broken bodies of patients flung about; a bank building and a smashed safe. Was it so long ago we called the Germans Huns for destroying civilian populations without mercy?'

Beals wrote a full description of the guerrilla leader, whose appearance was then almost unknown, even in Nicaragua:

Sandino is short, probably not more than five feet. On the morning of our interview he was dressed in a new uniform of almost black khaki and wore puttees, immaculately polished. A silk black and red handkerchief was knotted about his throat.

His broad-brimmed stetson, low over his forehead, was pinched
into a shovel shape. Occasionally as we conversed, he shoved
his sombrero far back on his head and hitched his chair
forward. The gesture revealed his straight black hair and full
forehead. His face is straight-lined from temple to sharp-angled
jawbone, which slants to an even firmer jaw. His regular
curved eyebrows are high above liquid black eyes without
visible pupils, eyes of remarkable mobility and refraction to
light – quick, intense eyes.

Beals then goes on to call Sandino, 'a man utterly without vices,
with an unequivocal sense of justice, a keen eye for the welfare
of the humble soldier ... In every soldier and every officer to
whom I talked, he had lighted fierce affection, blind loyalty; he
had installed in every man his own burning hatred for the "invader".'

Beals quotes some of Sandino's epigrams such as, 'Death is but
one little moment of discomfort; it's not to be taken too seriously.'
He notes the reference to religion in Sandino's talk, 'Several times
he referred to the Seventh Day Adventist book he had brought
from Mexico. Frequently he mentioned God: "God is the ultimate
arbiter of our battles." "If God wills it, we shall go on to
victory." "God and our mountains fight for us." '

His most frequent gesture was the shaking of his fore-finger, a
full-armed motion behind it. Invariably he leaned forward as he
spoke and once or twice took to his feet, emphasising a point
with his whole body. His utterances were remarkably fluid,
precise, evenly modulated; his enunciation absolutely clear; his
voice rarely changed pitch, even when he was visibly intent
upon the subject matter. Not once during the four and a half
hours while we talked, almost continually, without prompting
from me, did he fumble for the form of expression or indicate
any hesitancy regarding the themes he intended to discuss.
His ideas are precisely, epigrammatically ordered. There was

not a major problem in the whole Nicaraguan question that he dodged or that I even needed to raise.

The only critical note that sounds in Beals' admiring account, is really a compliment in disguise:

> In military matters, however, he was quite too flamboyant and boastful and exaggerated his successes. 'Where are all the aeroplanes I have heard so much about?" I asked. He smiled: "At ten o'clock they will fly over San Rafael,' he said, and at ten, as he had said, two bombing planes buzzed over the little town, circling lower and lower. Sandino's men were stationed in the doorways, rifles in hand. 'Don't fire unless they bomb' were his orders. On the last approach the planes roared over the very roof tops, then were gone.

Sandino had ordered, on his arrival at San Rafael, that any soldier who touched anything not belonging to him would be shot; and Beals learned from the local shopkeepers, that everything bought was paid for. However, as Beals remarked elsewhere, the Sandinistas confiscated the saddles and horses of Conservatives. Sandino also forbade the sale of alcohol in any place held by his forces; the penalty for a breach of this law was, for a man, shooting; for a woman, the burning of her house. Shortly before he left San Rafael to cross into the territory held by the government, Beals was approached by the nervous General Siquieros who told him, 'General Sandino is going to shoot me.'

'Nonsense,' said Beals; 'Sandino has talked with you. He's been courteous and thoughtful.'

'You don't know our people ...' Six months later Siquieros was shot for treachery. Beals appeared to believe the story that 'documents were found on him, arranging to betray Sandino to the Marines.'

General Sandino took his leave, giving Beals absolute freedom to speak and write about everything he had seen with the guerrillas, 'If you wish, ride straight to Jinotega, six leagues from here and tell the first Marine Commandant that you meet, everything you have seen and heard. In fact that would suit my plans admirably.'

9

SAN RAFAEL DEL NORTE

WHEREAS BEALS HAD got to Sandino the hard way, over the mountains by the Honduras border, I went by road to San Rafael del Norte. Beals had done the equivalent now of going to meet the Contra rebels, who operate in the same way as Sandino. They come from bases in Honduras, or just this side of the border, and spend most of their time in mountainous forest. Only occasionally do the Contras venture into the more inhabited regions of Nicaragua, round Matagalpa, Jinotega and San Rafael del Norte. In this region I did for the first time feel aware of the war. But even here I had no sense of impending danger, as I have felt in other countries engaged in this kind of warfare, Vietnam, for example, or parts of Northern Ireland. There are hundreds of troops around but they show no suspicion or even awareness of wandering foreigners. I did not see on the faces of village people, the fear and alarm that appear when guerrilla troops have entered the district. It was cool and refreshing up in the mountains. The driver who took me from Matagalpa would not go further than Jinotega. I went to the bus depot to look for someone to take me to San Rafael.

The driver I found was like one of those sinister-comic characters from a Hollywood film about Mexico. He did not actually call me 'Gringo' but he was unshaven, moustached, red

144

eyed and he cackled a lot, baring gold teeth. On his dashboard there was a statuette of the Virgin, as well as a curious plastic sculpture, in bright orange, showing two galloping horses pulling a wagon on which were seated a woman holding the reins and a man at the back with an old-fashioned machine gun, firing at his pursuers ... Red Indians presumably. It was suitable for this increasingly Indian country. I had just been staring at this work when there thundered towards us, moving at greater speed than our car, a bullock, closely pursued by a cowboy waving a lariat round his head.

It was the first time I had seen this outside a cinema. I had seen dude cowboys back in Managua with stetson hats and horses that did little dance steps; but here in the highlands, the driver told me, the cowboys were genuine.

San Rafael del Norte turned out to be one long street of adobe houses, with one dingy church. I got out of the car and asked the first man I met which was Sandino's old house. He frowned and pointed along the street. I tried again and received a scowl of hatred. A third man pointed and said coldly, 'That's his house. It's now a museum.' The museum was shut. When would it open again? Maybe next year. An old man came up and actually smiled in greeting. Did he remember Sandino? I asked. Yes, he remembered him as a small child. What did he remember? The old man pointed at his feet and said a word that I did not know and could not find in my pocket dictionary. This may have been 'puttees'. The old man said that Sandino's wife had lived in the house next to Sandino's. It was a billiard saloon and a soft-drink shop, but they would not sell me a bottle. I can only assume that they thought that anyone asking about Sandino must be a Sandinista.

At the only café in San Rafael del Norte, they served me an orangeade but refused to talk. The wall decorations proclaimed the landlord's views. There was a photograph of the Pope, three paintings of Christ and four of the Infant Samuel at prayer. I left

145

the café and was heading towards the church when an army truck, crammed with soldiers in combat gear, came roaring along the street, followed by six more, a total of nearly two hundred men. The citizens of San Rafael del Norte, once the headquarters of General Sandino, gave no greeting to the troops of the Sandinista army. The part of the country once controlled by Sandino, the huge north-east, is once more hostile to the government from Managua. But now it is Russia and Cuba, not the United States, that lend support to the government forces. In order to understand what has happened, one has to go back to the story of General Sandino, where we left him, after his meeting with Carleton Beals.

By the end of January 1928, the month of Beals' visit to the guerrillas, the strength of the US Marine force had doubled to three thousand, but still was insufficient to win victory. A Marine lieutenant, Moses J. Gould, wrote of a recent encounter, 'The discipline maintained, their morale and the accuracy of the fire of the bandits, as well as the tactical disposition of their troops, were far above anything displayed by them in any of their actions heretofore in the section, and leads to the belief that they are receiving training instruction from sources other than Nicaraguans, because of the up-datedness of their tactics.'

The combination of jungle and mountain gave all the advantage to the guerrillas who knew the terrain and how to move about in it. The Marines were tortured by heat in the day and cold at night, by almost daily rain, by insects, leeches and the continuous fear of poisonous snakes. The only means of transport, except on foot, were mules and aeroplanes. During a battle at Quilali, a plane was used for the first time in history as a 'Medivac', flying the wounded out of the improvised landing strip; in this case, on the main street of the village. The pilot, Lieutenant Christian Schilt, made ten landings under intense fire on each of which, 'Marines had to run out and grab the wings in order to slow the plane down and keep it from smashing off the end of the abbreviated runway.'

The discipline and valour of the Marines prevented any serious decline in morale. Nevertheless, one sergeant deserted and joined Sandino, while even an officer, First Lieutenant Richard Fayn was heard to exclaim, at a cocktail party, 'I'm an Irishman in the service of the United States, but as an Irishman, I say that General Sandino is a patriot.' As the war dragged on, most of the counter-insurgency work devolved on Nicaraguan troops of the National Guard under United States officers. Here again there were frequent desertions, or men sold their weapons to the guerrillas. There was one small mutiny and seven Marine officers were shot by their own Nicaraguan troops.

One Marine veteran of the Nicaraguan war said many years afterwards in an interview with Macaulay, 'We were too nervous. One of those fellows could live in ambush for a week when you couldn't do it for two hours. You'd get to worry why nobody came along.' The Marines, however, had a striking success with 'Company M', a special anti-guerrilla patrol consisting of thirty Nicaraguans led by two very gung-ho officers. Most of the Nicaraguans in 'Company M' came from the very small minority of almost pure Indians who felt at home in the jungle and liked nothing more than the chance to kill people of Spanish or partly Spanish origin. The Sandino troops and their foreign admirers often accused 'Company M' of using terror and torture and cutting off the heads of enemy dead and prisoners.

Sandino himself made an institution of terror in his *cortes*, a Spanish word that can mean both 'courts of justice' and 'cuts'. The earliest of these *cortes* was the *corte de chaleco* or 'waistcoat court', in which the culprit's head was lopped off by a machete, after which his arms were removed and then a sign was carved on his chest with slashes. One of Sandino's henchmen invented the *corte de chaleco*, but later grew bored with it and ordained instead that all 'traitors' suffer instead the *corte de cumbo* or 'gourd court', in which a skilful machete man sliced off a bit of the victim's skull, exposing his brain and leaving him to suffer hours

147

of agony and convulsion before death. If there was no executioner expert enough to perform the 'gourd court', the guilty man suffered the 'bloomers court', by which his legs were cut off at the knee and he bled to death. Sandino sometimes had people shot, but, as he said in 1931, 'Liberty is not conquered with flowers and for this reason we must resort to the *cortes* of "waistcoat", "gourd" and "bloomers".' The Sandinistas normally mutilated their enemy corpses, shoving the penis into the mouth.

Sandino was safest up in the jungle near El Chipote, but every so often he ventured into more open, populous regions in search of provisions, horses and mules, recruits and, above all, cash. When Beals met him early in 1928, Sandino was just about to embark on a lucrative series of raids on the coffee plantations around Matagalpa. Among his victims was the Conservative plantation owner, Leopold Salazar, who barely escaped the 'waistcoat court'.

About a dozen of these plantations were owned by citizens of the United States and most of the others by Germans, Englishmen and other foreigners. The planters were vulnerable, not only to theft of their goods or cash, but the threat of scaring away their workforce. Sandino's first victims were one English and two German planters, whom he relieved of their money, mules and any portable equipment, giving receipts for everything he took. This Robin Hood touch should not blind one to the fact that Sandino was practising banditry. It cannot be seen as an act of social justice in robbing the rich to feed the poor, since most of the money was spent not on food, but on arms and ammunition. Sandino himself was the son of a prosperous landowner, he always believed in the virtue of private property for himself. The enterprise of the German and English coffee planters had opened up and brought prosperity to the Matagalpa region, as Rubén Darío remarked in his *Voyage to Nicaragua* twenty years earlier. Indeed Darío went out of his way to state that Nicaragua needed more, not less, foreign planters.

148

The articles and the book by Carleton Beals had made Sandino into a world celebrity. The Comintern took up his cause in 1928, although they already knew he was not a Marxist. At the first International Anti-Imperialist Congress that year in Frankfurt, a Sandinista representative held up a captured Marine flag to applause from such dignitaries as Jawaharlal Nehru and Madame Sun Yat Sen. Perhaps because of that lady's recommendation, the anti-imperialist troops of the Kuomintang carried a portrait of Sandino on their victorious entry into Peking. One of the units of Chiang Kai-Shek's army was renamed the 'Sandino Division'. The most telling sign of the fame and popularity of Sandino came from Hollywood where Cecil B. de Mille proposed making a movie about his life. The idea was crushed by objections from Washington.

Nicaragua went to the polls in a general election in 1928, under the eye of nearly a thousand US polling officials, determined to see fair play. In order to stop the practice of double or multiple voting, each elector, on casting his vote, was made to dip one finger in a Mercurochrome dye. General Sandino, who had denounced the poll as a fraud, said that the dye was dangerous. In the areas he controlled, he was able to use more forceful methods of stopping people from voting. In spite of Sandino, one hundred and thirty-three thousand people cast their votes, or, fifty thousand more than in 1924 in the last election supervised by the United States. The result was a victory for the Liberal General Moncado, and this time the incumbent Conservatives had the grace to acknowledge that they had lost in a fair election; something unprecedented in Nicaraguan history.

Fair elections would not survive the departure of the US Marines. Far more significant to the future of Nicaragua was the setting up of a National Guard, intended to be a non-political body, but one that became the private police and army of the Somoza family. The United States was proud of the National Guard it had formed in the Philippines; but the Philippines were

149

a colony and the Guard was run by the United States. In Nicaragua the Americans had only a temporary status, so that although they managed to form and train an efficient National Guard, it still remained vulnerable to the local politicians. Both Parties tried to manage the National Guard, even while the United States maintained a presence in Nicaragua. When the Conservatives were in office, the American Chief of Managua police complained, 'The people were against our methods at first because they could not bribe us to act blind or look the other way. I asked the lady next to the police station to present our case to the President whenever we had to lock up some prominent Conservative, or, once in a while, his nephew, or brother or secretary.'

The frustration of the Americans sometimes showed itself in outbursts such as this from Captain Bleasdale, the National Guard Intelligence Officer, writing in 1928 to his Commander:

> If, as a people, the Nicaraguans had any sense of law, order, honesty and common ordinary decency, there would be no occasion for the United States to lend its assistance to them to straighten out the pathetic mess they have made of their efforts to negotiate the complicated machinery of modern civilization. This is a sorry country and a sorry people and the better Nicaraguans know, that when it becomes a better land, it will be because of the United States and your Marines.

The Liberal President Moncado proved worse than the Conservatives in using the National Guard for his own ends. In April 1929 he imprisoned sixteen opponents. In spite of protests from the United States, he went on to arrest forty more, deporting six of them, including the editor of *La Prensa*, then as now the leading Conservative newspaper. He justified his actions with the unlikely tale that the Conservatives were in league with Sandino to have him assassinated. Next year he arrested a number of Communists, or alleged Communists, and gaoled them with the

Conservatives. The American chief director of the Guard said at the time, 'Moncado is a difficult man to do business with. He is hard drinking and despotic and erratic to a degree when he is in his cups. He dislikes Americans.'

The Marines had few good Spanish speakers and had to deal with the President through a Nicaraguan intermediary. This role came to be filled by a bright young man with a fluent command of English, Anastasio Somoza García. Increasingly, American officers took their problems first to Somoza, who passed the messages to Moncado, and often suggested how the replies should be phrased. The Guards Chief of Staff, like the majority of American officers, felt that Somoza 'always played the game fairly with us'.

Back in the Nicaraguan civil wars of the 1840s, one Barnabé Somoza, was said to have been renowned for his charm and excessive cruelty. He hated the English and wanted to rule Nicaragua with help from the United States. His grand-nephew, Anastasio, was born in 1896 at San Marcos, very near to Sandino's home and, like Sandino, he studied at the Granada Commercial College. He married in 1919 into the wealthy Debayle family and, thanks to his father enjoying a good coffee crop, was able to study in the United States where he got his useful command of the English language.

When his father's coffee failed, Somoza was not above taking such jobs as boxing referee, baseball umpire, electric meter reader, and lavatory inspector for the Rockefeller team, which was carrying out a programme of technical aid in Nicaragua. During the civil war of 1925, Somoza started a not very glorious rising on behalf of the Liberal Party at San Marcos. He fled the day after hoisting the Liberal colours. However, he met and greatly impressed the American special envoy, Stimson, who was to be Hoover's Secretary of State.

When the Liberals won power in 1928, Somoza became a General, then Governor of León province; a junior foreign minister and finally, head of the National Guard, the power base of his family for the next half century. Somoza was stocky and tall, a giant by Nicaraguan standards; an extrovert; an expert dancer of the tango and rumba and always ready to smile and laugh. He had the bonhomie that North Americans often confuse with charm; but he had charm as well, and a power for dissembling that was to outwit Sandino. He was a cruel and envious man, acting the part of the bluff hearty soldier; a modern version of 'honest, honest Iago'.

Meanwhile, General Sandino's insurrection was running out of steam. He had proved from the start his ability to maintain his army safe from attack in the mountains and jungle near Honduras. He had shown he could make the occasional raid on coffee plantations or mines. The fact remained that he could not show his face in the cities and plains of west Nicaragua, where nine-tenths of the population lived; nor is there evidence that he had any popular sympathy. His standing in the outside world depended on friendly journalists such as Beals and in this respect he suffered a grievous blow when his friend, the Honduran poet, Turcíos, gave up left-wing politics to be his country's Ambassador in Paris. This defection broke Sandino's propaganda machine. For a time in 1929, he decided to circumvent the press and address himself direct to the chancellories of the world. He wrote a letter to President Herbert Hoover of the United States, closely modelled on Rubén Darío's poem *A Roosevelt*, 'I am not unmindful of the material resources at the disposal of your nation, you have everything, but you lack God.'

This letter was sent to the US legation in Honduras, but the officials there refused to accept it when they noticed Sandino's seal, showing a Nicaraguan with a machete cutting off a Marine's head.

Discouraged by his lack of publicity coming on top of a lull in the fighting, Sandino decided to take up an offer to visit Mexico. He imagined he would be given some arms and a base for his operations, but Mexico's President Gil was offering only political refuge, such as he afterwards gave to Leon Trotsky. When Sandino reached Mexico, he could not get permission to visit the capital and had to reside in the charming but distant city of Mérida on the east coast. The absence of their chief disheartened the Sandinistas who had remained in Nicaragua; they turned increasingly to pillage, rather than fighting the US Marines. The Americans in Nicaragua set up the first of a number of 're-located villages' by moving the population from areas where they might give food and support to the guerrillas. The modern Sandinistas have 're-located' tens of thousands of peasants from Contra regions.

By April 1930 Sandino was feeling so frustrated in Mexico that he gave his hosts the slip, and returned to Nicaragua. This decision brought to a head the long-rankling quarrel between Sandino and the Marxists. In May that year, a Communist Party statement accused Sandino of treachery to the anti-imperialist cause, and going back to Nicaragua to 'sell out to the highest bidder, to fight on the side of petty bourgeois groups.' Among the Communists who denounced Sandino was his own private secretary, the El Salvadorean Augustín Farabundo Martí, whose memory is now revered by the left of his country. In 1932, a peasant revolt in El Salvador was put down by a massacre that is said to have taken at least twenty thousand lives, including that of Martí. Although Martí believed Sandino's flag was 'one of independence . . . not of the Communist program for which I was fighting', he added shortly before he was shot by a firing squad, 'I solemnly swear that General Sandino is the greatest patriot in the world.'

Today, the Central American left maintains that Communists and patriots have one common enemy, the United States; that the struggle of Nicaragua and El Salvador are the same. One might draw a different lesson from what occurred in the early thirties. In El Salvador, an eccentric dictator backed by the rich

Salvadorean coffee planters, felt free to kill tens of thousands of poor compatriots, in the confidence that the rest of the world would not hear of the crime, or would not care.

At the same time, in Nicaragua, Sandino was leading a small peasant revolt against the central government. This government did not respond by a massacre or the wholesale use of torture and terror. Its counter-insurgency operations were carried out under the law, and in the light of publicity from the foreign press. Why were the two countries so different? Surely because in Nicaragua the presence of the United States Marines restrained the local politicians from killing and beating their own people after the Central American fashion? As soon as the US Marines left, Nicaragua went back to despotism.

In June 1930, shortly after returning from Mexico, Sandino decided to make his presence felt with an assault on El Saraguesco mountain, near Jinotega. His four hundred men were well trained and armed. Some of their war material had been captured from the National Guard, but most was purchased in the United States, Nicaragua and neighbouring Central American countries. At least three boatloads of ammunition had reached Sandino from Mexico.

During the battle of El Saraguesco, Sandino was hit in the leg by shrapnel. One of his nurses, Teresa Villatorio, had been Sandino's mistress up in the mountains. Once, when Teresa was hit in the head, Sandino had taken a chip of her skull and set it in gold on a signet ring, which he always wore as a memory of their friendship. This cannot have pleased his legal wife, Blanca, but she had been 're-located' by the Marines to León. Both of Sandino's women were hell-cats. We know from Beals that Teresa was in the habit of offering round American cigarettes she had lifted from dead Marines. Sandino himself complained of his wife, 'My little Blanca has her point thirty-two pistol and her point forty-four Winchester rifle and I cannot stop her from shooting up much ammunition daily; she is manly, like Mary the

154

wife of Joseph was, and all I can do is permit her to do everything she likes.'

A Sandinista, made prisoner by the Marines, said, 'We would have captured Jinotega if it were not for the aeroplanes.' In the judgement of an official history:

> Air was an integral part of the Marine expeditionary force, not a separate arm. Operating under the direct control of ground force operations, Marine pilots in Haiti and Nicaragua worked out many techniques of World War II, during the 1920s.
>
> Air drops of supplies, aerial casualty evacuations, message pick-ups and signalling by ground patrols, were an old story by that time, and Marine fliers initiated dive-bombing in combat nearly two decades before Nazi aviators of the Luftwaffe were accredited with the 'innovation'.

Nicaragua was also the testing ground for the prototype of the combat helicopter. In May 1932, an OP 1 autogiro arrived at the US Marine corps base in Quantico, where it drew enthusiastic crowds. 'The turkey-hen was admired for a long time by curiosity seekers,' reported *Diario Moderno*. 'But if OP 1 offered some diversion, it also claimed the serious attention of the Marine pilots putting it through the paces,' writes Lynn Montross in *Cavalry of the Sky: The Story of Marine Combat Helicopters*.

American air power could not help in the operations to stop the supply of food and arms to the rebels from over the frontier with Honduras. The border was five hundred miles long; the terrain was mountainous; the visibility often obscured by cloud; and the vegetation thick. Even if the Marines succeeded in blocking the roads and the main trails, there were countless paths available to the experienced tracker. In this border land, the Americans were always in danger of ambush; eight out of ten Marines who went to repair some telephone lines near Ocotol were surprised and killed. The Nicaraguans of the National Guard did little better, since most of them came from the western plain and felt just as strange in the mountains as the Americans did.

However, American air power did deter Sandino from plunder raids into the coffee country of Jinotega and Matagalpa. This, more than anything else, decided him in 1931 to make an attack on the east, which he justified by saying that most of the mines and plantations there were American property. Moreover, the economic depression after the Wall Street crash of 1929 had upset the banana business, causing social unrest around Bluefields. The growers association was withholding its produce in order to keep up the price, and using force against peasant farmers who wanted to sell their bananas to the ships. In January 1931, a crowd had sacked a Chinese store and two depots of the United Fruit Company. In March, Sandino ordered attacks on American property near Puerto Cabezas, and on the mines further inland.

As in the previous century, the coastal Mosquito peoples regarded themselves as separate from the Ladino or Spanish-speaking Nicaraguans. Almost all were of mixed Indian and Negro race. If a man was more black than brown, and spoke English, he called himself Creole. If he was more brown and spoke the indigenous language, he called himself Indian. Creoles and Indians got on well with each other, but not with the west coast Nicaraguans. General Sandino therefore chose as his two lieutenants on the Mosquito coast, a mulatto, Abraham Rivera, and a half-Mosquito, half-Scottish politician, Adolfo Cockburn. The Sandinistas attacked the Standard Fruit Company, taking prisoner and beheading an American and two British employees. The raids were lucrative and did not result in a backlash of feeling from the American public. The left said that the American fruit companies cheated Latin America; the right said they encouraged mixed marriages; the US government did not like them, because they demanded protection but did not pay the US tax.

While Sandino was down on the Caribbean coast, there took place one of those natural intrusions into the human folly of

Nicaragua. On 31 March 1931, Managua, the capital, was wrecked by an earthquake and subsequent fire that destroyed thirty blocks and left only a dozen buildings upright. Many of the thirty-five thousand inhabitants, especially the middle class, had gone to the mountains or to the sea for the holiday of Holy Week. Nevertheless, the toll of the dead was one thousand four hundred and fifty-four, of whom four were United States citizens. The rising politician, Anastasio Somoza, was praised by Americans for his work in fire-fighting, helping the homeless and burying the dead. Although it was known by now that Managua lay on a geological fault, the government rebuilt on the same position, between the lake and the hill of Tiscapa, so that forty-one years later, Managua was once more destroyed; though on that occasion nobody praised the role of the son of Anastasio Somoza. In 1931, as after any earthquake, the wiseacres and soothsayers drew from it all kinds of meaning. Sandino said that, 'it clearly demonstrates to the doubters that divine gestures are guiding our actions in Nicaragua.' He told his men to, 'tremble before these things of divine origin, precisely for the reason that our army itself has sprung from the same invisible impulse.' Meanwhile, his army continued to murder and loot along the Mosquito coast.

The Sandino revolt came nowhere near victory, but it spurred the United States into ending its long involvement in Nicaragua. By the time the Marines departed at the end of 1932, General Sandino held no more territory than he did six years earlier, and he had if anything less support in the rest of the country. On the other hand, the Marines and their Nicaraguan protégés had not managed to kill or catch Sandino, in spite of their much superior numbers and arms, and air power. The US decision to leave Nicaragua without having achieved a clear-cut victory was very much due to the unpopularity of the war at home. Not all Americans took the heroic view of the Sandinistas put forward by Beals and the liberal Senator Borah, but many disliked a war in which the United States was made to look like a bully.

As early as 1928, the fervently anti-Communist Secretary of State, Frank B. Kellogg, complained to the US Commander in Nicaragua:

There is a great deal of criticism in this country about the way in which these operations are being dragged out with constant sacrifice of American lives and without concrete results. So far as anybody here can see, what is now taking place can and will go on indefinitely. People cannot understand why the job cannot be done and frankly, I do not understand it myself.

The next United States Secretary of State was the same Henry L. Stimson who had negotiated the Nicaraguan peace treaty only to see his efforts wrecked by the intransigence of Sandino. However, he was a realist, who bore no personal grudge and was all too aware of the problems of Nicaragua. His President, Herbert Hoover, knew something of Latin America and its sensitive feelings towards the United States. Before his inauguration in March 1929, Hoover had taken a Latin American cruise during which he had spent a day in Corinto. Both he and Stimson planned to withdraw from Nicaragua as soon as this could be done without throwing the country back into civil strife or despotism. They agreed to keep on some Marines for the war against Sandino, but pushed ahead with handing over the rest of the National Guard to Nicaraguans. After the general election of 1932, the US Marines would leave the National Guard to its first Nicaraguan Commander-in-Chief, Anastasio Somoza.

The economic depression and discontent at home, strengthened the will of Hoover and Stimson to wash their hands of Nicaragua. Congress had caught the public mood of irritation with Nicaragua, a mood that could quickly turn to anger, as when the eight Marines were killed at the end of 1931. Congress not only called for withdrawal of US troops, but would not vote the money for US officials to supervise the general election of

1932. In the Sandinista histories of the period, it is claimed that the United States did not withdraw from Nicaragua until it had found a suitable puppet, Somoza, to guard its interests. In fact, the United States just wanted out. General Somoza was left (and glad to be left) to his own devices.

On New Year's Day 1933, the newly elected liberal President, Dr Sacasa, took office. Next day the Marines finally left Nicaragua, after a six-year war in which they lost one hundred and thirty-six lives, of which thirty-two were killed in action; fifteen died of wounds; eleven were murdered (seven of them by their Nicaraguan troops); fourteen were killed in air crashes; twelve committed suicide; one was shot while resisting arrest, and the rest died of disease. The rebels published casualty lists, but according to Mr Macaulay, 'The total numbers of the Sandinistas killed at Ocotal (July 1927) and the El Sance railroad (a battle of 28 December 1932), their first and last battle, was probably greater than the Marine and National Guard figure for the entire intervention.' For the US Marine Corps, the Nicaragua imbroglio provided a training in jungle warfare that was to prove invaluable in the coming struggle against Japan in New Guinea, the Philippines and the smaller Pacific islands.

With the Marines gone, Sandino had no more justification for his rebellion, but he was wary of the Managua government. In return for disbanding his army, he asked for a *de facto* rule over the northern and eastern territories he controlled, as well as a small military guard to protect his safety. His demands included an agricultural settlement on the Coco River, which for much of its course is the frontier between Nicaragua and Honduras. He did not advocate land reform in the sense of appropriating private land and distributing it to the poorer peasantry. On the contrary, he said there was plenty of unused land; as there still is.

Sandino made peace in a mood of foreboding, 'I woke up today feeling romantic and tragic,' he told his friends on the 1 February 1933. 'I think I have to make peace in the next five days, or I'm dead, and the way to do it is for me to go to Managua and deal directly with Dr Sacasa.' He arrived in Managua by plane the following day, to be met at the airport by General Somoza, the newly appointed head of the National Guard. The two men embraced with apparent affection. Both were liberals, Generals, old boys of the Granada Commercial College, and Freemasons. They went to the palace, where Sandino met and embraced Dr Sacasa, the President. An agreement was signed, allowing Sandino to have his agricultural colony and a guard of a hundred men.

Demobilisation took place on 22 February 1933, here in San Rafael del Norte. Among those present was José Romain, a young Nicaraguan journalist who admired Sandino and worried about his safety. Would it not be more prudent to take a diplomatic appointment rather than trusting himself to enemies here at home? To which Sandino replied that he had invitations to go to Paris, Buenos Aires and Mexico but did not want to exhibit himself 'like a movie actor, tango singer, politician or showcase ambassador'. Another witness at San Rafael was Leo Salazar, the Matagalpa coffee planter who had been robbed by Sandino's men and threatened with death by the 'waistcoat court'. His account of Sandino is understandably waspish:

> He was a very nervous fellow, a little dinky fellow, nothing to him. And he had this whip . . . he was always snapping the whip, and nervous. And always wearing the hat. And he talked . . . a funny way of talking. He was not brave but had what you call in the United States the gift of the gab. He could stand on a tree stump and talk and talk, and send his men off to fight.

Three months later, Blanca Sandino died in childbirth. The General left for his settlement on the Coco River, no doubt grief-stricken, but taking Blanca's niece as his bed companion.

Down in Managua, the capital, General Somoza's National Guard was gaining power from Dr Sacasa, the President. In November 1933, the Vice-President told the American Minister that Somoza was planning a *coup d'état*. Sandino, too, said that the National Guard was 'unconstitutional' when he came to Managua again on 16 February 1934. However, he met and appeared to get on well with Somoza. But already his murder had been prepared. General Somoza and his officers met that evening and gave their signatures to a document called 'The Death of Caesar'. Somoza assured them he had the backing of Washington for his plan to execute Sandino. Whether he did or not, we do not know. The next evening, General Sandino and his aides had dinner at the Palace. Afterwards, at the gate, they were held up at gunpoint by members of the National Guard and ordered off to the airport, where a firing squad was in readiness. General Somoza did not witness what followed, perhaps because it embarrassed him to kill a fellow Mason; so the work was left to some junior officers. Before his death, Sandino played for time by smoking a cigarette and asking to give his change and effects as souvenirs to the firing squad. He put his hands in his pockets and said, *'Jodido* [screwed]. My political leaders have picked me clean.' They were the last words he spoke before he was shot.

'Fifty years later – Sandino lives!' are the words you now see all over Nicaragua, painted or stamped on the plaster of the adobe houses. In the hagiography of the revolution, General Sandino appears as a folk hero comparable with such ancient figures of legend as William Tell, Robin Hood, Davy Crockett, Spartacus and the Three Musketeers; as well as more recent ideological warriors such as Tito, Mao Tse-tung, Che Guevara, Jose Martí, the Cuban revolutionary in the nineteenth century, and Augustín Farabundo Martí, the El Salvadorean Communist in the twentieth. Does Sandino deserve this adulation?

For a start, we must answer the question, would there have

been a Sandino revolt without Sandino? The answer is surely, no. All the other Liberal Generals in 1927 were willing and eager to lay down their arms and await the result of a fair election. No other general, nor any political leader, took Sandino's side. The area he controlled looks very big on the map, but contains less than a tenth of the population, of whom most are Negroes, Indians or a combination of both. These inhabitants of the mountains, the rain forests and the Atlantic coast had never truly belonged to the Nicaraguan body politic, which is crammed into a narrow, lowland strip beside the Pacific. There is no reason to think that Sandino had followers outside the territory where he ruled. The Conservatives were against him as a Liberal. The Liberals formed the government against which he rebelled. There was no Sandinista political group in the towns. Few, if any, supporters came from the towns to serve in his army. The North American Marines were as popular as any troops can be in a foreign country. Far from resenting the culture of the United States, the Nicaraguans developed a liking for jazz and a mania for baseball.

His enemies at the time called Sandino a bandit, because he earned his living from robbery; but he was scarcely a criminal. He had political views and ambitions to govern. He was sincere in wanting the North Americans out of his country, yet because of his rebellion, the North Americans stayed in Nicaragua six years more than they at first intended. Sandino liked to compare himself to the Mexicans, Pancho Villa and Zapata; but those who joined Sandino's army were neither poor nor landless peasants. They came from a part of Nicaragua where there was ample land and virtually no landlords.

The man Sandino most resembled was William Walker. He was a soldier of fortune, a filibuster, whose banditry was combined with a crude but plausible set of opinions. Both men were courageous, determined, self-confident, vain, and pitiless, though Walker allowed his foes a quick death by shooting rather than torturing them. Both men were small in stature and huge in their own estimations. Both men exacerbated the violence in what is a country always ready for violence. Both ended their days in front of a firing squad.

When reading about the Sandino affair half a century later, we find ourselves constantly making comparisons with later counter-insurgency wars, above all, Vietnam. Such analogies are usually made by those who admire Sandino but sometimes, too, by opponents, such as Robert Debs Heinz, Jr, author of *Soldiers of the Sea: The United States Marine Corps*. Writing in 1962, Mr Heinz declared that Sandino was,

> ... a modern style guerrilla demagogue in his articulacy, his talent for agitation, his deft intrigue, his cynical disregard for political commitments, his vanishing powers across 'neutral' frontiers ... [he] is far more recognizable in the 1960s than in the 1920s ... Fund raising drives in Lower Manhattan amassed contributions to buy arms with which Sandino terrorized his fellow countrymen and killed US Marines. Such phenomena as these – and Carleton Beals's grossly partisan articles for *The Nation*, date-lines in the camp of enemies of United States troops – came under the absurd heading of 'Liberalism' in the 1920s. The 1960s had another word for it.

That was written three years before the United States dispatched the Marines to Vietnam. The subsequent war from 1965 to 1973 when the last American troops withdrew, had further resemblances to the Sandino affair. In Vietnam, as in Nicaragua, American troops did much of the fighting in mountain and jungle against an enemy more experienced in the terrain. Their enemy, once again, was obtaining arms and supplies from 'sanctuaries' in the adjoining country, helped by the Communists. The US troops had difficulty with their allies, the army of South Vietnam, and much preferred to use special guerrillas, the Green Berets, supported by tribespeople who did not like the Vietnamese. The Americans tried to explain the skill and fortitude of 'Charlie' their

163

Vietcong enemy, by stories that they were officered by the Russians, French mercenaries or American renegades. Still more than in Nicaragua, the US troops in Vietnam depended on aeroplanes and helicopters for transport, evacuation of wounded, and bombing support to the troops. The Americans even bombed towns like Ben Tre, which had been overrun by the enemy. In Vietnam, as before in Nicaragua, the Americans never knew if the country people were friendly or 'peasants by day and guerrillas by night.'

In both cases the war drew opposition within the United States. The failure to beat Sandino and later the Communists in Vietnam, produced the idea that these were 'the kind of war the United States cannot win.'

All analogies are misleading; and Sandino's revolt differed in many ways from Vietnam. For one thing, Sandino's army never was Communist in its motivation. It got little backing from outside powers. At the start of the Vietnam war, most of the Vietcong were indeed, 'peasants by day and guerrillas by night'. But by the end, most of the country people as well as the townsfolk were hostile, or at least indifferent, to Communism. The army that took Saigon in April 1975, was formed of conventional North Vietnamese troops, supported by a superior power in tanks and artillery. Throughout the Vietnam war, including the period of American involvement, the majority of the fighting against the Vietnamese Communists was carried out by anti-Communist Vietnamese.

On the day after Sandino's murder, the National Guard attacked his camp at Wiwili, killing more than three hundred of his supporters. For the next three years, the National Guard pursued a campaign of 'pacification' in the Segovia mountains and other forest regions where people were living beyond the reach of Nicaraguan law. The 'pacification' consisted of punitive raids with rape, murder, torture, the burning of huts and crops, and, sometimes, the taking of hostages. The last of Sandino's

Generals, Pedro Almirante, was hacked to death, so legend goes, after a relative betrayed him. Most of the 'pacification' took place in the north and the east, whose people had never really considered themselves as Nicaraguans. In the populous western plain of Nicaragua, few had supported Sandino during his lifetime, and fewer still remembered him after his death, or honoured his memory.

Anastasio García Somoza purged the National Guard of any officers and men who showed disloyalty to his person. The Liberal President Sacasa stayed in power until the general election of 1936, when Somoza thought it was time to remove him. The constitution said that a President could not be replaced by a relative for at least six months. Somoza was married to Dr Sacasa's niece, and thought at first of divorcing her to comply with the constitution. Then he arranged for an interim President to delay the election for six months. By the end of 1936, Somoza had transformed the old Liberal Party into his own Liberal Nationalist Party, backed by a force of political strong-arm men called the *Camisas Azules* or Blueshirts, after the style of the European Fascists. After the general election, held in December 1936, General Somoza beat his only opponent by the impressive margin of 107,201 votes to 169.

When the Second World War broke out in 1939, Somoza grasped that the government of the United States was favourable to the British and French, so he dissolved the Blueshirt gang and became a vociferous Democrat, friendlier than ever with Franklin D. Roosevelt. The American author, John Gunther, who toured the region in 1940 writing his *Inside Latin America*, was charmed by the jovial, cigar-chomping Somoza. When the United States entered the war, Somoza did likewise and confiscated the coffee plantations owned by Germans. He added them to his private estate.

Like other American autocrats – for instance, Perón in Argentina – Somoza the first was popular with the mob of Managua and other cities. He scattered money around from his limousine; he took the side of the lorry drivers against their employers; he had the demagogic gift for remembering names of wives and children. When the Communists of the Moscow faction founded their Nicaraguan Socialist Party (PSN) in 1944, they gave their support to Somoza, just as they did to his sons until late in the 1970s; just as the Cuban Communist Party supported the local dictator, Batista.

The opposition to the Somozas came from what Communists like to call the 'bourgeoisie', the capitalist and shopkeeping class. In 1944, a part of the old Liberal Party formed an independent group (Partido Liberal Independente) to resist Somoza's bid for a third term in office. Somoza's friend, Franklin D. Roosevelt, stood in 1944 for a fourth term as President of the United States. In the same year, some brave Conservatives took part in street demonstrations which were suppressed with great brutality. Among these was Pedro Joaquín Chamorro, the editor of *La Prensa*, whose murder thirty years later sparked the final revolt against the Somoza dynasty. A few years later, another member of that persistent family, General Emiliano Chamorro, tried a barrack revolt (or *cuartelazo*), of the kind that had once been efficacious in Central America; it failed because of the discipline of Somoza's National Guard.

However, in spite of his loyal bodyguard, Anastasio Somoza García was vulnerable to a determined assassin. On 21 September 1956, he arrived at León to accept the Liberal Party nomination for yet another presidential term, when he was shot in the street, at night by Rigoberto López Perez, a poet, like so many citizens of León, the home of Rubén Darío. It was planned that as soon as López fired, his accomplices would switch off the lights at the main, allowing him to escape. They failed, or forgot to do this; López was seized and killed; the wounded dictator was flown to the US Military Hospital in the Panama Canal zone, where he died after a week. The succession passed at first to the eldest son,

Luís, and with his death from a heart attack, to the last and nastiest of the clan to be President, Anastasio Somoza Debayle, a West Point graduate with an American wife and the same extrovert charm as his father.

Through forty-five years, the Somoza family stayed in power because of the loyalty, the efficiency and the ever-increasing ruthlessness of the National Guard. The Somozas exploited this power to amass a family fortune valued at hundreds of millions of dollars. The first Somoza expropriated the Germans in 1944 and became Nicaragua's largest landowner, with fifty-one cattle ranches; forty-six coffee *fincas* and eight sugar plantations, to which wealth could be added the income from brothels, gambling and illicit alcohol, contraband in such things as machine-tools and electrical goods, as well as control of legitimate import and export licensing. After the Second World War, Somoza went into cotton, mining, cement, textiles and dairy production; he owned the national air and shipping lines.

After the murder of the first Somoza, his two sons diversified into property, construction, finance and insurance, later attracting businessmen from the 'sunbelt' of the United States, such as California, the South West, especially Las Vegas, and Florida, mostly the Cuban exiles in Miami. Among the wealthy Americans who visited or settled in Nicaragua were; Bebe Reboso, Robert Vesco, Frank Sinatra and Howard Hughes, the last-named making a hideaway in the top two floors of the Intercontinental Hotel in Managua. Much of the 'sunbelt' money went into tourism, hotels and casinos. The Somozas may have had a share in the sale of plasma to the United States from blood extracted from drunks and down-and-outs. The business premises in Managua were known as 'The House of Dracula'.

The commercial acumen of the last Somoza was shown after the earthquake struck Managua, just after midnight on 23 December 1972, knocking down seventy-five per cent of the city's houses and killing some twenty thousand people, including the patrons of the most fashionable night spot. The Intercontinental Hotel survived, though Howard Hughes on the top floor was rocked about in a frightening manner. After the earthquake, Somoza did not actually pocket the foreign aid, as some of his enemies claimed, but he cornered the business of reconstruction. His companies had a monopoly or a near monopoly in demolition, estate agency, cement, roofing, asbestos, plastics and building metals. The new streets were made with paving stones from one of Somoza's factories.

Somoza's business, while enriching him and his family, also created an economic boom, and many new jobs. Nicaragua's cotton industry, during the 1950s was held up as a model for underdeveloped countries. There was desperate poverty in the lake-side slums of Managua, but most Nicaraguans came to the cities in hope of a better life than they had in the countryside. The urban working class and even its politicians, such as the Communists, were by and large loyal to the Somoza dynasty. The opposition came from the middle class. The old Conservative Party did not like the Somozas because they were Liberals. Private businessmen resented Somozan monopoly of so much of the wealth of the country. Professional people could not stomach the fraud, injustice and lack of political freedom. The Roman Catholic Church was influenced by the ideas of Christian Democracy, a much more potent force in Central America than the much publicised 'Popular Church', based on the Marxist ideas of the 'liberation theologians'. The various elements of this opposition came together in 1967 to contest the election of President Anastasio Somoza Debayle. The opposition candidate was Dr Fernando Aguero, but then, as usual, the true opposition leader was Pedro Joaquín Chamorro, the editor of *La Prensa* and a Christian Democrat, although he stuck to the label of the Conservative Party.

Chamorro and others called for a mass demonstration to march on the Presidential Palace in Managua on 22 January

1967. More than fifty thousand people gathered, whereupon the National Guard opened fire with machine guns and tanks, killing at least two hundred and probably nearer a thousand demonstrators. Afterwards, Chamorro was put in prison, but he remained the centre of opposition to the Somoza family. It was he who put together a new coalition of protest in 1974. It was Chamorro's murder by gunmen, possibly under orders from Anastasio Somoza Portocarrero, the head of the National Guard, and next in line for the Presidency, that sparked off the final revolt and civil war. Until right to the end, it was the bourgeois politicians not the Sandinistas who posed the real opposition to Somoza.

Nicaragua was slow to join in the left-wing revolutionary politics that swept through Latin America in the 1960s and early 1970s. The craze began with the revolution and rise to power of Fidel Castro in Cuba in 1959. Although Castro accepted aid from the Soviet Union and nearly started the Third World War when he allowed the installation of Russian rockets, he did not appear to the rest of the world as an orthodox Moscow Communist. With his wealthy background, flamboyance and dash, Castro was anything but a commissar; he rather resembled his arch enemy, John F. Kennedy, even down to such details as his reliance upon a tough and less popular younger brother.

The early career of Castro also had interesting parallels with the career of Sandino thirty years earlier. The fathers of both were wealthy, pure-blooded Spanish landowners. Both experienced and detested the power of North American business interests. Neither developed a clear political ideology. Just as Sandino dabbled in Yoga, Socialism and Seventh Day Adventism, so Castro toyed with Perón's and even Hitler's ideas before becoming a Marxist to please the Russians.

Sandino and Castro both saw armed revolution not as a substitute for, but as something inherently better than constitutional government. Each began his career with an unprovoked and deliberate act of violence; Sandino against the garrison at Jicaro and Fidel against the Moncade barracks in Santiago. After the failure of these attacks, both men took their bands to the highest available mountain range, where both proved brilliant guerrilla leaders.

Both Sandino and Castro were gasbags, stuffed with inordinate vanity, both comparing themselves with Julius Caesar, but having much in common with his successor, Mussolini. Although both men loathed the United States, they sprang to fame after the visits paid to them by admiring North American journalists; Beals to Sandino and Herbert Matthews to Castro.

These comparisons come to mind on reading Hugh Thomas' huge and magnificent *Cuba: The Pursuit of Freedom*. Of course there were many differences in the characters of the two men, and still more in the countries they wanted to rule, but it is worth bearing in mind how Sandino foreshadowed Castro, just as Castro foreshadowed the Sandinistas.

Cuba appealed not to the old-fashioned Communists, but to the new left which had rediscovered Trotsky and more recent ideologues such as Herbert Marcuse and Frantz Fanon. The new left cried out for revolution, not so much in the great industrial countries where Marx had prophesied that it would come, as in 'underdeveloped' third world countries, especially former or actual colonies of the West. The archetype of the 'Fidelista' was Che Guevara, a wealthy Argentine who had taken part in the Cuban revolution and dedicated his life to spreading the faith among the dispossessed of the continent. He went to agitate among the Bolivian peasants, who promptly turned him in to the army. He was shot and became a martyr to all the revolutionary youth. The cult of Guevara flourished among the students of Paris in the *événements* of 1968; the agitators against the Vietnam war; the friends of terror in Palestine and Northern Ireland.

Student militancy was the rage in most of Latin America. In 1965, I went to visit Caracas University and found it under the armed occupancy of the students, many of whom were in their thirties. Pilots would not fly over the campus because of the anti-aircraft fire they received. Most of these revolutionaries were the sons and daughters of Venezuala's rich; bored; and excited by violence. The fun revolutionaries were mostly in the countries like Venezuela, that still enjoyed democracy and an open society; things they denounced as 'repressive intolerance'. At the end of the sixties, fun revolutionaries in the more tolerant countries such as Venezuela, Uruguay and Argentina, also in Italy, France and West Germany, turned to 'urban guerrilla' action, like kidnapping, the murder of businessmen, the planting of bombs in shops or cafés. In Argentina and Uruguay, 'repressive intolerance' soon gave way to brutal military dictatorship and death squads. Most of the revolutionaries had the money to flee the country or to obtain legal help and support from abroad, but thousands of harmless people who had not dabbled in Marxism, were murdered or tortured.

The Latin American new left was almost by definition, hostile to the United States. Indeed, as I wrote in a book published in 1967: *The Gringo in Latin America*, 'The Americans and the Communists are over-afraid of each other and greatly over-estimate each other's powers. In a sense, they also thrive off each other. Whenever riot or revolution threatens, the Americans are ready to offer aid or arms to stop the danger of Communism. Whenever the Americans intervene, the Communists can play on instinctive anti-gringo feeling.'

For a quarter century after the death of Sandino, his name was scarcely remembered by the Nicaraguans. Then, in 1958, one of Sandino's former commanders, General Ramón Rondales, brought a group of guerrillas from Honduras, most of them university students and most of them armed with guns from the 1930s. They were soon dispersed and Rondales shot. However, his brave example, followed soon afterwards by the triumph of Castro in Cuba, inspired the formation of what is today the

171

ruling group in Nicaragua, the Sandinista National Liberation Front, known by its Spanish acronym of FSLN. The three founder members who met in Tegucigalpa, the capital of Honduras in the summer of 1961, were all university graduates, and sons of the bourgeoisie. They were Silvio Mayorga, Tomás Borge, now one of the rulers of Nicaragua, and Carlos Fonseca Amador, its principal martyr, whose bearded, spectacled face appears on thousands of hoardings, next to the face of Sandino himself. Like many Sandinista luminaries, Fonseca came from a family that was not just rich, but intimate with the Somozas.

The new Sandinistas followed the old Sandinistas into the mountains and jungle near the Honduran border, where they could hope to avoid the National Guard. But whereas the former Sandinistas were mostly peasants or migrant coffee pickers, who knew how to use the terrain, the new Sandinistas were strange to this part of the world. 'There was nothing to eat, not even animals to hunt', wrote Tomás Borge; 'there was no salt. It wasn't just the hunger that was terrible, but constant cold twenty-four hours a day, because we spent all our time in the river. We were always wet through with the clinging rain of that part of the country; the cold a kind of unrelieved torture; mosquitoes; wild jungle animals and insects. No shelter, no change of clothes, no food.' Moreover, most of the locals were either indifferent or downright hostile, as is acknowledged in George Black's pro-Sandinista *The Triumph of the People*. 'Old sympathies for Sandino did not prevent a percentage of peasants from being convinced Somocistas, while many others were at least superficially under the sway of the dictatorship's ideological control . . . For most of the *guerrillos*, urban middle-class youth, it meant abandoning the class of their birth, with no turning back.'

Although the new Sandinistas always maintained a handful of fighters up in the north and east, this was not one of their strongholds, even when most of the country rose in arms against the Somoza family. The east-coast Mosquito people, of Indian and Negro origin, may once have been friendly to General Sandino but not to these new, ideological Sandinistas. The new Sandinistas attracted support and recruits from the class that had scorned General Sandino; the schoolchildren and university students from better-off families in Managua, León and other towns of the western coastal plain. By the 1970s, Pedro Joaquín Chamorro, himself a Conservative, guessed that seventy-five per cent of the university students were Sandinistas. If they had failed as guerrillas up in the mountains, the university radicals excelled at making their protest heard in the cities. They robbed banks; they kidnapped and held to ransom a cocktail party of the Somoza establishment; one revolutionary holed up in a villa of west Managua, defied the helicopters and tanks of the National Guard for hours, before he was finally gunned down; all of which happened under the television cameras. Another, luckier, Sandinista, the former Conservative, Edén Pastora, led a band of men that stormed the National Palace, taking the deputies hostage, and using them to release from prison fifty Sandinistas, including Borge. The loss of Fonseca, killed in an ambush in 1976, was more than recompensed by his later services as a martyr. In all revolutions, the dead hero has this advantage over the living, that he cannot change his allegiance like Danton, Trotsky, Tito, Djilas, or in the case of Nicaragua, Edén Pastora, who broke with the Sandinistas and went into exile in Costa Rica.

The eventual downfall of the Somozas was due almost entirely to their own megalomaniac greed and cruelty. The National Guard had become the uniformed branch of Somoza's economic empire, enjoying its own luxurious housing estates, schools, hospitals and shops. Extortion and graft were institutionalised so that in fact the police ran the rackets like gambling, smuggling and prostitution. The growth of unrest in the cities and countryside was used as justification for brutal, anti-terrorist units, who were allowed to rob, rape and torture and even kill, without fear of reprimand. In 1978, Anastasio Somoza Debayle appointed his son, Anastasio Somoza Portocarrero as head of the Guard's infantry training school, whose graduates soon became hated and feared, even by other Guardsmen. The school's magazine, *El Infanta* published photographs of Nazi troops. Trainees on the parade ground were made to partake in a question and answer drill:

¿Quiénes somos?	Who are we?
¡Somos tigres!	We are tigers!
¿Qué comen los tigres?	What do tigers eat?
Sangre.	Blood.
¿Sangre de quién?	Whose blood?
Sangre del pueblo.	The blood of the people.

Anastasio Somoza Portocarrero, nicknamed *El Chiguín* (the tough brat), may have given the order to murder Chamorro, the editor of *La Prensa*, on 10 January 1978. The explosion of rage that followed had nothing to do with the Sandinistas, who were taken entirely by surprise ... Mobs attacked and burned down factories of the Somoza family and friends, beginning with the plasma firm, the infamous 'House of Dracula', which stood conveniently next to the offices of *La Prensa*. They burned a Somoza textile factory, then fifteen other buildings, including banks and finance houses. Next, the crowd turned on and burned the First National City Bank of New York. On the third day after the murder, fifty thousand people followed Chamorro's coffin on the road to the cemetery. The funeral was succeeded by a strike and a great volume of protest, embracing every interest from the trade unionists to the capitalists, and from radical priests to the Archbishop of Managua, Obando y Bravo, now a Cardinal. The Somozas stayed in power only because they had arms, and the people did not.

The focus of violence then moved to the town of Masaya, whose Indian quarter of Monimbo is famous for artisan skills. The people of the quarter held a series of masses and demonstrations to honour Chamorro, and then, on 21 February 1978, they marked the anniversary of Sandino's death. The National Guard launched an air attack on one procession, then killed a boy at the door of the church. The Monimbo people used their mechanical skills to produce 'contact bombs' from black aluminium, sulphur, petrol and nails, with which they fought off a Guard attack with tanks, armoured cars, helicopters and heavy machine guns. The Somozas and the National Guard had opened a civil war against their own people.

Once again, the revolt had little to do with the self-styled revolutionaries. As George Black, the Sandinista historian says: 'The Monimbo insurrection proved to the FSLN that the war between the people and the dictatorship would not always follow the time-table set by the revolutionary vanguard.'

The Sandinistas had staged a spectacular *coup de théâtre* with Edén Pastora's raid on the National Palace on 22 August 1978. It caught the imagination of the world. Nevertheless, the revolts and civil war that broke out all over the country during the coming year, owed little to Sandinista planning. They were spontaneous expressions of rage against a dictatorship that had alienated all but its own dependents. The brutality of the National Guard produced a revolt in Matagalpa, the major town in the coffee country, where the people fortified the churches against Somoza's tanks and planes. 'The Frente (FSLN) had not chosen the time of the insurrection, but once the masses began to act autonomously,' writes Black, 'the Sandinistas faced a stark choice; either to block the insurrection or to support it. In September the fighting spread to León, Estelí and Chinandega, the "Guernica" of Nicaragua.'

The final assault on the Somozas' dictatorship began at the end of May 1979, with insurrections all over the country, as well as a full-scale invasion by Nicaraguan troops based in Costa Rica, under the leadership of Edén Pastora.

They advanced against the Somozas along that narrow strip between the Pacific and Lake Nicaragua, where once General Walker had tried to control the inter-ocean route. The town of

Rivas, where Walker had fought in three successive years, was once more a battleground. On 20 June, rebels captured León. Managua itself was a hard city to conquer because the earthquake had left huge patches of open ground which were vulnerable to air attack and machine-gun fire. However, the eastern suburbs rose in revolt and were bombed and shelled. After three days of appalling casualties, thousands of families from Managua stole away in the night and trekked to Masaya, now in rebel hands.

The press and those functionaries who had not escaped observed the war from the Intercontinental Hotel, which stood close to Somoza's heavily guarded bunker. On 21 June, an American television reporter, Bill Stewart, was shot dead deliberately by the National Guard; an act that was filmed and shown in the United States. The incident was later woven into a fictional movie about the Nicaraguan revolution – *Under Fire*. The hero and heroine, a photographer and a radio journalist are asked by the Sandinistas to help in concealing the death of a Sandinista chief, whose loss might take the heart out of the revolution. They therefore fake a photograph showing the corpse apparently still alive and reading a current newspaper. This photograph rallies the insurrectionists and helps to bring down the dictator, Somoza. The journalists excuse their lie by their eagerness to bring down a dictatorship which had killed their friend.

It is a specious argument, to say the least. By exalting the Sandinista leader, the journalists therefore imply that only the Sandinistas could topple Somoza. And this, of course, is what the Sandinistas now claim. The overthrow of the Somozas came from a popular movement, led at first by Conservatives like Chamorro, and backed by the Roman Catholic Church under Archbishop Obando. The Sandinistas followed rather than led the revolution. Their main contribution was a supply of guns from Cuba and Eastern Europe. When Somoza was overthrown, the Sandinistas used their weapons to maintain power. The Sandinistas hijacked the revolution.

10

MANAGUA

COMING BACK TO Managua, in 1988, I made sure that my US visa was up to date for the overnight stay in Miami. This time I discovered that LACSA, the Costa Rican airline, was running a late-night flight that stopped in Nicaragua. By the time I arrived here, at midnight local time, I had spent a full day either in aeroplanes or airports, and was feeling ready for sleep, until I discovered a party in progress. Since it takes three hours for passengers to embark or disembark at Managua airport, most of them go to the airport bar, which is one of the best in town. On this occasion, I fell into talk with a friendly and very amusing group, who filled me in on recent events in the country. From there we progressed to Rubén Darío, the want of a proper history book on William Walker and, then, to a favourite Nicaraguan topic, the origins of the Chamorro family. Although most of the group were Sandinistas, or claimed to be, and did not agree with my point of view, they were friendly and jolly, and would not allow me to buy any beers. This hour or two at Managua airport brought back to me just how fond I am of the Nicaraguans, whatever I think of the Nicaraguan government.

Awaking, at noon, in my room at the Seven Seas, I still felt some of the early morning euphoria. It was soon dispelled by an afternoon in Managua. The first indication I got of economic

177

disaster was seeing child beggars and people obviously under-nourished. The exception, of course, are the well-fed soldiers who eat and drink at the Seven Seas. Everyone that I spoke with complained of the worsening shortages and inflation, how one month's wages went on a shirt, and two months for a pair of shoes. Doctors report that more than half of the children suffer from malnutrition. Doctors themselves have joined the ever-increasing emigration. In the last two years, more than half of the thirty-nine gynaecologists at the main women's hospital have resigned. Of the 750 engineers who were working in Nicaragua, three years earlier, only two hundred remain.

Already, three years ago, there was a 'diplomatic shop', where foreigners and the new nomenclature could buy imported goods with dollars. Now Nicaragua has followed the lead of Communist countries in Europe by putting a 'dollar shop' in the Interconti-nental. Here you can buy American cornflakes, tinned ham, jello, *Newsweek* and the *Miami Herald*, a welcome change from the bookstall trading in Nicaraguan money, which runs mostly to works on Colonel Gaddafi and Winnie Mandela. Although the country is starved of dollars to buy much-needed machinery, fertiliser and pesticide, the bar of the Intercontinental now serves only imported American beer.

The downtown part of Managua teems with soldiers. Convoys of trucks roll by, day and night. A photograph in *Barricada* shows some of the '240 girls handling the anti-aircraft guns in the north'. All this military preparation is still more senseless now that the US has withdrawn support for the Contras, and Colonel Oliver North has been sent for trial for his part in funding them through a deal with Iran. Although the Sandinistas have beggared the country with military spending, they still have not brought in a terror against their opponents. They have, it is true, imprisoned a great many politicians, and possibly murdered some more; but Nicaragua has not become a police state like Cuba. Nor, to be fair, has she copied such right-wing regimes as Argentina, Chile, El Salvador and Guatemala, terrorising opponents by kidnapping, torture and execution. Although the regime has closed the Catholic radio station, *La Prensa* is back, and easy to buy. People speak out openly against the regime, careless of whether or not they are overheard. Once a complete stranger approached and warned me, 'That man you were talking to yesterday is a Sandinista.'

As ever, political argument centres around the Cardinal, Archbishop Miguel Obando y Bravo. The abuse of him in the Sandinista press has plumbed new depths. 'Why does he hate us?' asks the headline over an article in *El Nuevo Diario* by Gustavo Antonio Ortega Artole:

> Seeing the picture of Cardinal Miguel Obando y Bravo published in *El Nuevo Diario* on Monday, the tenth of this month, caused me great worry, pain and fear. It is well enough known that the eyes are the mirror of the soul, and that by the expressions of the face, we show dislike, hate, bitterness and love. And in this photo, the eyes of his Eminence reveal hatred, but hatred of whom? Would it be hatred for his flock who every day are demanding from him a speech about those murdered by the Contras? Can it be hatred for those mothers who, every Thursday go to the Curia asking him for a few minutes to raise the question of their children, kidnapped by the Contras? . . .
>
> And that sneer, your Eminence, if any painter or sculptor wanted to do a work that represents the full magnitude of hate, that photo would be a perfect model.

The Sandinista newspapers love to confront Obando with sayings or incidents from the Gospels. For instance, the Party organ *Barricada* wrote of one of the Cardinal's sermons, critical of the Russian presence in Nicaragua, that 'if Christ had encountered Obando in the temple, he would have chased him out with blows of the whip'.

One of the most marked changes in Nicaragua over the last

179

few years is the falling away of the 'Sandalistas', the foreign admirers of the regime. Los Antojitos and cafés around the Plaza España, are no longer crammed with left-wing nuns from Pennsylvania, ancient, crop-haired Canadian Trotskyists, Swedes with deep blue, sorrowful eyes, and West Germans in Nelson Mandela T-shirts. An English journalist here, who supports the Sandinistas, talks of a loss of heart in the British solidarity group. If foreign supporters do not come here so much, they seem to have kept their loyalty. A newspaper reported in May 1988, 'At dawn on 4 February, Harold Pinter and Antonia Fraser opened a bottle of wine and drank a toast. They were celebrating the news which they had stayed up to hear on the radio, that the American Congress had voted against a request by Ronald Reagan for aid to the Contra rebels.' The novelist Salman Rushdie wrote an approving book on his sojourn here. The playwright, Nick Darke, who came to write a work for the Royal Shakespeare Company, was quoted as saying that 'leaving England and arriving in Nicaragua was like walking out of a cupboard and emerging into light'. The Royal Shakespeare director, Roger Michell said that his play would highlight the optimism and energy he found here.

The American, as well as the English left, has begun to lose interest in the Nicaraguan Revolution. Sandinista politicians and publicists no longer draw crowds of admirers in the United States, even at East Coast universities. The Democrat candidate in the 1988 election, Michael Dukakis, tried in vain to whip up feeling on Colonel North and his aid to the Contras. This falling away in sympathy for the Sandinistas corresponds to a more balanced coverage by the press and TV. Reporters would not now slant or even fabricate stories, as they were shown to do in the film *Under Fire*. An excellent book by Shirley Christian, *Nicaragua: Revolution in the Family*, now offers a clear and balanced account of the rise to power of the Sandinistas.

If the US newspapers and TV now give a fairer picture of Nicaragua, Hollywood has produced a grotesque distortion in

Walker, 'The Major Motion Picture from Universal', accompanied by the book of the film by Rudy Wurlitzer, *Walker: The True Story of the First American Invasion of Nicaragua*. Even the title endorses the Sandinista version of history, that Walker came to this country for the United States government.

The film-makers had the chance to make an exciting but truthful film about Walker, which could have enlightened us all on the roots of the present conflict. They could have produced a film as interesting as Pontecorvo's *The Battle of Algiers*. Walker's career was thrilling and strange enough not to require embellishment and distortion. The Nicaraguan government gave permission to film in the very towns, like Granada, where Walker went. The film-makers could, had they so wished, have hired Nicaraguan actors to play the parts of their ancestors; and any amount of extras, cheap. The actor, Ed Harris, who played the title role, actually looked like Walker and could have given a fine performance, if he had had a proper script. Instead, the producers made a kind of burlesque, or comic strip, with many facetious references to the modern United States, the Contras, the Vietnam War and present-day racial politics. We see a copy of *Time* magazine, with Walker featured as 'Man of the Year'. In a reference to the fall of Saigon, Walker and men are lifted out of Granada by helicopters. The dour and puritanical Walker appears at different times as a ranting hysteric, a pansy, a cannibal and a Don Juan, engaged in naked revels. The tastelessness and vulgarity of the film are very depressing.

Sergio Ramírez, the Nicaraguan Vice-President, wrote that if *Walker* became a commercial success it might open some eyes and change some minds. In fact, *Walker* propagates lies and misconceptions on what is a serious matter to the United States: her quarrel with Nicaragua. The film not only implies that Walker came here as agent of the United States government. It says explicitly that he was hired to take Nicaragua by the American capitalist, Cornelius Vanderbilt. In a preposterous confrontation, beside a train in the desert, Vanderbilt says to Walker:

'Nicaragua is a tiny, insignificant country somewhere to the south of here. But this worthless piece of land happens to control the overland route to the Pacific . . . What I want is for some man to go down there and take over. I need that country stable for my business interest and I want it done now . . . Do you think you can handle the job?'

This scene in the film is not just fabrication. It turns the whole story on its head. The facts are that Vanderbilt never met Walker; that Walker first interfered with, then commandeered Vanderbilt's inter-ocean traffic; it was Vanderbilt who financed the army that beat Walker. In short, Walker was acting not for but against Vanderbilt and, ultimately, the United States government. In as far as he represented anyone, this was the government of León. One can, of course, say that *Walker* is only a film and that nobody takes Hollywood seriously. However, as both Hitler and Stalin knew, films are a potent means of spreading lies and hatred.

The film does not show how Walker eventually met his death in front of a firing squad in Honduras, the neighbouring country to the north. Here again there were curious parallels with modern Nicaragua. Like the modern Sandinistas, Walker had been at odds with all the surrounding countries, Costa Rica, El Salvador and Honduras. A coalition of all their armies, backed by Vanderbilt and the British, had forced him out of the country. The Sandinistas today are on constant guard against the real or imagined threat of Contra forces, possibly backed by American troops, over the border in Honduras.

When he left Nicaragua in 1858, Walker still regarded himself as President, and still intended to come back. However, his former patrons, the Liberal faction in León, were now unable or unwilling to pay for Walker's return. But in 1860, when he had just completed his memoirs, Walker received an invitation to come to Central America, from Roatan, one of the Bay Islands, off the coast of Honduras.

The Sandinistas always describe Walker as *'filibustero'* yet at the same time they boast of their own success in that odious modern form of piracy, hijacking aeroplanes. In October 1970, a group of Sandinistas in Costa Rica pulled off one of the first and most successful hijacks, to win the release from prison of some of their comrades, including their founder and chief, Carlos Fonseca. On the eighteenth anniversary of this hijack, *Barricada* carried a tribute to its perpetrators by none other than Tomás Borge, the Minister of the Interior. Its gloating and self-congratulatory tone, as well as the pulp fiction language, reveals the mind of the people running this country:

> That 21st of October 1970, the sky was clear in spite of the rainy season. The TI-1024 of LACSA Airways had taken off two minutes earlier from sweltering Puerto Limón to the cool capital of Costa Rica. The North American employee of the United Fruit Company consulted his watch. It was 7.35 in the morning.

The American takes a furtive look at the young woman next to him, with the face of a college student. It soon turns out that she is the Sandinista who smuggled the firearms on to the plane. The hijackers force down the plane at San Andrés, an island owned by Colombia. As they wait there, while the hijackers bargain for the release of their comrades, the American sweats from heat and fear. He feels an itch in the sphincter. (How does Borge know this?) When a group of reporters venture too near the plane, the principal hijacker threatens to shoot all North American passengers. At last Somoza agrees to release his prisoners, and the plane continues to Cuba.

One can just understand how, twenty years ago, foolish and young revolutionaries thought it clever to hijack an aeroplane. That was before a whole series of deadly and harrowing crimes by Palestinian and other terrorists. It is simply revolting that such crimes are boasted about by a man who is not only now in his fifties, but Minister of the Interior, the man responsible for upholding the law.

This same Borge is claimed as a friend by Graham Greene. Constantly, during my stays in Nicaragua, or reading and writing about it at home, I find myself puzzling over Greene's attitude to this country. One cannot say about Greene, as about so many other visitors, that he speaks out of ignorance, vanity or stupidity. He has known Latin America for more than fifty years; although it amuses him to mix with people like Chu-Chu, the Panamanian Marxist, and General Torrijos, he never allows himself to be lionised; and although in his eighties, Greene is as sharp and perspicacious as ever. Nor has he suddenly turned left wing. He is just as suspicious as ever of isms and ocracies. He does not believe in revolution as such. What brought him to Nicaragua was, I think, his lifelong dislike of most things from the United States, especially its liberalism. The other is a religious feeling, which started with sympathy for a church under persecution, and ended as a rebellion against the hierarchy, including the present Pope. Greene's Latin American books, which I have brought with me on the present journey, are quite indispensable to an understanding of Nicaragua.

Greene tells us that his fascination for Spain and Latin America dates to his childhood reading, when he had envied the fate of William Ewart who had been shot accidentally during the Pancho Villa rising in Mexico. Later, he obtained an advance to write on the persecution of Christians in Mexico. Early in 1938, Greene travelled through Texas and northern Mexico to the backward provinces of Tabasco and Chianas, where the religious persecution continued, out of the sight of tourists and other inquisitive foreigners. To make the region still more unpleasant for those, like Greene, who enjoy a drink, the red-shirts and *pistoleros* imposed a ban on liquor as well as the Catholic religion. This helps to explain why a 'whisky priest' is the hero of Greene's subsequent novel, *The Power and the Glory*.

This was the book that established Greene as a major writer, and also created the legend of 'Greeneland', that hot, corrupt and dangerous country, where men despair, and vultures crouch on the tin roofs. While not disputing the excellence of *The Power and the Glory*, I like still better Greene's Mexican travel book, *The Lawless Roads*, which came out first, and was indeed the intended report on religious persecution. For one thing, it is a very personal book, probably more revealing about himself than anything Greene has written, including his memoirs. At least one critic has said that *The Lawless Roads* is a left-wing book. I cannot see this. In a new introduction, Greene says that, 'All successful revolutions, however idealistic, probably betray themselves in time, but the Mexican revolution was phoney from the start.' This is not a case of old age mocking the indiscretions of youth, for Greene as a young man was quite as contemptuous of the 'dawnists', the people who wanted to build a better society, whether in Russia, Spain or Mexico. In *The Lawless Roads* we see the first signs of two obsessions: a sense of divided loyalty and, closely related to it, antipathy to the United States. The first pages go back to Greene's childhood at Berkhamsted, where his father was the headmaster of a local public school. As a schoolboy there, young Greene felt himself to be an inhabitant of two different countries. He spent the week in a dormitory with his fellow schoolboys, the weekends with his family on the other side of the baize door. 'How can life on a border be anything but restless?' he asked. 'You are pulled by different ties of hate and love.' Some critics see in this schoolboy division of loyalties the reason for Greene's later, notorious, loyalty to the Soviet spy Kim Philby. In *The Lawless Roads*, the border between his family and the school is also the border between the United States and Mexico.

Two other English novelists of the twentieth century shared this anti-American feeling, D. H. Lawrence and Evelyn Waugh, and both were attracted to and also repelled by Mexico. Both disliked American liberalism. One of the best Lawrence essays was an attack on Benjamin Franklin, while Waugh especially loathed President Woodrow Wilson, who wanted 'to teach the South American republics to elect good men'.

Although he does not mention it in *The Lawless Roads*, Greene had experienced trouble in getting to the United States. Before becoming a Roman Catholic, he briefly joined the Communist Party and therefore came on a US blacklist. Until long after the Second World War, Greene met with problems at US ports. Even today, he likes to avoid the United States when making his way to Central America.

During his first visit to Latin America, Greene had been roughing it in the hills of south Mexico, among xenophobic and surly *pistoleros* who had made life still more unpleasant by placing a ban on alcohol. When Greene returned to Latin America, in the early 1950s, he opted instead for the sybaritic delights of Batista's Havana. In Cuba, Greene started to work on a book that had been in his mind for at least ten years, of a spy who sets up a network of bogus agents. Although *Our Man in Havana* appeared to predict the missile crisis of 1962, the book was written and published before the overthrow of Batista. When, in the late 1950s, Greene got down to writing *Our Man in Havana* he went out of his way to study the politics of the country, even venturing to sinister Oriente province; however, he says it was not a political book, and it did not please the Fidelistas.

A kind but absurd American couple appear in Greene's novel of Haiti, *The Comedians*. Writing later about that book, Greene blamed the United States for keeping in office the tyrant 'Papa Doc' Duvalier. By the time *The Comedians* appeared in 1966, Greene had become a friend of Fidel Castro and sympathetic to his plans for revolution throughout Latin America. At about this time, Greene started to take an increasing interest in the southern part of the continent, especially Argentina, Chile and Paraguay,

186

where President Stroessner held his malevolent sway. The hero of Greene's entertainment *Travels with my Aunt* (1969) goes up to Paraguay on the river boat, where he meets an American CIA man.

The CIA and the other Americans play a less comic role in Greene's novel *The Honorary Consul*, where enmity to the United States for the first time sounds intemperate. The book was published in 1973 when there was turmoil in the zone. While Stroessner had tightened his grip on Paraguay, left-wing 'urban guerrillas' were waging terror in Uruguay, which was a democratic welfare state, and Argentina, where Juan Perón was returning to power. In Uruguay, the rebels, or 'Tupamaros' were mostly sons of the middle class, stuffed with the theories of Marx and Marcuse, and angry at what they described as the State's 'repressive tolerance'. They waged a campaign of bombings, murders and kidnappings including, in 1971, the British Ambassador in Montevideo. In Argentina, the rebels failed to start a peasant revolt and instead turned to terrorist acts in the cities. In Chile, another country, like Uruguay, with a long tradition of tolerance and democracy, the left succeeded in bringing to power the government of Allende, whom Greene was to meet before his overthrow and death, in 1973.

At the time of *The Honorary Consul*, South America was in the grip of the same student and middle-class revolutionary movement, which Europe and the United States had endured in the 1960s, the period of the Vietnam War, the *événements* in France and growing terrorist movements in Ireland and Palestine. Soon after *The Honorary Consul* was published, Argentina, Chile and Uruguay came to be ruled by right-wing dictators even more brutal than Stroessner in Paraguay. While Pinochet in Chile still, at the time of writing, survives, Argentina and Uruguay have returned to some form of democracy. But in the whole zone, there is nothing left of the radical terrorists and guerrillas.

In the winter of 1976, Greene got a telegram at his home in

Antibes which started him off a new string of adventures, the more remarkable since he was now in his seventies. General Omar Torrijos, the ruler of Panama, had invited Greene to come as the guest of his country. Greene did not hesitate before accepting, for Panama had appealed to him since he learned 'Drake's Drum' as a child.

In his visits to Panama before Torrijos's death in a plane crash, Greene spent much of his time in jaunts round the countryside, swimming, attending parties and drinking rum punch with Torrijos and Chu-Chu. He became a confidant and also a kind of agony aunt on the General's problems with women, his colleagues and, most of all, the United States.

Because Torrijos trusted Greene and perhaps understood his publicity value, he asked him to join the Panamian mission to Washington, for talks on the Panama Canal. Greene enjoyed this, and only a pressing engagement in France kept him from joining a military mission to Fort Bragg, North Carolina, dressed in the uniform of the National Guard. Greene says that Torrijos wanted to be his tutor in the affairs of Central America, not just Panama, and as part of this education, sent him to meet George Price, the Prime Minister of Belize. 'You will like Price,' Torrijos told him, 'he is a man after your own heart. He wanted to be a priest, not a prime minister.' Greene did like Price, who also had read and admired Greene's books.

Greene's increasing involvement in the affairs of Central America, brought him in touch with people not nearly as pleasant as Price. He met the Salvadorean Marxist Salvador Cayetano, and remarked to a friend that he had the most merciless eyes he had ever seen. When Salvadorean guerrillas kidnapped the South African Ambassador, Pretoria asked for Greene's help in getting him freed, for his health was poor and his wife dying of cancer. Greene failed in his efforts to mediate. Later the guerrillas claimed to have 'executed' the diplomat, but the South Africans thought he had died from the hardship of his captivity.

When Greene went back to Panama in 1983, after Torrijos' death, he resumed his role as some kind of diplomat for the new President, Ricardo de la Espriella. It seems that Espriella did not trust the head of the National Guard, General Paredes, whom he considered too right wing and friendly to the United States. He asked Greene to visit Cuba and Nicaragua, now under the Sandinistas, to tell them that the ideals of Torrijos lived on. 'After seeing the President I had drinks with Colonel Noriega, the Chief of Staff. He too was keen on my visit to Nicaragua. It was obvious that the right wing slant of General Paredes embarassed him as much as the General . . .'

In Nicaragua, Greene brought greetings from Noriega to Lenin Cerna, the Sandinista head of security, or chief of secret police, and Cerna gave Greene an invitation to Noriega to visit Nicaragua. In Managua, Greene met friends he had known as exiles in Panama, like Tomás Borge and Father Cardenal. He went to León and Granada, where Chu-Chu had a quarrel with a journalist from *La Prensa*.

Greene's latest novel, *The Captain and the Enemy*, culminates here in Managua and Greene has reverted to sombre mood, the atmosphere not of a nightmare but a bad dream, fraught with anxieties and obsessions, many of which are concerned with Latin America. The principal character and, for most of the book, the narrator, starts as a twelve-year-old boy in a boarding school at a place that might be Berkhamsted in the 1960s. One day a stranger, claiming to be a friend of his father, comes to take the boy out for the afternoon. The boy is glad to be free of his hated school and makes no objection when, in a dreamlike series of incidents, he finds himself going to London. The stranger, always known as the Captain (though he is wanted by the police under an alias as the Colonel) intends the boy as a surrogate son for his mistress, who lost her own child. The Captain has won the boy at backgammon (or maybe cards) from his true father, known as the Devil, who comes across as a figure of menace. The only hero of the book is the Captain, a con man and fantasist who can nevertheless feel love and suffering.

Some ten years pass. The boy is now a young man and a journalist. The Captain is living in Panama where, from a secret airstrip, he flies arms and supplies to the Sandinista rebels in Somoza's Nicaragua. The Captain's mistress is killed in an accident in London. The narrator goes to Panama City to tell the Captain the bad news. He funks this duty; he is a cold and graceless individual; he sells out to Mr Quigly, a journalist and a CIA agent who wants to spy on the Captain.

The hotel where the narrator stays has vague resemblances to the one where Greene stayed in *Getting to Know the General*. The narrator is given a bodyguard, not like Chu-Chu, but nevertheless sympathetic. The Captain is under the care of the Panamian National Guard, especially one Colonel Martínez. At last the ungrateful narrator confronts the Captain and tells him brutally of his mistress's death; he then betrays to Mr Quigly the site of the Captain's secret airstrip. The news comes too late. The Captain has flown on his last, suicidal mission. As Mr Quigly recalls, 'His plane crashed near the bunker in Managua where Somoza stays at night these days. The plane must have been as full as he could make it of explosives, but all he did was kill himself and break a few windows in the Intercontinental Hotel across the way. No one else was hurt – only himself.'

Like *The Lawless Roads*, written fifty years earlier, *The Captain and the Enemy* begins with the horror of school life and a sense of divided loyalty. Although he is glad at getting away from school, the narrator shows no gratitude to the Captain. He dislikes his father, the Devil, but does not hate him. All his emotions are faint. There are all sorts of echoes from earlier books. The Captain insists that when the narrator comes to Panama he must not go via New York, but instead use the long route from Amsterdam. We even encounter, briefly, that archetypal 'Greeneland' figure – the kindly secret policeman.

190

In Panama, as they go near the Canal Zone, the narrator asks his bodyguard who are the Captain's enemies, '. . . his reply was a silent one – a wave of his hand towards the golf house and a putting green and a group of officers in immaculate American uniforms, watching the players.' The CIA man, Mr Quigly, provides his thumbnail sketch of Central American politics, 'The people here hate the Zone. In Nicaragua they are fighting Somoza and in Salvador they are fighting the death squads – and both Somoza and the death squads are helped by the United States.'

When I finished reading *The Captain and the Enemy*, I was actually in Managua, close to the Intercontinental Hotel. Perhaps this was what made me think that the novel was unconvincing, a little contrived, perhaps even an exercise in self-parody. Of course, I should have remembered that Greene always gets it right; life always imitates the art of his novels. Time and again in Vietnam, I found myself living some incident from *The Quiet American*. Not long after the publication of *Our Man in Havana*, in which a reluctant spy had passed off pictures of washing machines as Russian rockets, the President of the United States showed the Press photographs of what turned out to be genuine Russian rockets, starting the Cuban missile crisis. During the opening week of the stage adaptation of *The Power and the Glory*, concerning religious persecution in Central America, Archbishop Romero was shot dead in San Salvador, and the following Sunday, twenty-seven people were killed while attending his funeral. Within days of reading *The Captain and the Enemy*, I found myself meeting its characters, or rather, two of the characters rolled into one.

One evening, I went to the Intercontinental and took a place at the bar, near to the table where I had first spotted Greene with Tomás Borge. A strange American took the seat on my left. He was in his late fifties, a friendly, quiet-spoken man, who nevertheless looked out of place. He did not talk like an idealogue or a politician. He was not self-important enough to be a diplomat from the Embassy. He lacked the assertiveness of a businessman, and anyway there is little business left in Nicaragua. I was not surprised to learn that he was a farmer from the Middle West, a region where, as he kept complaining, 'all those big, beautiful, blue-eyed women keep taking the Pill, and ain't breeding no more'. I asked Jim Denby, for that was his name, what he was doing in Central America, and he told me he had a cattle ranch in Costa Rica, one of the few countries, south of the border, that welcomes North Americans.

Then he started to talk about William Walker. He had read Walker's autobiography, published in 1860, the year of his death, and everything else he could find on that odd career. Delighted to meet a Walker buff, I asked Jim Denby if he had seen the resemblances between Walker and Colonel Oliver North, the man arraigned before the United States Congress for organising the shipment of arms from the Middle East to the Contra rebels here in Nicaragua. Both men were short, humourless, self-righteous and vain to the point of speaking about themselves in the third person. For reasons I did not understand, Jim Denby winced at the very mention of North.

'Are you staying here at the Intercon?' I inquired.

'No, I've checked in to one of those Sandalista hotels. It's costing me all of four bucks a night. You know those young foreigners who come here? You really meet some most interesting people.'

'You meet some jerks as well.'

'*And* you meet some jerks,' he agreed.

I became still more curious. Why should an elderly, mid-Western farmer want to stay in a kind of left-wing youth hostel? What was he doing here in Managua? I tried a roundabout approach.

'Have you spent much time in Nicaragua in the past?'

'Yes, I was here last year for a few months.'

192

'On holiday? Or business?'

'No, I was in gaol.'

'Really. May I ask why?'

'I was overflying Nicaragua in my plane. I wanted to land in Costa Rica but it meant coming in from this side. I made three runs and afterwards I was told that the soldiers fired three hundred rounds at me. Only eleven hit the plane but one of them got the carburettor. I was forced down. Even then I thought I might get away with it. I'd even persuaded the soldiers to help me start the plane and take off again. Then an officer turned up, and I knew this was the end.'

There was something I had read in the papers about an American airman shot down in Nicaragua. A genuine CIA man. 'Were you the man . . .?' 'No, hell no! That was one of Oliver North's tricks. That was bad for me, though.' This explained his antipathy to North.

'Where were you in prison?'

'Right here.' He indicated the hillock behind the hotel, the place which had once been Somoza's command post and bunker, and now serves the same function for the Sandinistas. 'Hell! I could have looked right down into this hotel . . . It was real boring in there. So I showed them how to redesign the cell. One day Tomás came to see me, you know Tomás Borge? He's the man that really matters here, I reckon. We talked for forty-five minutes. He was telling me about his time in gaol under the old regime, how bad it had been for him. So I said, if you know how bad it is, why don't you let me out? . . . They were going to trade me off. You know how they let you out to a US politician? He gets political mileage from freeing you. This government gets his support. They were going to trade me off with Jesse Jackson. You know, the coloured preacher?'

'Why didn't they?'

'Because when the trial came up, I was found not guilty. I had a smart lawyer, a black man from the Atlantic coast and a damned smart lawyer.'

193

One thing still puzzled me. If he had had such a bad time here, why did he want to return?

'To get my plane. And before I can do that, I've got to pay off my lawyer. The plane's still there. When the hotel manager saw it, he was so impressed he gave me the bridal suite. I've got to get a truck to take it down to Costa Rica.'

Jim Denby felt amiable to the Nicaraguans. But he thought their agriculture was ruined and birth rate too high. This brought him back to those big, blue-eyed American women who swallowed the Pill instead of breeding.

One evening, when he was staying in the Intercontinental Hotel, Greene started to talk of his friend, Evelyn Waugh. For the benefit of one of the Nicaraguans present, Greene gave a résumé of their relationship, 'He was also a novelist, now dead, and a very good friend of mine. But we were totally different in our opinions. He was very conservative, while I've always been on the left. He was also a Catholic, but very orthodox, while I've always been, well, a bit of a heretic.'

One can guess what Waugh would have thought of Nicaragua under the Sandinistas, for we know what he thought of Mexico under the Marxists in 1938, the same year that Greene went to that country. While Greene was there to study the persecution of Christians, Waugh had obtained a much bigger advance (sufficient to take his wife with him in comfort), to write a book on the nationalisation of British oil wells. One observation that Waugh made about Mexico, fifty years ago, could equally well be made about modern Nicaragua. Besides the holidaymakers and the sentimentalists, he noticed a third group of foreign visitors. 'These are the ideologues; first in Moscow, then in Barcelona, now in Mexico these credulous pilgrims pursue their quest for the promised land; constantly disappointed, never disillusioned, ever thirsty for the phrases in which they find refreshment, they have flocked to Mexico in the last few months for the present rulers have picked up a Marxist vocabulary.' After the Second World War, these 'credulous pilgrims' moved on to Eastern Europe, especially Tito's Yugoslavia, and then, with Tito's disgrace, to China, Vietnam, Cuba, little Grenada, and now Nicaragua, whose present rulers have also picked up a Marxist vocabulary.

The friends of revolution today take no interest in a bloodless reformation like that which followed the death of Franco in Spain, or the overthrow of the Marcoses in the Philippines. The foreign friends of the Sandinistas were not content with the overthrow of Somoza, if indeed they had heard of Somoza; what excited them was the carnage of war, a war protracted in order to let the Sandinistas win control of the army, its weapons and ultimately of the government. When Somoza had fled, and the great majority of the people hoped to enjoy their freedom in peace and prosperity, the Sandinistas determined to make the struggle go on – *la lucha sigue*. It is one of their favourite slogans. But since Somoza had gone, and his cronies with him, the Sandinistas found themselves lacking in enemies. They therefore had to create them.

The Sandinistas robbed and harried the propertied class; they picked a quarrel with the Church; they gave arms and support to rebels in neighbouring countries; above all they ranted against and provoked the United States, befriending her enemies such as Cuba, Libya and Russia. Within two years of the overthrow of Somoza, Nicaragua was again at war. The ubiquitous uniforms and guns, the constant, hysterical war propaganda, most of it aimed at the United States, delight the ideological tourists as much as they sadden most Nicaraguans.

Because revolution in Russia, Vietnam or Nicaragua brings war and misery to the people, it does not mean that the new regimes cannot survive. 'It is not to be imagined because a political system is, under certain aspects, very unwise in its contrivance, and very mischievous in its effects,' wrote Burke in 1791 in *Thoughts on French Affairs*, 'that it therefore can have no

195

long duration ... What can be conceived so monstrous as the republic of Algiers? and that no less strange republic of the Mamalukes in Egypt? They are of the worst form imaginable, and exercised in the worst manner, yet they have existed as a nuisance of the earth for several hundred years.'

Burke went on to prophesy and, alas, how right he was, that France alone could not make a counter-revolution; that the longer the system lasted, the greater its power to suppress opposition at home; 'thirdly, that as long as it exists in France, it will be the interest of the managers, and it is in the very essence of their plan, to disturb and distract all other governments, and their endless succession of restless politicians will continually stimulate them to new attempts'. *La lucha sigue.*

In the new French Assembly, a number of seats had been allotted to representatives of the clergy, or politician priests such as we have now in Nicaragua. While disapproving of priests who went into politics, Burke still more condemned those who brought politics into church. Nicaragua furnishes proof that the Church is weakest when it brings politics into the pulpit, and strongest when it confines itself to religious duties. The Anglican Church, over the last thirty years, has abandoned not only its Bible and Prayer Book, its doctrines and moral code, but almost its sense of right and wrong, in order to fall in line with modish political theory; and yet congregations continue to fall away to the point where the faithful are now outnumbered by Roman Catholics and by Islam.

In all Latin America, Nicaragua alone is gripped by religious fervour. I have seen something comparable in only two other countries, both Roman Catholic, both loyal to the present Pope, and both hostile to Marxism and 'liberation theology'. These countries are the Philippines and the Pope's own Poland. The Philippines, under Ferdinand and Imelda Marcos, had much in common with Nicaragua under Somoza. There was wide discontent with the greed and arrogance of the ruling family. Both

196

countries had at one time fought against and been ruled by the United States, towards which they have ambivalent feelings. Just as opposition to Somoza was led by Archbishop, later Cardinal, Obando, so in the Philippines, the opposition to Marcos formed round the strangely named Cardinal Sin. It was Sin who encouraged, and some think directed, the presidential election campaign of Mrs Corazón 'Cory' Aquino. But whereas in Nicaragua, the Marxist Sandinistas took control of the popular opposition, the Marcoses were overthrown by a bloodless revolution, in which priests and nuns were in the front ranks defying the guns and tanks. The Filipino left-wing guerrillas took no part in the overthrow of the Marcoses and now make war against Mrs Aquino.

In Poland, nine tenths of the population go to church in a spirit of solemn, even severe devotion, free of the jokes and pleasantries that you find in the West. Each year, three hundred thousand miners march in pilgrimage to a shrine of the Virgin Mary, for Poland, like Nicaragua and the Philippines, is strongly Marian in its religion. In front of the Lenin shipyard in Gdansk, there is a triple crucifix rising one hundred and twenty feet in the air, commemorating the workers shot there during the strikes. A text from the Psalms stretches along the shipyard wall. There are always flowers on the monument to the martyred Father Popielyszko. At the start of the Solidarity campaign there was a photograph of the Lenin shipyard strikers kneeling in prayer. It was a fine example of what G. K. Chesterton called the joke of the Christian message, ridiculing the aspirations and pride of man. In a shipyard named after the cruel and presumptuous Lenin, the workers knelt to a very different leader.

By the same kind of paradox, the Church in Poland, the Philippines and in Nicaragua, just because it does not meddle in politics, has won enormous political power. This power comes from spiritual authority. The Church goes about its own business, the care of souls and the guardianship of morality. This may and

197

almost certainly does mean confronting the State on matters concerning the Church, such as the education of children, divorce, sexual morality and abortion. The politicians are eager to have their say on these matters; the Church considers them as its own business.

Even Burke would have agreed that the Church must defend its own interests. The Church of England led the opposition to James II, who locked six bishops up in the Tower. The Church also speaks for the nation against its foreign oppressors. As Graham Greene said about Poland, 'The Church represented the nation against Russia in the days of the Tsar, it represented the nation against Hitler and now it represents the nation far more than the group of men who rule it in the interests of Russia.' The same could be said of the Church in Nicaragua.

Because the Pope, Cardinal Sin and Cardinal Obando are, almost by definition, hostile to Marxism, an atheist ideology, it does not mean they are 'right wing', in the sense of siding with capitalism, the rich, or the white race. When Graham Greene was in Texas in 1938, he praised the recent encyclicals which had condemned capitalism quite as strongly as Communism. Fifty years later, Pope John Paul II published another encyclical *Sollicitudo rei socialis*, which seemed to equate the 'imperialisms' of East and West, liberal capitalism with Marxist collectivism. 'Each of the two blocs harbours within it, in its own way, a tendency towards imperialism,' the Pope wrote.

The encyclical brought down on the Pope the fury of many Americans who had previously been his admirers, conservatives such as William Buckley and William Safire. The latter wrote in the *New York Times*:

As a political manifesto, the encyclical's purpose is obviously to align the church with the downtrodden, which is proper enough. In so doing, the Pope curries favor with the third world — mainly dictatorships, oligarchies and juntas — in a way

198

that enshrines the rhetoric of resentment. It's not your fault that you are poor, the Pope is saying – nor the fault of your socialist system or your corrupt leaders. No, you were unfairly treated by the imperialists, and deserve right now a share of what the developed world has earned.

I think the encyclical *Sollicitudo rei socialis* does have special relevance to Nicaragua, the Church and 'liberation theology'; also to Poland and the Philippines, two other countries with similar circumstances. Coming from a country under the heel of Russia, and beggared by its political system, the Pope is fully aware that the Soviet Union is an obnoxious tyranny, and socialism does not work. But when we look at the Philippines, we get a different picture. Ferdinand Marcos held power for twenty years very much thanks to the military and financial help of successive United States Presidents. He leased to the Americans their largest air and naval bases in the Pacific. President Johnson called him 'my right arm' in Asia; Nixon and Reagan treated him as a special friend. American banks made huge loans to the Philippines, most of which money was squandered on useless projects if it was not actually stolen by Marcos, his family and his friends. In twenty years under the Marcoses, the Philippines declined from being the second most prosperous country in East Asia, after Japan, to being the second poorest, after Bangladesh. The economy is still crippled by debts incurred by Marcos to the American liberal capitalists.

The latter did good business with the Somoza family here in Nicaragua. It is fair to say that even the last Somoza did not steal to the same extent as Marcos, and left a share of the wealth to the rest of the country. The economy grew and Nicaragua prospered as it had not done before and has not done since. But Nicaragua was a fairly unpleasant dictatorship.

American conservatives such as Buckley and Safire would doubtless call this the fault of the Nicaraguan people. They may be right. Liberal capitalism and the ideas of Locke, Jefferson, Lincoln and Churchill work well in the Anglo-Saxon countries from which they sprang. They do not work so well in the 'third world', a euphemism for all those peoples in Africa and in Latin America who, before they were colonised, had not enjoyed a civilisation, with written language, law, education and private property. In most of the 'third world' countries of Latin America, the great majority of the people come from the Indian race.

It may be that these 'third world' countries, whether in Africa or America, are not really suited to liberalism, democracy or even self-government. Nicaragua, for example, has been a disaster since independence. But independence is a fact. And as far as Nicaragua goes, I think the Pope is right. The imperialisms of East and West, 'suspicious and fearful' of one another, as the Pope says, have turned this country into a cockpit of rival ideologies, neither of which is useful or relevant. Somoza's capitalism and Sandinista socialism are equally undesirable in this agricultural country.

The one Nicaraguan truly representative of his country is Cardinal Obando y Bravo. He is an almost pure Indian, in contrast to the Sandinista leaders, most of whom come from the white ruling class, as did the Somozas. Although here in Nicaragua, unlike for instance Mexico and Peru, the Indians feel little resentment against the whites, they have a sense of their separate identity. Rubén Darío was very aware of it in himself. It helps to explain his awe of the physical Nicaragua, its lakes, volcanoes and luxuriant vegetation. He was Indian in his religious passion and special love for the Virgin Mary; also, perhaps, in his drunkenness, Rubén's gentle nature expresses the Indian, not the Spanish, side of the Nicaraguan character. Whereas, in most Spanish countries, the word *macho* means male, boastful, aggressive, here it conveys the same meaning as *gringo*, a North American in an unfriendly sense.

It is very much thanks to Obando and to the higher authority of the Pope that Nicaragua has so far been spared much of the horror of civil war. Although both the Contras and Sandinistas have performed atrocities, and accused each other of more, the toll is not high.

Although I happened to be in Rivas when a bomb went off, this was an unusual incident. Neither the Sandinistas nor Contras go in for violence. I think this is due to the Pope, who has been implacable in his condemnation of terrorism, or what the Anglican bishops call 'the armed struggle', whether in Latin America, Africa or Ireland. The Poles themselves, who have suffered far more grievous oppression than have the Latin Americans, Irish or Africans, have not resorted to terror against their tormentors. Not one person was killed during the Solidarity agitation.

In Nicaragua, as in the Philippines and in Poland, one can understand why the Pope is against 'imperialisms', both liberal capitalism and Communism, the United States as well as the Soviet Union. Both systems are, in their different ways, a threat to the family, and therefore the Church, the one by an excess of freedom, the other by oppression. The fiercest enemies of the present Pope are not the Communists of the East but the liberal ideologues of the West, the feminists, Freudians and advocates of divorce, abortion, pornography, legalised drugs and homosexual behaviour. Again, this is not a question of left and right. Most Communist countries come down hard on, for instance, homosexual behaviour and drug abuse. Hitler was a pioneer of abortion and euthanasia; his party organ *Der Stürmer* thrived on sadistic pornography. The Philippines in the Marcos age was a hunting ground for homosexual paedophiles.

The Pope and Obando stand firm against all assaults on the family and traditional Christian morals. They are against the state perversion of education. The Church in Nicaragua would not allow the kind of abuses considered permissible in England: the indoctrination of children with feminist, 'gay' or racial propaganda; the snatching away of children into care. In Nicaragua, as

201

in Poland, I sense that, however poor they are, the people have kept their dignity and a grace. I never yearn for Miami.

Although we can see in Nicaragua the clash of great principles like conservatism and revolution, the church and the libertarian ethos, such things probably matter little to most of the people. Revolution cannot for long repress the deeper feelings of family, clan or national loyalty, as we now see in the Soviet Union or Yugoslavia.

Likewise, in Nicaragua, under the Sandinista slogans, we see ancient rivalries dating to Independence or even earlier. The Sandinistas, with their aggressive military stance to the other Central American countries, follow the lead of William Walker and also the Liberal President, General Zelaya, the patron of Rubén Darío. The Contras, drawing support from the north and east of the country, especially the Blacks and Indians, are heirs, though they would not like to admit it, of General Sandino.

The Conservatives, and their newspaper *La Prensa*, speak for the opposition, but also, perhaps, the Chamorro clan. The more I have seen of this country, the more I suspect that some of the feuds and rivalries date to before the Spanish Conquest, to things that the Indians still remember but will not say to a European. In this ancient and rather mysterious land of lakes and volcanoes, the brief ten years of a Sandinista government may come to be seen as of only passing importance.

Nor do I think that the country has suffered irreparable damage. Nearly a decade after the Sandinistas came to power, the Revolution has little to show for itself except poverty, inflation at up to 36,000 per cent, and an exodus of the professional class. Although the Sandinistas have an enormous army and try to keep up a war hysteria, there is in fact little fighting. Neither side has gone in for terrorist bombing, murder and torture, as both sides have done in El Salvador.

The Sandinistas have not committed the kind of crimes that

demand revenge in blood. If they fell from power, the leaders would have to leave the country, but peacefully, in traditional fashion. In all the civil conflicts in Nicaragua, the winners of *coups d'état* have seldom slaughtered the losers. Nor do I think that the fall of the Sandinistas would mean the return of Somoza's men, who are still unpopular.

The gravest threat to the Sandinistas is not from their enemies in the United States but from their friends in the Soviet Union. As part of his *glasnost* reforms, Mikhail Gorbachev has already withdrawn troops from Afghanistan, threatened to stop paying his surrogate armies, the Vietnamese in Cambodia and the Cubans in Angola. He will not want to continue subsidising a very expensive regime in Nicaragua, whose bellicose policies also upset his new, friendly relationship with the United States.

Reports from El Salvador suggest that the Communist rebels may be winning their struggle for power. A victory for those rebels, by all accounts a most sinister bunch, could bring intervention from the United States, and might involve Nicaragua. But there are also signs that the Soviet Union does not want to commit itself to the Communists in El Salvador.

La lucha sigue, the fight goes on, but not, surely, for ever. Young revolutionaries grow into married and middle-aged men and women. They tire of slogans and waving AK-47s. Bliss was it at that dawn to be alive; but dawn is succeeded by midday, evening and night. Eventually people get bored with the Revolution.

EPILOGUE

MY LAST EXPERIENCE of Nicaragua was true to the country's stormy character. On 15 October 1988 I read in *La Prensa* that Hurricane Joan was heading for Nicaragua. The report, which had no doubt come from the International Hurricane Centre in Miami, said that Joan was now in the Caribbean, near Colombia, but was gathering strength and force, and might hit Bluefields early next day. The story proved to be true in every detail except the timing, which was a week out. The rate of a hurricane's progress is much more difficult to predict than its course or its strength.

Next morning, Sunday 16 October, both the government papers denounced *La Prensa*'s story. 'With ignorance and pre-meditation, *La Prensa*'s perverse scare over a tropical storm', was the heading in *El Nuevo Diario*. A spokesman for the Meteorological Department at Sandino Airport described *La Prensa*'s report as 'distortion and alarmism'. He scoffed at the thought of danger to Nicaragua from what he described as 'the tropical storm Johan'. A tropical storm is less severe than a hurricane. 'Johan' was the first of many spellings used by the Sandinista regime to avoid the North American 'Joan'.

On Wednesday 19 October, *La Prensa* counter-attacked. It pointed out that the Nicaraguan Meteorological Department was now calling Joan a hurricane and had said it was heading for Bluefields. It published a blown-up version of Sunday's *El Nuevo Diario*, over the caption, 'they put their foot in it'. Now who are the perverts, now who are the ignorant, it inquired. The next day, Thursday 20 October, the government banned publication of all information about the hurricane, except from official sources. The decree, from the Ministry of the Interior, called the hurricane 'Johanna'. An editorial in *La Prensa* denounced the ban as absurd and illegal, 'If we were not aware of the dark political interests lying behind this order to silence us, it would be incomprehensible.' The editorial said that in neighbouring Costa Rica, also threatened by Joan, there was information available to help people guard themselves against danger, while here there were only official pronouncements, which generally said nothing. The newspaper pointed out that censorship on Joan would only be justifiable if the government had declared a state of emergency.

The next day, Friday 21 October, the government did declare a state of emergency. It seemed that *El Nuevo Diario* had taken to heart *La Prensa*'s comparison between Nicaragua and Costa Rica. The front page had two pictures from Puerto Limón, on the Atlantic coast of Costa Rica, suggesting that there was panic and, by implication, no cause for alarm in Nicaragua. One picture showed, in the words of the caption, 'townspeople desperately crowding round the door of a bus trying to get a place. Some inhabitants have decided to stay in the town, saying "Be it as God Wills".' The other picture showed an anguished woman, 'The government has told people to leave the town but transport is scarce. This Costa Rican lady is crying because she cannot find transport out of the zone menaced by Hurricane Juana.' The word 'Juana' is Spanish for Joan. In Mexico it is short for marijuana; it can mean 'whore' in Colombia; in Nicaragua, Juana was used for a woman camp follower, or perhaps a soldier, like those who were with Sandino fighting the US Marines in the twenties and thirties.

205

On that same day, Friday 21 October, *Barricada* carried a map, showing the progress of Joan, from the International Hurricane Centre in Miami. It also carried the Centre's forecast of torrential rain and flooding in Managua. That Friday, President Daniel Ortega flew to Bluefields and promised the help and expert advice of Cuba, not a popular country, least of all in Bluefields, whose population is mostly Black, Protestant and conservative.

The next day, Saturday 22 October, President Ortega came on the television to say he had gone to Bluefields as 'head of the country and of the revolution'. It was the first of many suggestions that Joan was in some way counter-revolutionary. Here in Managua, the local authorities ordered the mass evacuation of all those living in shanty towns, like Leningrado, close to the lake. By this time I had left the Seven Seas and moved down the road to the Hotel Morgut, a new establishment, much to be recommended, with friendly staff and a functioning telephone. The manager proved himself a Noah. He had built a cement wall across the front door to keep out the flooding, 'I've got hurricane lamps, and when the electricity fails there is one torch for each of us. We've got meat, eggs and bread. There's plenty of beer in the fridge, and three days' water supply. This is a well-built house. It's the only one round here that survived the last earthquake, as you can see. Look!' He slapped at a wall. 'It is solid. This house won't fall down.'

All through that day the rain fell, and when night came, turned into a hurricane with water bucketing down, and Joan shrieking around us. But here in Managua, Joan had done little damage. Next morning I noticed a few uprooted trees but nothing comparable with the devastation in Hyde Park in October, the previous year. In Bluefields, it was another story. Although only fifteen people were killed, not fifty as it had first been reported, the hurricane had destroyed virtually all the wooden buildings. On Monday 24 October, *El Nuevo Diario* devoted the whole of its front page to a photograph of the devastation wrought by Joan. Even the Sandinista press was now using the Anglo-Saxon version.

But even now, two days after the tragic hurricane, *El Nuevo Diario* could not refrain from political propaganda. Its headline over this front page picture consisted of just three words, but ones with peculiar import to Nicaraguan readers, '¡Aquí fué Bluefields!' 'Here stood Bluefields!' As all Nicaraguans and those who have read this book will no doubt recognise, these words echo the infamous boast by William Walker, after exacting revenge on the city which had betrayed him, 'Aquí fué Granada!' It is the most famous saying in Nicaraguan history.

As more news came through about the effects of Joan, it was clear the government had mismanaged the whole affair. The people of Bluefields so distrusted the Sandinistas that they refused to believe in Hurricane Joan and would not evacuate. Perhaps they were wise, for few if any of those who took shelter sustained any bodily harm. Most of the deaths were caused by flying zinc roofs that hit people foolhardy enough to stay in the open. Most of the hundred or so deaths caused by Hurricane Joan were in western Nicaragua, especially at Matagalpa and even at Rivas, near the Pacific. By minimising the danger of Joan, the government press gave a false sense of security.

Even after Joan had devastated the country, the government treated it as a matter of propaganda. President Ortega brutally spurned all offers of help from the United States although, as he himself said, Joan had caused more damage than the Managua earthquake of 1972. The Nicaraguan exiles in Miami hesitated to aid their fellow countrymen, for fear of lending support to the Sandinista regime. President Daniel Ortega became demented with hatred of the United States. On Sunday 23 October, *El Nuevo Diario* told its readers, 'Daniel affirmed that the country stood on maximum alert, with all its defensive mechanisms deployed, including the Supreme Council of Defence, the ministries of the armed forces and agriculture. It has an active plan to confront catastrophe or a North American military intervention.'

Here was a man so crazed by revolutionary rhetoric that he dared not only American military might but the forces of Nature; this is a country where Nature is terrible in its power to destroy. All the attempts by human beings to build a paradise on earth are vain and ridiculous, but especially here, where the earth quakes and erupts in mountains of fire like Momotombo. One might as well try to create the People's Republic of Pompeii, or the Soviet Union of Sodom and Gomorrah.

The greatest of Nicaraguans, Rubén Darío, understood and respected and feared the power of Nature and God. The words from his 'Canto de Esperanza', the 'Song of Hope', are carved on his statue here in Managua.

> Oh, Señor Jesucristo, por qué tardas, qué esperas
> para tender tu mano de luz sobre las fieras
> y hacer brillar al sol tus divinas banderas?
>
> Surge de pronto y vierte la esencia de la vida
> sobre tanta alma loca, triste o emperdenida
> que, amante de tinieblas, tu dulce aurora olvida.
>
> Ven, Señor, para hacer la gloria de tí mismo,
> ven con templor de estrellas y horror de cataclismo,
> ven a traer amor y paz sobre el abismo.

Further Reading

THERE IS NO proper history on Nicaragua nor even a travel book on Nicaragua alone. The best book on William Walker remains his own memoirs, published in 1860, shortly before his death by firing squad in Honduras. Charles Watland's life of Rubén Darío supplements the poet's own autobiographical writing. Carleton Beals's *Banana Gold* gives a vivid and memorable portrait of Sandino. His hero-worshipping tone needs the corrective provided by Neil Macaulay's scholarly researches. Richard Millett is excellent on the Somozas. Hugh Thomas's monumental history of Cuba and study of Fidel Castro helps to explain the rise of the Sandinistas. By far the best book on recent events is Shirley Christian's *Nicaragua, Revolution in the Family*. She also explains the relationship of Nicaragua with Panama, in which Graham Greene had a diplomatic role.

ACKNOWLEDGEMENTS

MY THANKS ARE DUE to the editors of newspapers who contributed to the cost of journeys to Nicaragua or nearby countries, including the *Mail on Sunday*, the *Daily Telegraph* and the *Independent Magazine*.

Above all I am grateful to Charles Moore, the editor of the *Spectator*; for financial support and for letting me use certain passages on Nicaragua and on the writings of Graham Greene.

Although I met with much helpfulness in Nicaragua, I should like to single out for thanks Mr Richard Owen, who was the British chargé d'affaires in 1985.

My thanks again to Mary Taylor, who typed some of the first draft; to my agent Maggie Noach for finding a publisher; to that publisher Vivien James; and above all to my wife, for bearing with me over four years of obsession with Nicaragua.

INDEX

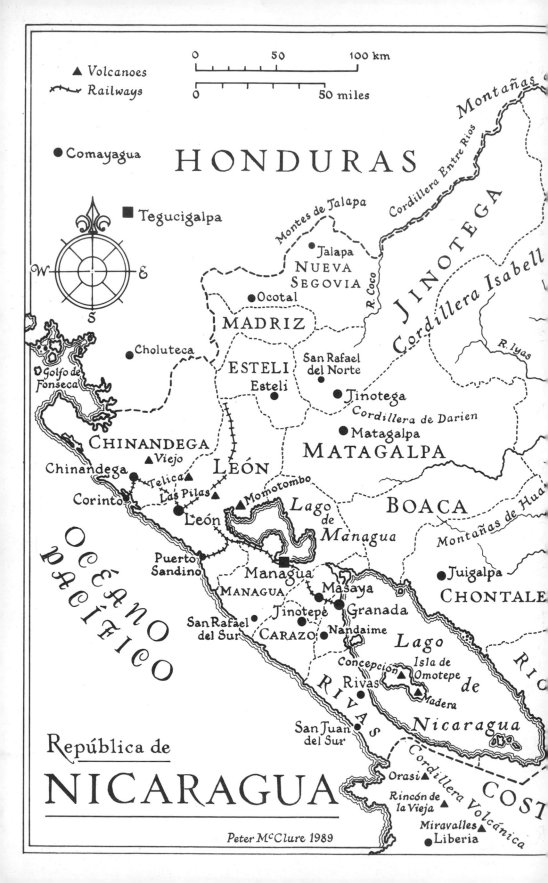